License to Do That

"I'm very much intrigued by the issues raised in this narrative. I also enjoy the author's voice, which is unapologetically combative but also funny and engaging." A.S.

"I love Froot Loup! You make me laugh out loud all the time!" Celeste M.

"A thought-provoking premise and a wonderful cast of characters." rejection letter from publisher

The Blasphemy Tour

"With plenty of humor and things to think about throughout, *The Blasphemy Tour* is a choice pick ..." *Midwest Book Review*

"Jass Richards has done it again. As I tell anyone who wants to listen, Jass is a comedy genius, she writes the funniest books and always writes the most believable unbelievable characters and scenes ... I knew this book was a winner when ... a K9 unit dog kind of eats their *special* brownies... and dances 'Thriller'. ... Rev and Dylan are not your ordinary guy and girl protagonists with sexual tension and a romantic interest, at all. They both defy gender roles, and they are so smart and opinionated, it's both funny and made me think at the same time. ... They tour around the USA, in their lime green bus that says 'There are no gods. Deal with it.' Overall, I highly recommend anything by Jass, especially this one book, which is full of comedy gold and food for thought." May Arend, Brazilian Book Worm

"If I were Siskel and Ebert I would give this book Two Thumbs Way Up. ... Yes, it is blasphemy toward organized religion but it gives you tons of Bible verses to back up its premises. And besides, it's pure entertainment. There's a prequel which I recommend you read first. *The Road Trip Dialogues*. ... I only hope there will be a third book." L.K. Killian

The Road Trip Dialogues

"I am impressed by the range from stoned silliness to philosophical perspicuity, and I love your comic rhythm." L. S.

"This is engaging, warm, funny work, and I enjoyed what I read. ..." rejection letter from publisher

"Just thought I'd let you know I'm on the Fish 'n Chips scene and laughing my ass off." Ellie Burmeister

"These two need stable jobs. Oh wait, no. Then we wouldn't get any more road trips. Fantastic book which expands the mind in a laid back sort of way. Highly recommended." lindainalabama

Dogs Just Wanna Have Fun

"Funny and entertaining! I looked forward to picking up this book at the end of a long day." Mary Baluta

"... terrifically funny and ingeniously acerbic ..." Dr. Patricia Bloom, My Magic Dog

"Jocko won't leave his property, Carson won't come into the house, Rosie is a depressed former race dog. Biscuit refuses to go on walks, and Winner is an over-achieving herder. Amber is a distraught search-and-rescue dog, Toby, a wall-flower unless he has his turtle costume on. Cookie, a puppy-mill casualty, sees the light of day for the first time in her life. ... Brett is funny in a caustic, quirky sort of way, with a heart for dogs in need and a propensity for knowing how to have fun with them." Mary Trimble, My Magic Dog

"I enjoyed this book IMMENSELY!" Deborah Titus, Smashwords

This Will Not Look Good on My Resume

"Ya made me snort root beer out my nose!" Moriah Jovan, *The Proviso*

"Darkly humorous." Jennifer Colt, *The Hellraiser of the Hollywood Hills*

"HYSTERICAL! ... There are really no words to describe how funny this book is. ... Really excellent book." Alison, Goodreads

"This book is like a roller coaster ride on a stream of consciousness. ... Altogether, a funny, quirky read ..." Grace Krispy, Motherlode: Book Reviews and Original Photography

"Brett has trouble holding down a job. Mainly because she's an outspoken misanthrope who is prone to turn a dead-end job into a social engineering experiment. Sometimes with comically disastrous results, sometimes with comically successful results. (Like pairing up a compulsive shopper with a kleptomaniac for an outing at the mall.) I don't agree with everything she says, but I will defend her right to say it—because she's hilarious!

"My favorite part was when she taught a high school girls' sex ed class that 70% of boys will lie to get sex, 80% won't use a condom, yet 90% are pro-life. She was reprimanded, of course. I think she should have gotten a medal.

"You will likely be offended at one point or another, but if you are secure enough to laugh at your own sacred cows instead of just everyone else's, this is a must read." weikelm, Librarything

"First, let me just say I was glad I was not drinking anything while reading this. I refrained from that. My husband said he never heard me laugh so much from reading a book. At one point, I was literally in tears. Jass Richards is brilliant with the snappy comebacks and the unending fountain of information she can spout forth. ... The quick wit, the sharp tongue, the acid words and sarcasm that literally oozes from her pores ... beautiful." M. Snow, My Chaotic Ramblings

"Wonderful read, funny, sarcastic. Loved it!" Charlie, Smashwords

"I just loved this book. It was a quick read, and left me in stitches. ..."
Robin McCoy-Ramirez

A Philosopher, a Psychologist, and an Extraterrestrial Walk into a Chocolate Bar

"Jass Richards is back with another great book that entertains and informs as she mixes feminism, critical thinking, and current social issues with humour ..." James M. Fisher, *The Miramichi Reader*

"I found myself caught between wanting to sit and read [*A Philosopher, a Psychologist, and an Extraterrestrial Walk into a Chocolate Bar*] all in one go and wanting to spread it out. I haven't laughed that hard and gotten to spend time with such unflinchingly tough ideas at the same time. ... [And] the brilliance of the Alices! ... I can now pull out your book every time somebody tries to claim that novels can't have meaningful footnotes and references. [Thanks too] for pointing me to the brilliant essay series 'Dudes are Doomed.' I am eagerly watching for *The ReGender App* ..." C. Osborne

TurboJetslams: Proof #29 of the Non-Existence of God

"Extraordinarily well written with wit, wisdom, and laugh-out-loud ironic recognition, *TurboJetslams: Proof #29 of the Non-Existence of God* is a highly entertaining and a riveting read that will linger on in the mind and memory long after the little book itself has been finished and set back upon the shelf (or shoved into the hands of friends with an insistence that they drop everything else and read it!). Highly recommended for community library collections, it should be noted for personal reading lists." *Midwest Book Review*

"We all very much enjoyed it—it's funny and angry and heartfelt and told truly..." McSweeney's

"If you're looking for a reading snack that has zero saccharine but is loaded with just the right combination of snark, sarcasm, and humor, you've found it." Ricki Wilson, Amazon

"What Richards has done is brilliant. At first, I began getting irritated as I read about a familiar character, or a familiar scenario from our time living on the lake. Then, as the main character amps up her game, I see the thrill in the planning and the retribution she undertakes for pay back." Cottage Country Reflections

Substitute Teacher from Hell

"I enjoyed reading "Supply Teacher from Hell" immensely and found myself bursting out laughing many, many times. It is extremely well-written, clever, and very intelligent in its observations." Iris Turcott, dramaturge

more at jassrichards.com

Also by Jass Richards

fiction

(the Rev and Dylan series)
License to Do That
The Blasphemy Tour
The Road Trip Dialogues

(the Brett series)
Dogs Just Wanna Have Fun
This Will Not Look Good on My Resume

*A Philosopher, a Psychologist, and an Extraterrestrial
Walk into a Chocolate Bar*

TurboJetslams: Proof #29 of the Non-Existence of God

stageplays

Substitute Teacher from Hell

screenplays

Two Women, Road Trip, Extraterrestrial

performance pieces

Balls

nonfiction

Jane Smith's Translation Dictionary

Sweet Sixteen pitch based on a short story by Peg Tittle. The pitch for *Exile* was actually made at the Great American Pitchfest, it received the described response, Tittle did rewrite it as a novel, and it has since been published (Rock's Mills Press). Go figure. Should she pitch it again, now that it's a published novel? Should she hire a man to pitch it on her behalf?

Thanks to FierceMild and Hekate Jane for Rev's response to cis-privilege, taken almost word for word from their lovely comments on *Feminist Current.*

Thanks to K.A. for the post on *I Blame the Patriarchy.*

All (or almost all) references to past events occur in the previous Rev and Dylan novels. (Enjoy … !)

And thanks again to Bill for his younger self.

The ReGender App

Jass Richards

Magenta

The ReGender App
© 2017 Jass Richards

jassrichards.com

First published in 2020

978-1-926891-68-2 (print)
978-1-926891-69-9 (pdf)
978-1-926891-70-5 (epub)

Published by Magenta

Magenta

This is a work of fiction. Names, characters, places, brands, media, and incidents are either the product of the author's imagination or are used fictitiously. The author acknowledges the trademarked status and trademark owners of various products referenced in this work of fiction, which have been used without permission. The publication/use of these trademarks is not authorized, associated with, or sponsored by the trademark owners.

Cover design by Jass Richards
Formatting and interior book design by Elizabeth Beeton

Library and Archives Canada Cataloguing in Publication

Title: The ReGender App / Jass Richards.
Names: Richards, Jass, 1957 - author.
Identifiers: Canadiana (print) 20200152300 | Canadiana (ebook) 20200152319 | ISBN 9781926891682 (softcover) | ISBN 9781926891699 (PDF) | ISBN 9781926891705 (EPUB)
Classification: LCC PS8635.I268 R44 2020 | DDC C813/.6—dc23

our last one.

and i—

i miss—

and cherish—

everything.

but most of all

kayaking with you (my greatest joy)

and your capacity for glee—

W hatcha doin?" Dylan said to Rev as he entered the screened-in porch with a cup of coffee and a couple slices of cold pizza.

"Watching the lake ice over." Rev was on the couch, her hands already wrapped around a cup of coffee, staring out at the lake.

"You can do that? You can actually see the moment the water turns to ice?" He set the pizza on the table between her couch and his chair, then settled in.

"No. Well, in all my years here, no. Which is why I'm watching now."

"But it's only November."

She looked at him.

Right. When she was deciding where to settle, where to look for her dream-come-true cabin-on-a-lake-in-a-forest, she'd narrowed it down to somewhere in B.C. and somewhere in mid-northern Ontario. She'd chosen the latter, thinking that if she lived in B.C., she'd miss the variety offered by the four seasons. She didn't know that mid-northern Ontario had just two seasons: winter and bug season. Each lasting six months. Though, it had to be admitted, the latter offered a variety of blackflies, deerflies, horseflies, mosquitoes, and no-see-ums.

"And what are *you* two doing?" he said to Froot Loup, the baby wolf who'd followed him out of the forest one day and then adopted him, and Corn Flake, her best bud from down the road, both of whom were sprawled out on their nest of blankets at the end of the porch.

Loup stared at him. Wasn't it obvious? They were chewing on his shoe. One of the new ones.

They sat in companionable silence, the four of them, for what was left of the morning. Rev and Dylan had fortuitously come upon each other a few years prior, after a twenty-year gap following their graduation from teacher's college. They'd gone their separate and, apparently, quite different ways. Rev had failed with a boom, Dylan with a fizzle.

They'd each sent a letter or two over the years, but because Dylan had quit his teaching job in Nelson to go on tour with A Bunch of Drunken Indians (he played tambourine), and Rev had been fired, more or less, from one teaching job after another and so went from one address to another, they never received each other's letters.

When they'd reconnected, it was like time had put a bubble around their relationship. It was intact and unchanged.

Dylan had turned his nomadic house-sitting lifestyle and his history not-quite-degree into a freelance sort-of-career as a travel writer. And although he still took off every now and then, he had become content, even happy, to hang out at Rev's cabin on a lake in a forest.

Rev had become an off-site item-writer for the LSAT, crafting the multiple-choice logical reasoning questions that went onto the test, making good use of her philosophy degree and her inability to get along with people.

At around one o'clock, just as they were finishing their breakfast—the forementioned coffee and cold pizza—it started snowing.

"Let's go kayaking," Rev said. She never started working until the evening. Most of her neurons didn't even come online until noon, and it took until then for them to warm up.

Dylan looked out at the pretty white thick flakes. "Yes, let's! It'll be so ... Option (B): delightfully incongruous!"

"Indeed." She grinned. Despite her hermit nature, Rev enjoyed having Dylan around. Somehow he didn't destroy or invade her solitude. And he made her life fun.

They changed into their kayaking clothes and headed down to the water, Froot Loup and Corn Flake bounding along with them. Because, hey, SOMETHING WAS GOING TO HAPPEN!!

Rev got into her beloved red kayak, tied to one side of the dockraft—a Rev construction, just an eight-by-eight raft permanently pulled up on shore but buoyed at the far end by two floats. It did the trick. Which was to give her, one, a take-off platform for her kayak, and two, a sit-down platform for her lounge chair, from which she watched the sparkles on the water on sunny days and moonlit nights. And three, because of the floats, it didn't have to be taken out every winter and put back in every spring; it just rose and/or fell with the ice instead of being bent and/or broken by it.

Dylan manoeuvred his recently-purchased lime green kayak from its spot on shore to the other side of the dockraft. They'd considered just tying it to that other side, but quickly realized that on windy days it would keep banging into the dockraft. And annoy the hell out of Rev.

She pushed herself away from the dockraft and—Corn Flake jumped in.

"Okaaaay," she quickly steadied her rocking kayak. Flaker quickly assessed the situation, but did not change his mind. He sat down, snuggling himself between her knees. *Did* want to go with her. Did *not* want to go overboard.

"Ready?" She turned to see that Loup had, similarly, jumped into Dylan's kayak. Cool. Or not. Dylan didn't have her kayaking skill. And Loup was a good twenty pounds heavier than Flaker. She watched as Dylan struggled not to capsize.

"Down!" she called out to Loup.

Instantly, Loup lay down in the cockpit. Dylan's kayak stabilized considerably.

"See what good teachers we could have been?"

Dylan opened his mouth, then closed it. It was true. They had spent a great deal of time teaching Loup how to ... survive. As a pet wolf in a neighbourhood full of rednecks with rifles. And they had, apparently, succeeded.

Even so, she was quarantined during hunting season. She didn't mind the bright bandanas—usually orange, but sometimes neon pink or neon green or, Dylan's latest purchase, bright turquoise with a bunch of yellow dinosaurs swimming about. She hadn't been so keen about being tied up for two weeks at a time. Now, however, she got to spend much of the two weeks with Flaker. At his place.

After the first hunting season, and after it was clear that Froot Loup and Corn Flake were best buds, he and Rev had offered to pitch in for half the cost of replacing Kit's ten-by-ten pen with something considerably larger. Kit gladly tore down the pen—it had been all she could afford since she'd just bought the house—and fenced in her whole property instead. It wasn't as large as Rev's lot. More importantly, it was level and rectangular. So that was where Loup now spent most of his time during hunting seasons. Safe, and happy, with Flaker.

They slowly made their way out of the cove and into the lake per se, wisely hugging the shoreline. Once they were past the stretch of cottages, Dylan let Loup get up.

"Steady ... " he said as Loup negotiated sitting in the kayak. "Good wolf."

A few minutes later, halfway across the widest part of the lake, a necessary crossing in order to get to the little river Rev was heading toward, Rev risked a glance behind her to see that Loup was sitting between Dylan's legs, following Flaker's lead, and being very still. Dylan was concentrating on paddling, compensating for Loup's weight, which was not quite evenly distributed. All was well.

Until Flaker decided that the view would be better from the prow.

Rev recovered quickly and grinned. Flaker sat there like a not-so-little hood ornament as they moved steadily along the water's surface through the falling snow.

"NO!" She heard Dylan shout a moment later. Just before she heard the splash. "REV!"

Resisting the urge to do otherwise, Rev made a slow, wide turn.

"She tried to jump onto the prow! Like Flaker! And didn't quite—"

"I see."

Loup had surfaced near Dylan, who was paddling haphazardly, in a mad panic, trying to stay close to her in case, in case—

"She's okay," Rev called out. "Look, she's swimming."

"But the water must be ice cold!"

"She's got a thick coat. She's moving. In fact—" Rev pulled ahead of Froot Loup with several strong, even strokes, despite the fact that Flaker was now *standing* on the prow, anxious about—or perhaps just curious. About. Rev intended to lead Loup to the nearest shoreline. Which was, fortunately, at the mouth of the river they'd been heading toward.

"Stay … " she said to Flaker. Who promptly jumped down off the prow, into the cockpit, and half onto Rev's lap. He shoved his head over her shoulder, trying to keep Loup in sight.

"Or don't," she grinned, counterbalancing with ease. Then barely breaking stroke, she turned the kayak and continued, paddling backwards. Flaker jumped up onto the prow again.

"STAY!" Rev said again, far more sharply. Flaker's coat wasn't nearly as thick. And though he wasn't as heavy as Loup, it would be awkward, possibly impossible, to pull him out of the water and back into the kayak if he decided to jump ship and help—or join— Loup.

No need. Loup swam toward Flaker. Of course she did. Kept swimming toward Flaker, as Rev kept paddling, backwards, toward shore. Dylan paddled behind, calling out calmness and encouragement. And, occasionally, a slight course correction. It was rather like that time in Algonquin Park …

A minute later—a *long* minute later—the procession touched shore. Loup immediately jumped into Dylan's kayak, and then— *then*—shook herself.

Dylan screamed.

"Ice cold, yeah?" Rev grinned.

Fortunately, Dylan had taken Rev's advice at purchase and his kayak clothes, like hers, were relatively waterproof, as well as windproof. So once Loup was done, and both she and Flaker were back on land—Flaker had flown from Rev's kayak into Dylan's to make sure Loup was okay—Dylan stood up and shook himself. Not as efficiently. But still.

They carried on then, up the pretty river, paddling in the falling snow, Loup and Flaker electing to run along shore. It was so quiet, so beautiful. And so delightfully incongruous.

"FUCKING SHIT!" Rev spat out the words. There, where the river became shallow enough for the ATVs to cross—they'd made a trail through the forest where none had been—and it was annoying as hell on humid days because the engine noise could be heard all the way to her cabin—they saw an abandoned fridge, a TV, and a car battery. Just sitting there. Dumped.

"Why go through all the trouble to bring it here, and not to the dump?" Dylan was perplexed.

"Because it's hazardous waste. You need to buy a ticket to take your fridge to the dump, and you need to wait until a hazmat day to take car batteries. The TV is electrical waste ... can't remember if they accept that all year long or if that's a special day too."

"Unbelievable."

"Actually, it's not."

Rev told him then about how she used to take a big garbage bag with her when she walked through the forest—once in the spring when the snow melted and all the garbage tossed by the snowmobilers was exposed, and once in the fall after the summer people had stopped coming and tossing *their* shit. She'd seen entire bags of household garbage dumped, old clothes, soiled diapers, and yes, car batteries and household appliances.

On the way back down the river, Loup and Flake elected to get into the kayaks again. And onto the prows again. All was well for a few minutes. Suddenly Flaker leapt off the prow to catch a snowflake, then splashed into the river, giggling. Loup followed suit. They both swam to shore and waited to be picked up. Rev and Dylan obliged. Once back in their respective kayaks, Flaker and Loup shook themselves. They both screamed. Rev and Dylan, that is.

Flaker and Loup positioned themselves back on the prows. A few seconds later, each made another spectacular launch to catch a snowflake. Then swam to shore, and waited for pick-up.

"Shake!" Dylan insisted.

Loup jumped in and shook.

"I meant *before* you got in." He smiled lovingly at Loup.

"Probably impossible to teach the concept of time to animals who live in the moment. So completely, so easily," she added with admiration.

"Yeah." He grinned. With envy.

Then he thought, hell, he was already soaked. So next time, Loup launched himself off the prow, *he* followed suit.

Easier thought than done. He didn't launch, so much as spill, overboard. Spectacular in its own way.

As evidenced by Rev's look of disbelief. Because the water *was* ice cold. Maybe not quite as cold here in the shallow river as out on the lake, but still. And their kayak clothes were kayak clothes, not drysuits.

When Dylan surfaced, he grinned. Tried to grin. Found he had little control over his facial muscles.

"Did you catch one?" Rev asked.

"One what?" Apparently also little control over his brain.

Okay, then. She climbed onto the prow, set her sights on a thick flake close to the water's surface, then dove for it. And looked like a soggy bologna sandwich sliding off a kitchen counter. Never mind. Caught it! Did she rock or what?! Aim low, *that's* the path to success!

Flaker and Loup stared at them as they struggled to shore, giggling, their clothes dragging. They were bedraggled. The word was meant for them right then, right there.

"Shake." Dylan said.

"I am."

"No, I mean—" He demonstrated.

Flaker and Loup stared at him. Pathetic.

Rev shook herself. Fell over.

Truly pathetic.

Flaker and Loup converged on them and started to lick them dry. They got their heads done, and then—the four of them stared at the kayaks floating down the river, out of reach.

"Oh yeah. Didn't think of that."

"If we run, maybe we can catch them before they get out onto the lake," Dylan said. "You run! You're fast!" Rev had indeed been a runner. Long-distance, but still.

She took a couple of swish-swashing steps.

"That's not running!"

"Nor is it fast," she agreed.

She rolled up her pants, unzipped her jacket, then tried to take off her soaked sweatshirt.

"Hurry!" Dylan urged. "They're getting away."

She glared at him. Settled for wringing out her sweatshirt as best she could.

She tried again. To take a couple steps. They still swish-swashed. But not quite as much.

"That's better. Lift your knees," Dylan called out as she swish-swashed away.

She turned and glared at him again. Flaker and Loup had, in the meantime, sat down. To wait for the humans to figure it out.

"You just need to catch one. Then you can get in and paddle after the other one."

"Or we can just walk home from here. Deal with the kayaks tomorrow. It's not like they're going to drift out into the ocean."

"Are you on speaking terms with any of your neighbours? One has a boat we can use?"

She glared at him yet again. Flaker and Loup had lain down.

"Eventually they'll hit shore *some*where," she said. "We'll just walk around the lake until we find them."

"Okay."

They both stared at the river then.

"We're on the wrong side, aren't we." Dylan asked the obvious.

"Wrong as in morally wrong or—"

"Wrong as in we're going to have to swim across."

"Yeah."

"Isn't there a shallow spot where we could just—walk across?" Dylan asked hopefully. His teeth chattering.

"Yeah. Back where the ATVs cross."

"Oh." That was at least a mile back.

After weighing the extra wetness, negligible, against the time saved, considerable, they decided to swim across. Then wrung themselves out. Then started walking. Loup and Flaker followed them across the river, shook themselves, then took the lead.

"Pity we didn't bring an extra set of dry clothes," Dylan said at one point.

"We did. At least I did."

"And—Oh."

"Do you think our clothes will ice over? You could watch and see. It happen."

"We should call the Coast Guard when we get home. Tell them we're safe, in case someone reports—Oh. Right."

"Besides, there is no Coast Guard."

"So did you catch a snowflake? As you sailed out across the water?"

"Yeah." She grinned. "You?"

"Yeah."

Two hours later—Loup and Flaker had taken the scenic route home—not that Rev or Dylan would know—both had spent considerable time in the forest, yes, but *on the trails*—they were warm and dry, sitting on the rug leaning against the couch in front of a fire, sipping hot fudge chocolate.

Loup and Flaker were lying a safe distance away.

"Oh, we forgot—" Dylan pushed away from the couch and crawled toward the pile of kindling, opening a little tin box tucked nearby. He took out a packet of something and tossed it into the fire.

"Oh yeah!" Rev said and smiled. The flames went turquoise and green and orange and red ... The packets were called Funky Fire and contained a mix of chemicals that coloured the flames by oxidizing— something. Dylan had found them at the hardware store, unbelievably enough.

A few moments later, he opened another little box that looked like it contained chess pieces and pulled out a baggie, rolling paper, and matches. He'd found an apparently abandoned marijuana patch in the forest one day, had tended it back to health, and now called it the Marijuana Meadow. M&M, for short.

As Rev took again the joint Dylan passed to her, she nodded at Loup and Flaker. "Whoever hypothesized that wolves became domesticated because they sought the Neanderthals' fires on cold nights … didn't know wolves." Almost lost the thought there for a moment. It had been such a long sentence. "Even most dogs are wary of fire."

Dylan agreed. "They'd much rather wear little hand-knit coats to stay warm. And booties. Little pink booties with white ribbons."

"Fifi flashbacks?"

He nodded. Dylan once had a dog, Bob, who left him for life on a farm with kids and—Fifi.

"Did you ever think that maybe Bob left you for the farm? Not for Fifi?" Because, frankly, she couldn't see *any* dog leaving Dylan for little pink booties with white ribbons. "Maybe he just wanted to run and run and roll around in the muck and run some more … "

"I never thought of that!" Dylan glowed. "I should've gotten him a farm!"

"Or at least a bunch of muck."

"Yeah," he drew in, "I probably couldn't afford a farm."

"But you could afford a bunch of muck?"

"I don't know. How much money does a bunch of muck cost? If a bunch of muck did cost … money?" He giggled.

"I don't know. Where would one buy a bunch of muck? If a bunch of muck could be bought."

"Oh—Oh—eBay!" She cried out. As soon as her brain had caught up. Because she bought everything on eBay. It was *so* much easier than going to a store.

"Do you think they sell it by the pound or square foot?"

"Which is more important, weight or volume?"

Dylan imagined being Bob. Not for the first time. "Volume."

Rev got up to go get her laptop. Fifteen minutes later, she returned.

"Did you get lost?"

"Oh shut up."

A few minutes later, "Oh, wow ... "

"It's expensive?"

"They're so pretty. Dylan, look at the sea butterflies ..." She turned her laptop toward him.

"They *are* pretty ... Oh, look at that one. With the feathery ... things."

It took another minute or two. "How did you get to sea butterflies? Weren't you going to look for muck on eBay?" He scrolled down to see more images.

Rev thought for a minute. Or two. "Oh yeah. I have no idea. But look at how pretty they are ... "

N ext noon, after their coffee and cold pizza, Rev called the
township to report what they'd found by the river.

"But it's hazardous waste," Dylan heard her say as he
entered the kitchen, Loup and Flaker trailing behind.
"Depending on when the fridge was manufactured, Freon could be
leaking out. The battery could be leaking too. Battery acid." It
sounded like she was trying to convince the guy it was important.
Nothing more was said. She hung up a moment later.

"Well?"

"He told me to go online and fill out a complaint form."

"Bureaucracy."

"Don't think so."

He looked at her inquisitively.

"I'll bet that if I were a *man,* the guy would've—*you* call. See what
happens."

"I've got a better idea." Dylan went into his room, rummaged in
his knapsack, and returned with his smartphone.

She stared at it. Then remembered that they *could* use their cell
phones at her cabin now. Without climbing onto the roof. Bell and
Rogers had finally improved their service and although her internet
access wasn't truly high-speed, it was now light years ahead of the
dial-up she'd had to use for far too long.

"Call again," Dylan said, handing the phone to her. "Use the voice modulation app. Choose James Earl Jones."

"Seriously?" She accepted the phone and explored the app.

"I prefer Alvin, myself," Dylan continued, "but ... "

She made the call. The same call. Dylan reached over to put it on speakerphone.

"Yeah, some woman just called about that. Where is it exactly?" the man asked. As if the woman had been unable to tell him.

"Where the ATV trail crosses the river."

"And what exactly has been dumped there?" As if the woman had been unable to tell him.

"A fridge, a car battery, and a TV."

"Oh, well, yes, we definitely want to get that taken care of. It's hazardous waste. Depending on when the fridge was manufactured, Freon could be leaking out. The battery could be leaking too. Battery acid." Rev gave Dylan a look.

"We'll send someone out this afternoon." A murderous look.

"Thank you." Rev handed the phone back to Dylan.

They were both quiet. Rev with anger, Dylan with disbelief.

"You know what we *really* need," Rev started to say, but Dylan had already left the kitchen again.

He returned in a few seconds with his laptop, sat at the small table, and started tapping away ... Rev waited, watching, wondering—

"It's already been invented." He tapped a few more keys, then turned the laptop so she could see as well.

"Holy shit."

It was an app called ReGender. It was Photoshop meets Holoshop.

"No surprise, really," Dylan said casually. As if the world hadn't shifted under his feet. "Remember when you started using a male name for your emails? And then went into a few chatrooms as a man? And remember that program we played with, the one that changed all the pronouns?" He started exploring the website.

"Yeah. I called it a Bechdel test for novels," she said. "If you could change the pronouns and not end up laughing, the work was truly non-sexist. And fantasy," she added.

"I know you're not into gaming," he said, tapping away, "but when women use male avatars ... "

Right. Because what woman *wouldn't* want to present as a man? To be taken seriously for one goddamned minute. The people in the chatrooms had not dismissed her out of hand. They'd actually engaged with her for what she said. Not for what she was assumed to be because of her sex.

"'Smartphones,'" he was reading the 'About It' page out loud, "'have been able to project miniature holograms since 2015.'" He looked up. "Did not know that."

While he thought of all the fun he'd been missing, Rev picked up where he'd left off. "'ReGender projects a hologram that completely masks the person holding the projecting smartphone.'"

Better pay, better performance reviews, promotions.

"This is going to make someone very, very rich." She turned to Dylan. "We have to buy stock. Now."

"But," he'd scrolled down, "it's only in the beta—They need people to test it." He looked over at her. Grinning from ear to ear. Daring her from ear to ear.

"Hell yeah!" She peered closely at the page he'd clicked to. "Oh."

They had to attend a two-week orientation and training session. Then commit to five months of testing. So five and a half months. She'd have to leave her beloved cabin for five and a half months. Their blasphemy tour had taken eight months. And that had been enough travel to last a very long time, as far as she was concerned. She'd started missing her cabin first week out.

"But it's in the winter. Mostly." He nodded outside to the still falling snow. "As soon as the lake freezes over, you won't be able to kayak anyway ... "

She considered that. In fact, she'd accompanied Dylan on a couple of his housesits during the previous winter. Because, yeah, she wouldn't've been able to kayak anyway. Or sit outside in the porch. But those trips had been for only a few weeks at a time.

"Where is it? Spending the winter in California would be nice. Isn't that where Google is?"

Dylan turned back to the screen. "It's not owned by Google."

"Yet." Rev got up and headed to the porch. Her laptop was on the little table beside her couch. She settled in, powered on, and found the site. Dylan followed, carrying his laptop, and settled into his chair. Loup and Flaker followed, glanced at the two of them, then at each other, then gently pushed their way out through the hanging strip of grocery-freezer plastic in the bottom half of the door. Early on, Dylan had modified the screen door so Loup could go in and out as she wished. Maintaining its function of keeping the bugs out had been a challenge, but after several failed designs, he'd prevailed. And then had the brilliant idea of changing the screen to heavy plastic once the temperatures dropped.

"It was created by some people in Halifax!" he said with surprise a few moments later.

"The home of *22 Minutes!* That makes so much sense! Dakey Dunn—Was Mary Walsh involved? I'll bet she was … " Rev scrolled and clicked …

"In any case," Dylan said, scrolling and reading, "It looks like they're wanting people to be, or go, all over. We choose five locations from a list and spend a month at each. All expenses paid."

"Really? Including the expense to get *to* those five places?" She explored the site trying to confirm that. "And *from* those five places," she thought to add.

"Travel, accommodation, *and* an honorarium!" Dylan kept reading. It did seem a little unbelievable.

"Are any of the places in California?" She was looking for the list. "The orientation is in California, right? Isn't that where Google is? Oh, no, wait, you said the app wasn't owned by Google … Okay, that doesn't make sense." She leaned back, thinking she'd identified evidence of a hoax.

"What doesn't make sense?"

"There's no way a start-up from the Maritimes, or, actually, anywhere in Canada, could afford what this is going to cost … "

"Hm." Dylan agreed. With disappointment.

"No, wait—" he said, returning to the 'About' page and reading. "They went to California to pitch it to Google, but instead ended up getting the beta test funded by a start-up in San Francisco."

"So they got bought out?"

"No … they still own it. I think. I don't really know how these things work … But they're still in California … In San Francisco."

"Okay, *that* makes sense. No sane person would spend winter in Halifax if they didn't have to."

"Which is why the orientation session is in San Francisco," Dylan grinned at Rev. "In January. Average temperature, 57 degrees. Rain. No snow." They'd stayed in San Francisco during their blasphemy tour, but only for a couple days. He wouldn't mind going back.

"But they still want to test it in both Canada and the States? That would make sense."

"It would, yes, if Canadians own the app and Americans are funding the test."

"Well, I was thinking it made sense because they intend to market it to both Canadians and Americans."

"Wouldn't they also want to reach the Asian market? So Japan and China should be on the list! We could go to Japan and China!" Dylan had already been, to *both* Japan and China, but—

The very thought of being among so many people made Rev sweat. "You can't speak Japanese, remember? Besides, Asians don't need the app. They aren't as sex-differentiated as we are."

Dylan raised his eyebrows. "You just can't tell them apart."

"That doesn't make me racist," she said quickly. Because he was right. She couldn't. She had trouble with black-skinned people too. "It just makes me inept at facial recognition. I can't tell white fat-assed crew-cut rednecks apart either. In fact, put snowmobile helmets over their heads and they *all* look the same."

"Still," Dylan said. "Asian porn," he added.

"Yeah." She conceded the proof of sexism in Japan and China.

"It's sort of a 24/7 thing," he said a few moments later, having resumed scrolling through the site, "having to test it. But you could probably keep meeting your LSAT quota … "

"Okay, that's good … " she was starting to warm up to the idea. Because 57 degrees. Not keen on so much rain, but. No snow.

"No, wait." She looked up from her laptop and at Dylan. "What about Loup?"

Oh. How could he have forgotten about his beloved Froot Loup?

"We can't take her with us. Can we? I mean, not only the travel, but a wolf in the city? Fraser made it work, but Loup's not Diefenbaker."

No, Loup wasn't Diefenbaker. Dylan set his laptop aside. Oh well, it was a good idea. While it lasted.

But Rev wasn't going to give so easily. Every year, the winters got colder, longer, and noisier. The guys who had a snowmobile were the same ones who had an ATV. And since all the ads told them they could go anywhere, everywhere, on their manly man-machines, they did. "OWN THE LAKE!" one ad actually commanded.

Which, now that she thought about it, explained their angry "You don't own the lake!" response when she'd politely requested that they at least turn around before getting to her cabin at the dead-end cove of the lake. She'd thought, naïvely, that their response had demonstrated an elementary understanding of public property. That, she'd thought, stupidly, she could build upon, with further discussion ...

"We can ask Kit if she'd look after Loup!" she suggested. "That way she and Flaker could be together. Which they are most of the time anyway."

On cue, the two of them walked through the plastic flap.

"Yeah ... " Dylan was coming back to the possibility.

"She'd take them for a run in the forest every day."

"Yeah ... No. She couldn't. When she goes on out-trips, Flaker stays with us."

"Oh. Right." Another reason they couldn't go.

Kit worked at a wilderness camp for so-called troubled adolescents. Once a month, several staff members went on a ten-day trip with several of the kids. The idea was that the kids would develop character. And what have you. Mostly they developed the latter.

"Well, it wouldn't hurt to ask. Maybe she'll have an idea ... "

Two days later, when Kit was due back from her current out trip, they headed over to her house to return Flaker and ask about Loup. Since she lived just a couple miles away, on dirt roads, they walked. Flaker bounced around, trying unsuccessfully to herd Rev and Dylan, while Loup, as was her habit, moved stealthily through the forest, about twenty feet in. It was an instinct they'd decided not to challenge. On the one hand, it made her more of a target. Should hunters break the rules and cruise close to the road for animals to kill. But on the other hand, it kept her otherwise hidden. In any case, she always had on one of her bright bandanas. Which sort of made both sides of the issue moot.

"NO!" Rev suddenly yelled as Flaker took off. There were half a dozen wild turkeys pecking about on the road some distance ahead. They needed to be herded. Around the wet spots of melted snow.

"NO!" Rev repeated, breaking into a run, Dylan on her heels.. "They can HURT you!"

Indeed they could. Standing three feet tall, with vicious beaks, and even more vicious claws, topped by spurs on their ankles, they'd actually put a man in the hospital some years back. Though god knows what he'd done to trigger their attack.

No need to worry. Froot Loup had also broken into a run. A far more impressive run.

"I didn't know turkeys could fly," Dylan said a moment later, coming to a stop beside Rev.

"I don't think that qualified as flying," Rev replied. "Looked more like running-for-your-life-while-hysterically-flapping-your-evolution-isn't-intelligent-design-either-wings."

They were close enough to see Corn Flake glare at Froot Loup.

Froot Loup looked apologetic.

Corn Flake forgave him. Because ever since he'd gotten caught in that trap—well, it had been a wake-up call for both of them. Injury, perhaps even death, was a possibility.

Five minutes later, they arrived at Kit's place to see her outside waiting. Joyously, Flaker flew into her arms. He was better at it than the wild turkeys, Rev noted. Kit caught him, swung around to absorb the impact, crooning while she turned in a circle. Rev became slightly dizzy. But did not fall over.

Once that part was done, Flaker lay down on the grass, belly up. Kit obliged, getting down on the grass beside him, and beginning an intensive belly-rubbing session. Flaker's tail thumped the ground.

Froot Loup had watched the whole thing. Timidly, she approached, and lay down beside Flaker. Also belly up. Not missing a beat, Kit started belly-rubbing Loup as well. Loup's tail started thumping as well.

Rev nudged Dylan. But didn't need to. Until now, Loup had done that only with him. And it had taken months. Dylan didn't know whether to be happy or sad that he was doing it now with Kit.

"Say yes," he eventually called out, grinning, but a little teary-eyed.

Kit looked up. "Yes?"

Once the belly-rubbing was, apparently, done—because, hey, first things first—Kit turned her full attention to Rev and Dylan. "Wanna come in for a beer?"

"Sure!"

Rev didn't like beer, but she was socially astute enough, now, to recognize that the question need not be taken literally.

"Loup too?" Dylan said at the door. Then chuckled. They used the French pronunciation of 'loup' so it triggered his inordinate fascination with the way words sounded.

"Of course, Loup too!"

As soon as the five of them settled in her screened-in porch—pretty much mandatory in that part of the province—Kit asked what the 'Say yes' was about.

"Well, we're thinking of going away. For six months. There's this thing … " He completed the explanation.

"Wow." Kit digested the information.

"And so we were thinking, we were hoping, now that your place is fenced in, that maybe—"

"What did you do with Flaker while you were on out-trips before?" Before he'd discovered Loup. And Rev and Dylan.

"I took him with me."

Okay, so they need not feel too bad about leaving Flaker without a second home for six months, but that was probably not a good option for Loup.

"If we had a bit more time to train Loup," Kit started thinking out loud, "I'd love to use her to scare the shit out of some of these baby-psychopaths I have to deal with … "

Dylan was confused. But Rev was not. Given her classroom

experience. "I'm not sure that'd be a good idea," she said to Kit. "Loup might not be able to understand faking it." Loup was definitely not Diefenbaker. Well, Draco.

"You're right," Kit easily changed her mind. "It would be confusing. And I wouldn't want to put Loup through that." She reached out to stroke her fondly. "Besides, honestly? I wouldn't put it past some of them to pull a knife on her."

"Okay, so a definite no to that idea." Dylan had caught up.

"Once I had to leave Flaker here," Kit said. "I can't remember why—oh yeah, we had an interim supervisor who said I couldn't take her with me. Anyway, I had a friend come over a couple times a day to let her out ... "

"But even if you left Loup outside ... Ten days is a long time ... " Rev said what was on Dylan's mind.

"Do you know anyone who ... " He trailed off.

"What about Dr. Theresen?" Rev suddenly thought of the vet they'd taken Loup to. Actually they didn't take Loup to her, she came to Loup. They'd heard about cats in cars, and had thought that wolves in cars might well be worse. Dr. Theresen was wonderful about the whole baby-wolf-adopts-Dylan thing. And the Flaker-caught-in-the-trap thing. When Loup had gone nuts.

"Or," Kit said, "I've been thinking ... "

They waited.

"I've been thinking it might be time to get out."

"You're thinking of quitting?" Dylan was appalled. Kit seemed to *love* her job.

"Not completely. Just stepping away from the front line. I've been offered a managerial position."

"You? Behind a desk?"

Rev jabbed Dylan.

Kit laughed. "No worry, I had the same thought. But, you know ... There comes a time ... "

"You're burned out. You don't care anymore. About the kids."

Kit looked at Rev, surprised to see the empathy in her eyes.

"No, I do, I just—No, I don't. Not really. Not anymore." She said it in a progressively smaller voice and looked down at her hands, hanging limply in her lap. She felt ashamed, sad, confused—She reached out and started stroking Flaker, snuggled beside her. "It's just … You try and try and put yourself out there again and again, and they call you a SAP. Sad and Pathetic," she translated. "Not to mention a bitch, a cow, a cunt, a—"

"It's a paradox," Rev interrupted. Because the litany was all too familiar. "Unless you harden, you keep getting hurt and die a death of a thousand cuts. But if you *do* harden, you're no good to them anymore. Lose-lose."

Kit nodded. "They shouldn't really call it being burned out. It's more like being … hollowed out."

Dylan stared at the two of them. After all, he'd been a teacher too, like Rev. He'd worked on the front line with kids too, like Kit. But he had experienced nothing like this. Were students harder on women? In the way they were talking about? Rev had told him about eventually having to brace herself before she entered the classroom because of the hostility. Every day at least one of the students would call her a bitch. He'd never been called a bitch. A wank, maybe, and a faggot, certainly, but not a bitch. And since he wasn't gay, it didn't hurt. Not in a real, personal way. But Rev and Kit weren't bitches either, so—well, yes, they were. Given that 'bitch' just meant, really, 'woman'. Hey, that was something they could test! With the app! Well, if they could get temporary teaching positions …

"Okay," Dylan turned back to the purpose of their visit, "so, if you decided to take the desk job, that would be, like, Monday to Friday, nine to five?"

Kit nodded. With some disgust.

"But it's a promotion, right?" Rev asked. "Better pay?"

Kit nodded. With a smile.

"And when would it start?" There was hope in his voice.

"January."

"Oh well, then." Could it be this simple?

"No talking about how it was meant to be," Rev said, to no one in particular, "or that it's fate or kismet or, heaven forbid," she grinned, "a sign from god. Think about it," she said to Kit. "And don't let—"

"But I *have* thought about it," Kit said. "The promotion, I mean.

I've been thinking about it for over a week. Actually, I think my heart decided as soon as the offer was made, and my head just needed to catch up. Or vice versa."

Dylan nodded. His head often needed to catch up.

"Honestly, I think this, your request, is just the nudge I need to say yes." She turned to Dylan, "So, yes. Yes!"

"Okay, then!" Dylan was delighted. "Thank you!"

"We haven't actually applied yet," Rev said, "so let's not get ahead of ourselves. Fun though that is," she turned to Dylan, anticipating his comment to that effect.

"And, but, if we do get accepted, we may need to leave a few days before January. To get to wherever we're going."

"No problem. I have a couple weeks' vacation I can use."

"Okay, then. We'll apply and let you know. If we get accepted, we'll figure out the details then."

"Okay. There is one condition though."

"We'll pay for her food, of course," Dylan quickly said. "We'll even pay for—how much does wolfsitting cost?"

"And any vet bills," Rev said, then turned quickly to Dylan, "not that there will be any."

"You remember Dr. Theresen?" Dylan asked. "She's Loup's vet."

"I remember," Kit smiled, assuring him. "I know. Are any of her shots due during your absence?"

"Oh. Good question. I'll check."

This was going to be okay, Dylan told himself. Kit was clearly responsible, and she clearly cared about Loup.

"Your condition?" Rev came back to that.

"Bring back one of the beta versions you guys will be testing. I wouldn't have to deal with half the shit I have to deal with if I looked and sounded like Schwartzeneggar."

They stared at her.

"You mean 'shit' figuratively, right?" Dylan asked.

Kit stared at him.

"One of these days, when we come back, I should do a story about—that."

o next day, in the screened-in porch with their morning coffee-and-cold-pizza, they returned to the ReGender website to fill out the application form. The snow had stopped falling, and it was sunny, and the lake was sparkling, but it was ... November.

"Why aren't we just snuggled in front of a fire instead?" Dylan asked. Rev was bundled in her bright red comforter, and he was cocooned in his sleeping bag. Loup was lying on the floor in a patch of sun.

"I like the fresh air. And that." She nodded to the sparkling water. None of the views from inside was quite the same.

"But you don't like the noise." Someone was chainsawing.

"True. Which is why I usually have my earplugs in and the stereo blasting."

"Oh."

"And do you usually have your fingertipless gloves on?" He nodded to her hands.

"When it's this cold, yes."

"But—"

"You're right." She got up with a sigh, then picked up her coffee and pizza. "I hate this day."

"But it's just begun!"

"No, the day I abandon the screened-in porch. The day the cold makes the noise not worth it, and I move my life indoors."

"Ah. That day. Today is that day?"

"Apparently."

He trailed behind her with his coffee and pizza. Laptops, comforter, and sleeping bag followed. And Loup.

She closed the door. "This afternoon, I guess I'll put the tarps over the screens."

"I'll help."

He set about making a fire. Which was another reason she'd agreed to make that day that day. She actually liked being inside with a fire. But she hated making a fire. It always took her forever and half the time she ended up with a back draft that filled the cabin with smoke. Better to just stay outside on the porch. Dylan, however, seemed to have the knack.

Eventually, snuggled in front of the fire, they returned, again, to the website to fill out the application form.

"You know," Dylan was looking to the right of the fireplace, "you could replace that little window with something considerably larger. Make the view from here as good as the view from your porch. It could be thermal, double-paned, whatever, so you wouldn't lose much heat."

She stared at him.

"What?"

"I've never thought of that. I can't believe I've never thought of that. Damn!"

"What?"

"Old habits! Being poor! I've never thought of that because I've never been able to afford that."

"But you can now. Right? Well, if you sold a bunch of LSAT questions."

"Yeah. By spring maybe." Or earlier, actually. She'd set aside her half of the blasphemy tour money for the next ten years of property taxes, but they were still getting royalty cheques from the book. True, sales had declined somewhat after the first year—Rev suspected that when it first came out, Christians everywhere bought every single copy in their local book store just so they could destroy them, not understanding that the publisher was using the print-on-demand model rather than the limited-run model—but the figures were still substantially higher than those for their book about the new parent licensing law, whereby people who wanted to become parents had to get licensed. In any case, the next royalty cheque would certainly cover a new window, she realized. Plus, they were still getting the occasional cheque from Kyle. Proprietor, Great Hands. (Not what you think.) (Or maybe exactly what you think.)

"Well, you wouldn't want to do it now anyway. What with us going away for the winter," he added.

"Yeah, *that's* why I wouldn't want to do it now," she said. Chances were good that whoever they hired, if they hired local, would remove the old window, and then it would be a week before the new one got put in. 'Course, in that case, she wouldn't want to do it during bug season either, so …

"Okay, so, you've found the application form?"

"I have."

"We know our names."

"We do."

They both started tapping away.

"Can I use your address?" Dylan asked. "It'd look better than 'not applicable.'"

"It would. Yes."

A moment later, he asked, "And what *is* your address?"

She snorted. "I think we need to get stoned for this. If only to justify—this."

Half an hour later, Rev exhaled. "Maybe we should mention how perfect we are." They'd gotten to the Personal Statement part. Amazingly enough.

Dylan giggled.

"I mean perfect for the study. Because you're in touch with your feminine side and I'm in touch with my masculine side."

Dylan considered that. "Just 'in touch'?"

Rev grinned. And burped.

"Actually, they might be looking for just the opposite," Dylan said. "People who are totally fem and totally stud, because if the app works for them, it'll work for anyone."

"Good point. You should mention how smart you are."

Dylan grinned. And took another toke.

"Maybe we should emphasize our age," he said a long while later. "I'll bet most of their applicants are in their twenties. And they'll be wanting to test this across all age cohorts."

"Really smart."

A long while later, during which she tried to figure out how old she was, she said, "Can I just say forty-something?"

"You're embarrassed about your age? You of all people?"

"No, I'm not *embarrassed* about my age. I'm just … pissed. About my age. I stopped keeping track once I hit forty, and I—can't do the math at the moment."

He giggled. "And you stopped keeping track because … ?"

"Because I wanna be 'Eighteen till I die!'" She sang it out. Loud. Dylan winced.

"Well," she corrected, "not eighteen. Twenty-four. Or twenty-seven. Thirty-two. Even thirty-five would be okay. But forty is old."

"But Bryan Adams is forty. Over. So is Tina Turner. And Sting. And Einstein. And Beethoven. And besides, you're over fifty."

"La-la-la, La-la-la," Rev put her hands over her ears.

"Beethoven's dead," Rev said a while later. "See? That's what happens after fifty."

"It happens after forty too. And thirty. That's how math works."

Rev thought about that.

"Really *really* smart."

"Actually," she corrected Dylan's previously implied point, "I think most people die in their forties. They just don't fall down."

"Plus," she knew there was something else, and had it now, "I have no desire to be subjected, relentlessly so, to our culture's attitudes about and consequent behaviours toward those over forty."

"Let alone those over fifty."

"It takes energy to keep saying 'Fuck you.' And my energy is limited. Now. Because I'm over forty."

"Fifty."

"Was that a circular argument?" she asked a moment later. "Because if it was, maybe I can write an LSAT question with it."

"You're smart too."

"Hey! I'll bet we can set the ReGenderApp to whatever age we want! It'll be able to derail not only sexism, but also ageism!!"

"That's the Regender app. Two words. Three if you count 'the'."

"The what?"

"The 'the'."

Rev considered that.

"I like the ReGenderApp better. One word. Well, two if. It's more … fluid."

"How apt! App-ed. Apt." He giggled.

She grinned at him.

"You could be Mrs. Eulalia!" he cried out then. "And I could be Mrs. Enid! No, wait, you're *already* Mrs. Eulalia!"

Rev glared at him.

"So … the point will be to be someone *younger!*"

Rev had stopped glaring. She'd realized she'd *love* to be Mrs. Eulalia. When she hit eighty.

She just wouldn't wear Mrs. Eulalia clothes.

A couple weeks later, Dylan received an email notifying him that he'd been accepted. By mistake, Rev's notice of acceptance had also been sent to him.

"We got accepted!" he called out from the couch as Rev came into the cabin, wrestled to get her winter boots off, and fell over. Only partly because she was favouring her right arm. Because she'd just torn her rotator cuff again. Trying to toss the snow onto the already-six-feet-high piles left at the end of the driveway by the snow plow. Which had been extra-annoying since it had taken her half an hour to *find* the damn shovel. Because the wind had moved it and the snow had buried it. On a patch of ice.

"So," he grinned at her uncertainly. It had been her turn to shovel.

She'd insisted on taking turns. "You're still good to go? To California?"

"Hey, I wonder if that magazine would be interested in an article," she said. A long while later. From in front of a fire. With a mug of hot chocolate. That contained a very large scoop of ice cream bobbing happily.

"Good idea!" He'd written an article for *That Magazine* about the new parent licensing law.

Dylan called the person he'd been dealing with at the magazine, told him what they were about to do, and asked if they were interested in an article. Rev listened to his half of the conversation. Which was pretty much just that. He hung up.

"Well?"

He glanced at her. Didn't want to say.

"He suggested you write a whole book about it, right? Said he knew someone at Penguin, or Pearson, and—"

"Yes."

She'd been trying her whole life to get published. And now ... she found herself near tears. Thinking about all the proposals she'd slaved over. Must've been dozens, over decades. She'd followed all the steps listed on the publishers' websites: she'd prepared an annotated table of contents; she'd written the complete first chapter which, since that was the last chapter one wrote, meant she'd pretty much completed the whole book or at least completed all of the thinking for the whole book (though of course the annotated table of contents requirement meant pretty much the same thing because 'annotated' meant the provision of a synopsis of each chapter); she'd prepared a marketing plan which included a comparison with similar books. All on spec. That is, without payment. With, instead, just hopes and dreams that were, apparently, delusions.

"No one actually does any of that," Dylan said, having heard her mumbling to herself. He decided not to point out that they themselves hadn't done that for their recently published book about their blasphemy tour. They'd been celebrities for a day, and that was enough for an offer to be made. No need for a proposal. Or even a high school diploma indicating a pass in grade nine English. He certainly didn't point out that he'd gotten asked—*asked*—to write a book about the Parent License Act. Solely on the basis of the articles he'd written.

"What? But *I* do! I *did!* They *ask* you to!" Again, near tears. "Why the hell do they ask for it if they don't really want it, don't really need it?"

He shrugged.

She was enraged. It was all just too ... devastating. The injustice of it all.

"You know, that's exactly—"

"One of the things we'll test," he cut her off. "Take one of your many proposals and walk into a publishing company regendered. See what happens."

She nodded.

But in the meantime, she called *That Magazine.* Right then and there. As Rev. A woman.

"Hi, could I please speak to—"

"Todd Markey," Dylan whispered.

"Could I please speak to Todd Markey." She waited a minute. Wondered if maybe she shouldn't've said 'please'. "Hello, I'm wondering if I could pitch an article to you. I see. Okay, thanks."

"Well?"

"He's not accepting any pitches at this time."

"But he just accepted one," Dylan pointed out. Unnecessarily. "Maybe it's because of my reputation. I mean," Dylan added hastily, "maybe it's because I've done articles for them before."

"But Markey didn't say he wasn't accepting pitches from *new* writers. Writers new to the magazine," she clarified. Because she sure as hell wasn't a new writer.

"Okay, call back. Use my phone." He handed it to her.

She looked at it for a very long time.

"Not Alvin."

"James Bond?"

"Hey I wonder how developed the voice modulation program of the ReGenderApp is. We can compare British with Bronxish. And expose ... classism? Culturism?"

Rev chose Brad Pitt, because one variable at a time, and repeated the call. Got Todd Markey on the line again. Said the same thing. *The very same thing.*

She listened to his response then suddenly looked a little panic-stricken. "Um ... 'Ecotourism: An Oxymoron.'"

Dylan grinned.

She provided her email address, then hung up. Looking a little stunned.

"Well?"

"Contract's on its way."

"So we leave when?" Rev asked. It was morning. Well, noon. They were having breakfast. Well, coffee and cold pizza.

Dylan consulted the acceptance letter he'd printed out and a calendar. "Two weeks. The orientation in California starts January 4."

"Okay, so first we should figure out where we want to go. For the five months."

"No, first we should call Kit to let her know."

"Oh right, good."

Dylan got up and used Rev's landline in the kitchen.

Rev raised her eyebrows when he returned. She knew Dylan was afraid Kit might change her mind.

"She said she'd already accepted the promotion," he grinned with relief, "and would let them know she wanted to take her vacation now. Well, starting in two weeks. Said it wouldn't be a problem."

"Cool. So we are indeed good to go!"

"We are! Okay," he sat down on the couch again and started a to-do list. "I'll make travel and housesit arrangements for California. We can decide once we're there, in January, where we want to go next. And next ... That'll be soon enough, right?"

"I guess. We should start at the bottom and work our way up."

Dylan stared at her.

"The bottom of the map. Because the top will be winter in February."

"Ah. Or we could just stay on the left. The whole time."

Rev thought about that. "Could do. Though it might be nice to get a trip out to the east coast. But not until May or June." It occurred to her then that the beta test period would cover not only winter but also bug season. Okay, so maybe it wouldn't be so bad ...

"Have you ever seen the aurora borealis?" he asked. "We could go to Yellowknife."

"No, I haven't, so yes, let's do that! But in June. 'Cuz Yellowknife is *way* at the top." Did she know her geography or what? "No wait, isn't March prime time for the aurora borealis?"

"I don't know. We'll find out."

"Okay. You're right. We should leave this for January. For now, you take care of what needs to be done with California, and I'll take care of what needs to be done with the cabin."

"And your car." It had survived the short month-long housesits Rev had gone on with Dylan, but when they'd returned from their considerably longer blasphemy tour, the battery was dead. She'd had to pay for a tow to the local garage.

"I was going to ask Kit if she'd be willing to come check the house while we're gone," Rev said. Technically, her house insurance policy required that. Practically, since everyone she knew was more than willing to trash her house ... "She might be willing to start my car a few times while she's here."

"That would work. We should ask her to bring Loup with her when she comes. So she can see that we're not here. That we're not back yet. That she should stay with Flaker at Kit's place." Leaving her was going to be hard.

"Good idea. Anything else?" Rev had started a to-do list as well. Because she sure as hell wouldn't remember all this. Being over fifty and all.

"Ask her if she'll drive us to the bus station? If our flight leaves from Toronto, we'll take the bus to the airport, right? Though," he started thinking out loud, "if they're paying for everything, we could fly from here to Toronto ... Ask her if she'll drive us to the airport. The one in Sudbury."

"Okay." She made a note. "Do we need to get anything special? For ... everything? Everywhere?"

"Don't think so. We can buy whatever special stuff we need ...

everywhere. Can't take much with us anyway."

"Right."

"We need to pack though," Dylan pointed out, then clarified, "our unspecial stuff. But that shouldn't be a big deal." They'd both kept their packing lists from their trips to Europe. In theory. Dylan didn't actually have a packing list, since he took pretty much everything he owned. It all fit into his knapsack. And Rev … after the first trip, she'd modified her list, then kept the revision. In order *not* to have to go through that again.

"Still. We should consider whether any changes to our packing lists are warranted."

"Just don't forget to pack your passport. And your cell phone. You don't use it here, but—oh." Dylan started another list. Things to do once they got to California. Because her cell phone wouldn't work there. Or would, but only at great expense.

Next day, Dylan found the perfect housesit. It was on the edge of the Haight-Asbury region, which was his first choice … because. It had originally been a B&B, called M&M, but then Mike died. His daughter inherited the house and decided to turn it into a housesit. Mike's dog, Moe, came with the house.

Of course he did, Dylan thought. It's his house.

Moe was used to having guests, the listing said. In fact, Moe *liked* having guests. He let them sleep in the guest room, use the bathroom, and even watch tv with him. But he drew the line at providing breakfast for them.

Hence a housesit instead of a B&B. Made perfect sense.

Day after that, Rev and Dylan went into town. Rev needed antifreeze for the pipes and a new tarp for the porch. Dylan needed a lot of new shoes. Apparently.

"They don't have shoes in California?"

"If I buy new shoes in California, it'll be too late."

"You won't have feet anymore? Once we get to California?"

"No, I won't have been able to wear them. Before I go."

"Ah." They'd surely be doing some hiking. He wanted to break them in to avoid blisters.

He also bought a new knapsack.

Soon enough, too soon, the day of their departure came. Well, the day before the day before the day of their departure came. They'd decided to take Loup over two days ahead of time, just to be sure the arrangement would work out. Also, since Kit had agreed to drive them into town to the airport, as well as check on Rev's cabin and start her car every now and then, they thought that taking Loup over, leaving her with Flaker in the pen, and then all *three* of them driving away right then and there would be too traumatic.

The day before (that is, the day before the day before), Dylan had gone with Loup for one last all-day-long bike ride slash run through the forest. Partly because they both loved it and he wanted to do it one more time—not one *last* last time, he assured Loup, because he'd be back—and partly to tire her out, a bit, so she'd be, perhaps, a bit less anxious about the move. And his departure.

Of course, they'd taken her to Kit's place before. And left her. During hunting season. But that was just for the daytime. Dylan always came and got her in the evening so she could sleep at home. At home with him.

Despite Loup's discomfort with riding in a car, they drove over. They thought that she'd accept their driving away without her more easily than their walking away without her. And they'd planned to drive away *not* back toward home, but in the other direction. It would mean a long detour to get back home, but no matter.

Loup jumped out of the car, happy to see Flaker, and Kit.

"Hey, the big day," Kit said, smiling at them. "Come on in and let's get her settled."

Once in the living room, Dylan shrugged his knapsack off his shoulder. "Her food and water dishes are in here," he explained. "And her blanket. And a bunch of bright bandanas. She likes the one with the yellow dinosaurs the best."

Kit smiled. "I'll bet she does." She turned to Loup. "You'd *love* to bring down a yellow dinosaur, wouldn't you?" She ruffled her neck fur.

They went into the kitchen and put Loup's dishes on the floor beside Flakers. Loup sniffed at the arrangement and looked up at Dylan.

"It's okay, Loup. You're going to stay here with Flaker and Kit, but just for a while. I'll be back."

Next, they put her blanket on the couch next to Flaker's blanket and encouraged Loup to jump up onto it. She did. But then jumped back down right away. Dylan set his knapsack on the floor beside the couch.

"It has my scent on it," he explained. "I bought another one to take on our trip."

"Okay, good idea. I'll leave it right there."

"And," Dylan handed over the garbage bag he'd been holding.

Puzzled, Kit took the bag.

"They're shoes. Old shoes of mine. Loup chews on them."

Ah.

Kit peeked into the bag.

"There's one for each month."

Rev snorted. Loup could chew through one in a day.

"I'll send more. As I get them."

"Okay ... "

As Dylan took one out and gave it to Loup, Kit wrote her mailing address on a piece of paper and gave it to him. She wouldn't be surprised if they'd never noted the number on her mailbox. After all, she'd never noted theirs.

"The new ones don't have as much 'me' on them, so maybe keep them in the bag for last."

"Understood," Kit nodded.

It was the wolf sanctuary all over again. At one point, they'd thought it best if Froot Loup found a pack, lived with her own, and they actually drove to a wolf sanctuary to make that happen. But the decision, and the drive, tore at Dylan's heart. How could he leave her? How could he possibly just walk away from her ...

But Loup had been terrified. She cowered, leaning against Dylan's legs. Turned out wolves form packs with their relatives. And they don't adopt outsiders. So they happily brought her back home with them.

A couple days later, Corn Flake showed up, and it was packmates-at-first-sight.

"She'll be fine," Rev assured him. "It's not like the wolf sanctuary. Her pack is here. Corn Flake."

Dylan nodded.

"And she knows Kit. Look, she's not clinging to you. She's okay with this."

It was true that Loup wasn't clinging to Dylan, but whether she was okay with what was going on …

"I'll take her, the two of them, for a walk in the bush every day when I get home," Kit assured him.

"Okay, good. She'll want that."

"So will I. After eight frickin' hours at a desk … " She didn't regret accepting the promotion, but it was going to take some getting used to.

"And she'll be safe during the day," Rev pointed out. "Half an acre safe."

"I know, but—"

"In fact," Kit had been thinking, "I'm going to miss the out-trips, so I think the three of us will have to go camping every weekend in the forest. Think she'll like that?" Kit reached out to stroke Loup.

"She'll *love* that!"

"Camping? In the middle of winter?" Rev said. What she meant was 'Are you nuts?'

Kit grinned. "Our trips have been once a month, remember?" It was true. Once a month, they'd been looking after Corn Flake. "Year-round. So that means … "

"Oh. Right. See?" Rev looked at Dylan.

"I've got all my gear," Kit continued. "It'd be a shame not to keep using it."

"But don't go during hunting season," Dylan said anxiously.

"Of course not," she said. What she meant was 'Are you nuts?'

"She'll send pictures," Rev tried again. Not because she really really wanted to go on their planned trip, but because she knew Dylan did. And he also really really wanted to be with Loup.

"Videos," Kit upped it. "In fact, now that we've got frickin' high-speed, sort of, the two of you can have regular skype calls."

"Yes!" That hadn't occurred to Dylan. "Wait—do you think Loup can see—I mean—"

"We'll find out. For sure she'll hear your voice though."

"She will!" He crouched down beside her then and tousled her neck fur. She licked his face. "I have to go," he said the words he always said when he left, and came back. "You stay here. I'll be back." Loup looked into his eyes. Then sat down.

"Good wolf." Dylan stood up. "You stay here," he repeated. "I'll be back." He tried to say it like he was just driving into town. Then he knelt down and put his arm around her one more time. She could smell his anxiety. He wasn't just driving into town. Still. He said he'd be back. Okay then.

"Is it all right if I call you every now and then?" he looked up at Kit. "Just for an update?" Because this would be their first overnight apart.

"Of course," Kit smiled. She understood. She'd been the same when she first had to leave Flaker.

He stood up again, turned toward the door, then turned back to Loup again. "Stay here with Kit and Flaker. I'll be back, I promise!"

Rev nudged him gently out the door.

"Don't you dare look back," she said. "You'll start crying."

"I will, yes." He looked back, saw Loup at the window, watching him leave. Dylan waved. As he always did. "I'll be back," he called out one last time. His eyes watering.

As soon as she saw Dylan drive away, Loup went to see what Flaker was up to.

And Kit told him that. When he called for an update an hour later.

"She's okay? What's she doing?"

"She's fine. The two of them are lying in the sun."

An hour later.

"She's still okay?"

"She's fine. They're investigating the tree."

Dylan was both relieved and upset that she wasn't howling at the gate in the direction of Rev's cabin.

"Hey, me again, she's—"

"Sleeping. Because *it's two o'clock in the morning!*"

O ddly enough, the flight from Sudbury to Toronto cost as much as the flight from Toronto to San Francisco. The airlines obviously weren't figuring in the environmental damage when they calculated their air fares. Used to be, that would have been a consideration that might have made the two of them choose the bus instead, even though the ride would have been much longer, but they both figured the planet was already past the point of no return. Unlike Trump, they'd both read Klein's *This Changes Everything*.

As soon as they landed at Pearson Airport, Dylan called Kit. Loup was fine.

They checked in and were given a form to fill out. Whether it was for customs or security or the airline, Rev didn't know. Or care. She was tired. And not looking forward to the next five hour flight. Especially after the last two hour flight. When was someone going to invent a Transporter app?

She stared at the form in front of her. First in frustration, then in disbelief.

"What?" said Dylan, ever sensitive to her—to her.

"It's asking for my gender. Not my sex. My *gender.*"

"You don't have one."

"Not only that—and there's no box for 'None' or 'N/A'—but what business is it of theirs what my personal preferences are? 'Gender' refers to 'masculine' and 'feminine' which just refers to some arbitrary composite of preferences, from clothing choices to career aspirations."

"You could tell them that."

She ignored him. "*And* the boxes are labelled 'male' and 'female'. That's sex, not gender." She corrected the question, replacing 'male' and 'female' with 'masculine' and 'feminine' then wrote 'None of your goddamned business' beside it. Dylan replaced 'gender' with 'sex' and also wrote 'None of your goddamned business'. Together they'd fix the world after all, goddamn it.

The person who took the forms back from them didn't even look at them. Which, they realized, truly they did, was probably a good thing.

"You know," Rev said, once they'd gotten a couple of milkshakes and started looking for a couple of empty chairs, "they've got the app named wrong too. It should be called the ReSexApp. It changes our appearance from male to female or vice versa."

At first, she walked right past two empty chairs near a trio of heavily-made-up women with jangling bracelets and long polished fingernails, but since she couldn't detect any perfume, and all of the other chairs seemed taken, or at least claimed, by big, gaudy purses, she circled back.

"Does it?" Dylan settled in beside her. "I mean, will it give you an Adam's apple, make your hands a bit larger, your hips narrower ... I was thinking it would just change our appearance from masculine to feminine. And vice versa."

"But how will it do that? Does it change our clothing? Will it put make-up on your face? Put some feminine jewelry on you?"

They hadn't really thought about this.

"If it doesn't change our clothing, we're going to have to choose our attire very carefully. Maybe that's included in the training."

"I'd think the app would have to. Change our clothing. I suppose it could change just the visible parts of our physical bodies and leave the rest, but wouldn't it be *easier* to change everything?"

"So it's both? A ReSexApp *and* a ReGenderApp?"

"Well, no, it can't *be* a ReSexApp. It can't actually change our biological reality."

"But an Adam's apple isn't part of gender, so if it puts an Adam's apple on me, isn't it changing my sex? Or at least changing the visible, secondary sexual characteristics?"

"Yeah … " Dylan thought it through. "And if it doesn't change our clothing—and it certainly can't change our personal preferences about—*anything*—it isn't really a ReGenderApp. Either."

"Hmm. I wonder why, how, the word got messed up. Sex. It was very clear in the 70s that 'sex' referred to one's biology and 'gender' referred to the social construct."

Dylan nodded. "It was also very clear that the two needn't be related."

"More than that, it was clear that gender was used to support sexism. Which is why so many thinking women just said fuck it. Fuck being feminine."

"Maybe in the 80s or 90s, something—When did this happen?"

"When I wasn't looking, that's for sure."

Dylan grinned.

"Maybe in the 80s or 90s," he suggested, "people became prudish. Again. Didn't want to say 'sex'. Because 'sex' also means, like, '*having* sex.'"

"Well, they should've changed *that* word. Phrase. Not replaced it with another word already in use for something else. In fact, I've always hated 'having sex'."

Dylan grinned again.

"I mean, the phrase doesn't even *mean* anything *right*. One doesn't *have* sex. One *can't—have* sex. One can engage in sexual behaviour. But I suppose that's too many words."

"Maybe 'having sex' is just a short form for 'having sexual intercourse'. Did 'gender' start replacing 'sex' when sexual intercourse stopped being the norm?" No, that wasn't the critical question. Besides, *did* sexual intercourse stop being the norm?

"I don't know. *You're* the historian."

"Am not. Didn't actually finish my degree, remember? Not that a history degree makes one a historian. Besides, most history degree programs don't study the history of—what are we talking about?"

"The history of linguistic fuck-ups."

"Yeah. That."

Dylan was silent.

"You were talking about when the phrase 'having sex'—"

"Oh yeah. Maybe when sexual intercourse stopped being the norm and other forms of sexual engagement became common, such as blowjobs—"

"*Another* stupid word. It's got nothing to do with *blowing*."

"And pity it's called a *job*."

"Well ... " Rev didn't finish that sentence.

"The whole concept of 'trans' is messed up too," she said a while later. After she noisily finished her milkshake. "I mean I can understand 'transsexual'. That just describes, or *should* just describe, someone who wants sexual body modifications. No different than, though perhaps the most extreme of, all sorts of body modifications we make. From losing or gaining weight to piercing to cosmetic surgery to steroids to beta blockers to—"

"But taking beta blockers just makes just a temporary change. Shouldn't we differentiate between temporary and permanent body modifications?"

Rev thought about that. "Why?"

"Don't know. You were saying?" He grinned.

"That I can understand 'transsexual,' but what the hell is 'trans*gender*' except wanting, doing, what society says you shouldn't? Because of your sex. Every woman who refuses to wear make-up and shave her legs is transgendered."

"Doesn't transgender refer to people who think they've been born into the wrong body?"

"No, that would be, *should* be, transsexual. More precisely, thinking you've been born into the wrong body would be a motive for *becoming* transsexual. Though if a man, say, feels he's been born into the wrong body and wants to act like a woman, whatever the hell that means, and usually it just means acting feminine, which is *completely* different, then why doesn't he just act feminine? You don't need a uterus and breasts to wear mascara and a pink dress. Or whatever.

"Getting hormone treatment and surgery suggests they want to *change* their sex, not that they were born with the wrong sex."

"But if you think you've been born into the wrong sex, wouldn't you want to change your sex?"

"Yeah, but don't they say they feel like they're a woman in a man's body? That's impossible. Unless you're intersex, you're a woman *or* a man. What they *should* be saying is they feel *feminine* in a man's body."

"Okay ... "

"And to that I say, big wup. I mean I feel masculine half the time, given the ridiculous gender dichotomy, and I've got a woman's body. That doesn't mean I'm going to run out and get a hysterectomy. Or a penis." She shuddered. At that last part.

"Even if sex is brain-based," she continued, having gotten up, disposed of her empty milkshake container, then returned to her chair, "and they feel like they have a female *brain* in a male *body*— apart from brain is body, it's the brain that produces hormones! The pituitary gland controls the chemicals our ovaries and testicles produce. So are they saying they have a pituitary gland that sends signals to ovaries that don't exist? Signals that, even though not resulting in the production of estrogen, make them feel like people who *have* estrogen? How the fuck does *that* work?"

Dylan had no idea how the fuck that worked.

"And let's say they *do* have a female brain—whatever the hell that might be—and somehow absent ovaries, it *does* produce estrogen. At the level that distinguishes females from males. Which makes them feel like a woman inside a man's body. *Then there would be no need for the hormone treatments!*"

"So," Dylan was trying to keep up, "are you suggesting that most transsexuals change their gender *and* their sex? Or want to? Change their gender and their sex?"

Rev nodded.

"Interesting. Because they're being radical and conservative at the same time," Dylan mused. "Radical in making such an extreme body modification, and conservative in embracing not only the concept of gender but its alignment with sex."

Rev looked at him. That *was* interesting.

One of the three heavily-made-up women a few chairs down leaned forward and gave Rev a haughty look. "You don't know what the fuck you're talking about," she said. Then leaned back. Case closed. Apparently.

Rev stared. So much for conversational engagement. Then she intensified her stare. Saw an Adam's apple. Noticed the size of 'her' hands and feet. Ditto the other two. And the several 'women' who had, in the meantime, returned to their claimed chairs.

Was there a trans convention somewhere? She looked around for some FtMs. Nada. Of course not. They wouldn't be allowed in the tree house. Because contrary to their protestations, MtFs were still Ms. They still had testosterone and/or a lifetime of be-a-man pressure and/or whatever it was that made them aggressive assholes. Because it was unlikely a woman would have—

"Are you all on your way to a convention?" Dylan asked cheerily. He loved when Jehovah's Witnesses came knocking on his door. Always invited them in. Sat them down. Made a pot of tea.

"No, we're all on our way to LA for surgery," one of the others replied. "Top surgery, bottom surgery ... " s/he giggled.

"Why?" That was Rev. Of course.

"Because we were born into the wrong gender, dear."

Dylan winced. Rev ignored it. For now.

"Gender's just sociocultural pressure," she said. "We're not born into it. We can take it or leave it."

"Well, not that easily," Dylan interjected, then took a sip of his milkshake.

"True. Most of us were conditioned relentlessly from birth. But there's a lot to which we can just say no. So," she turned back to him/her, "why don't you just say no? Grow a—spine. Dear."

The MtF huffed and puffed and gasped. "Bitch."

Rev turned to the one beside the one who had huffed and puffed. And gasped. "How do you know?"

"Know what?"

"That you were born into the wrong gender?" Rev genuinely wanted to know.

"Oh, well," s/he fluttered her fake eyelashes, "I've always felt like a woman. Deep inside."

"And how does that feel?" Rev asked. "Deep inside."

"Don't you know?" s/he asked, smiling at her.

"No. I don't know what it's like to be a bat. For the bat."

S/he looked at Rev. Yes, as if she was crazy. Bat-shit crazy.

Dylan grinned. He was familiar with the problem. Nagel's problem. Well, he was familiar with Rev's problem too, but—

"I know what it's like to feel healthy," Rev continued, "only because I've been sick. But I've never been male, so I can't really say which bits of what I feel like are due to being female and which bits are due to being human. Except for a few obvious things. For example, I can say what it feels like to have a uterus because the damn thing made me feel like crap once a month. But you don't have a uterus, so that can't be what you mean when you say you feel like a woman.

"I can't even say what it feels like to have estrogen. Maybe what I feel like is because of the dopamine and vasopressin coursing through my body, and not the estrogen. If I started taking estrogen-blockers, I guess I'd know. But otherwise—

"Are *you* referring to how it feels to have all that estrogen coursing through your body? Is that what you mean when you say you feel like a woman? No, wait. You *don't have* much estrogen coursing through your body. And won't, until you start with the estrogen shots. Until you start changing your *male* body *into* a female body."

The MtF she'd been speaking to also huffed and puffed. And gasped. Two down, Rev thought, turning to the third. The Haughty One.

"You've always felt like a woman too? Deep inside?"

"Yes, I have," his/her smile dripped disdain.

"Okay, are you using the word 'woman' to refer to sex or gender? Because if you aren't, in fact, biologically female, you can't possibly feel female.

"And if you're using 'woman' to refer to gender, then why do you need to change sex? As I've said, gender is a social construct; it isn't dependent on sex. If it *were,* how do we explain effeminate men and tomboys? Which is," she turned to Dylan, "*another* really stupid word. Tomboy. It should *at least* be 'tomgirl'."

"Or 'agnesboy.' 'Lilyboy'? No, 'bettyboy!' I like that one best. Bettyboy." He grinned.

"Effeminate men and tomboys were born into the wrong gender," the MtF said, fluttering his/her scarlet fingernails in the air. For some reason.

"You mean the wrong sex," Rev said. "And—oh! You want gender to match sex! It's like wanting your shoes to match your purse!" Because his/her shoes did indeed match her purse. They were both neon pink with little bows. "Why? Why is that so important?"

"It just is!"

"Ah," Rev leaned back, with great satisfaction. "Thank you. That was a very clear explanation. 'It just is.' You've obviously thought about this a lot."

S/he glared at Rev. In a very unfeminine way.

"Since sex is binary, and you want gender to match sex, you must want gender to be binary too. You want there to be masculine males and feminine females and everyone else be damned. Surgically and pharmaceutically altered."

Rev turned to one of the other MtFs. "You too have always felt like a woman? Deep down?"

S/he nodded.

"And by that you mean ... "

"Oh, you know," s/he smiled. And it was such an infuriatingly patronizing smile. She was definitely *not* a woman.

"No, I don't. I know what it feels like to be *treated* like a woman in a sexist society. But that can't be what you mean either because you surely haven't been treated like a woman."

"A girl can hope," one of the others piped up, and they all tittered.

Seriously? Were they so deluded? So naïve about sexism? Rev set that aside. For the moment.

"She's talking about your gender identity," one of the others joined in. So very unhelpfully.

"My what?"

"Your gender identity!"

"I don't have one of those. Do I?" she turned to Dylan.

"Don't think so."

"Then what do you call yourself?"

Rev thought long and hard about that. So many answers to choose from.

"Well, I don't call myself a woman, if that's what you mean, assuming 'woman' means 'feminized human' instead of 'female human.' Actually, either way … "

"So what *do* you call yourself?" That was the one who had called her a bitch.

"Generally speaking? A person. Though sometimes I call myself a genius."

Dylan grinned.

"The problem is other people," Rev said. Sartre was *so* right. "*Other people* call me a woman. *Other people* identify me as female. Whether or not it's relevant to the situation at hand. And their doing so enables a hierarchy based on sex in which women, females, are subordinated.

"And that would be the only time I refer to myself as a woman and/or female: to call attention to people's sexist treatment of me. But, as I said, generally speaking, I call myself a person."

"Yeah, but what about all the things you do to make yourself pretty?"

Dylan choked on his milkshake.

"When *I* say I feel like a woman," another MtF spoke up, "I mean that I feel like I've got a woman's brain."

"A female brain? A small brain?"

S/he glared at her. Yup. Definitely a man. Thinks size matters.

"One, how do you know? Two, could you give me references for the research that shows there are differences—significant differences of the kind you're probably thinking of—between male and female brains?"

"Honey, I don't need research."

Right. Why complicate the matter with, oh, facts and stuff.

"Even if you were born with ambiguous genitalia," Rev said a moment later, "and the doctor announced that you were male, and it turned out that you're female—In that case, you'd already have the 'right' body."

"In that case," one of the others spoke up, "the doctor should have shut the fuck up until they did a saliva test. For chromosomes."

"The doctor should have shut the fuck up anyway," Rev suggested. "Might help us move away from THERE IS NOTHING MORE IMPORTANT ABOUT A PERSON THAN HIS OR HER—SEE?—SEX."

"Okay," Dylan had been busy, very busy, working it all through, "so what about intersexed people?" He looked at the one who'd mentioned, surprisingly, chromosomes. "They're born with a sort of mismatch between chromosomes, chemicals, and body parts, right? *Then* it would make sense to say you were born into the wrong body, wouldn't it?"

"Not really," Rev replied. "I mean, suppose you *were* born into an intersexed body. How can you say that feels wrong? What can you possibly be comparing it to? Bat."

"Right ... "

"I'm not saying body dysphoria isn't real," Rev said to the ... people. "In fact, I experience every day the mismatch between what's inside and what's outside: I look like a woman over forty—"

"Fifty."

"But I don't feel like a woman over forty."

"Fifty."

"I still feel energetic and impassioned, not bland and resigned. But don't you see? I'm using as a reference all the stereotypes society has crammed down my throat and all my personal experience, which is rather limited, of other people who are over forty."

"Fifty."

"Then again, I *do* feel like a woman over forty."

"Fifty."

"I must. Because I *am* over forty."

"Butter."

"So this must be what a woman over forty—" She waited.

He just grinned at her. She grinned back.

"—can feel like. So," she got to her point, because she did have one, "if you're in a male body, what you feel like *must* be male. Maybe it doesn't match the stereotypes or what you see around you, but that's a whole different issue."

"But," Dylan backed up a bit, "you can see how having a mismatch between the various bits might motivate the desire for surgery. To make the bits match each other."

"Yeah," Rev conceded, "if you *wanted* the bits to match each other. See? It's a problem only if you believe the gender bits *should* match the sex bits."

"But if you've got bits of both … Bits of both *sexes* … "

"It would be interesting to find out why the bits that are considered more … definitive *are* considered more definitive," Rev mused. "And whether it matters how many or how much of any of the bits one has. For example, is a female who has undergone a hysterectomy and a bilateral mastectomy still female? Is a post-menopausal and thus low-estrogen female still female?"

"Maybe we should just use chromosomes," Dylan suggested, nodding to the person who'd mentioned the saliva test. "XX is female, XY is male, other is intersex."

"Yeah. Any of you intersexed?"

Everyone studied their nails.

"If you were intersexed," Rev continued without anyone else's input, because she could do that, "wouldn't that just mean you get to choose, with more freedom than the rest of us, what gender shit you want?"

"Wouldn't that depend on which bits were which?" Dylan suggested. "Which bits were visible? And how visible?"

"Yeah. I could be intersexed," Rev said then. "I mean, all my secondary characteristics could be female, and my body parts could be female, but I could have XY chromosomes."

"Could you?" Dylan asked. "Don't chromosomes *determine* secondary characteristics and body parts?"

"I don't know. Maybe. Any of you know?"

Everyone continued studying their nails.

"And if you, *you* you," Dylan looked at Rev, "*did* have XY chromosomes," he was thinking out loud, "that could explain … nothing," he concluded. "There is nothing you are that's incompatible with female. It's just incompatible with feminine."

"Yes!" She glared at everyone. Well, everyone except Dylan.

"Honestly?" she summarized, "I think you all just don't like the way you were genderized. Well, again, big wup. Welcome to my world."

"Why do *you* do things to make yourself pretty?" Dylan turned to the one who'd mentioned pretty.

"Yeah, why the over-the-top get-up?" Rev added. "I mean, really, you all look like you've just come off the set of *The Rocky Horror Picture Show.*"

"Oh, I *love* that show!" Dylan said. "'It's just a jump to the left,'" he jumped up. And everyone jumped up with him. Well, everyone except Rev. And except for Dylan, the jumps weren't really—they were all wearing fuck-me heels.

"'And then a step to the right,'" they all shouted along, stepping to the right.

"'With your hands on your hips.'" A dozen overly manicured hands slammed onto virtually non-existent hips.

"'And—' I forget the rest," Dylan sat down, sadly.

"Madness takes its toll." That was Rev. When one of the MtFs fell over.

"Easy for you to criticize!" s/he cried from the floor. "You don't have to prove every day that you're a real woman!" The others nodded their agreement as they helped her up and into her chair.

Rev stared at her. "You're wearing *fake* eyelashes to prove you're a *real* woman?" Too rich.

"It, this," she waved her scarlet nails, at her ensemble, "lets us *pass* as women."

"Oh, well, that's completely different! Why do you want to *pass* as women? Do you actually want to be *treated like women?* Are all of you ready to take a 40% cut in pay? To have your contributions to society mocked? To be forced to be an incubator? You're getting awfully angry with my rational challenges. How the hell will you survive the irrational ones?"

"Oh don't worry about us, dear, we will survive!"

Dylan winced again.

"'At first I was afraid, I was petrified,'" a voice piped up from the other end.

"'Kept thinking I could never live without you by my side,'" two more joined the song.

"STOP!" Rev glared at them. "Just—stop. You do *not* get to appropriate that song! It's for all the women who need to leave shitty men. It's not for you! None of you is such a woman.

"You have no idea what it's like to be a woman in an abusive relationship. To have been fed lines all your life—that is, for ten, twenty, thirty *years*—about standing by your man, making him a better person, being a doormat, being a fucking martyr.

"And then, when finally, *finally*, you work up the courage to leave, because he's beaten you to a pulp once too often—though once *is* too often—to be absolutely terrified to do so because he will find you and kill you—"

Dylan stared at her. Surely she—Then he remembered she'd worked at a women's shelter.

"If you want people to think you're a woman, then act like one!" she resumed. Angrily. Loudly. "Make polite requests, not demands. Take 'no' for an answer. Do not resort to insult or threat. Be quiet. Be small. Be subordinate. Be apologetic. Do not feel entitled to ... anything.

"And do *not* sing that song until you've come out the other side. After years of being told to sit down and shut up, after years of understanding that your opinion doesn't count, after years of assuming you know less than everyone else, after years of being told to be sensitive to everyone else's feelings, to respect them, to accommodate them.

"And Caitlin Jenner?" Rev was on her feet, looking around the terminal. "If you're listening? *Give back all the endorsements you got when you were Bruce!*"

Everyone stared at her. What?

"I don't think you're respecting our feelings," the one with the turquoise purse and matching shoes said a few moments later.

"You're right."

She saw that she needed to say more. Sigh.

"If I *feel* handicapped, should that entitle me to use the designated-for-handicapped-people parking spaces? If I *feel* like I have a learning disability, is that enough for me to get extra time on exams? No. I need to *prove* it. I need to have documentation for my handicap and my learning disability. *Feeling* like a woman is not enough to get access to women's restrooms." Rev stopped. "And what else? What else is it you're clamouring about? What else do you want?"

"We want to be treated like women!"

Rev sighed. And, so, ignored her.

Him.

"But how exactly do you want to be treated?" Dylan asked. "What is it about being treated like a man that you do not want to happen anymore? And what instead do you want to *start* happening?"

"I want ... ," one of them said, searching for the answer, "I want to be part of a gentler world."

"I don't want the shit beaten out of me because of my feminine nature," another added.

"News flash," Rev said quietly. And tiredly. "Men beat the shit out of women every day."

In the long silence that followed, Dylan stepped away, around a corner, then down the terminal, further than he anticipated, to get a good signal in order to call Kit once more before they boarded. Loup was fine. Yes, she was eating. Yes, she was playing with Flaker. No, she hadn't taken down a deer.

When he returned, all of the MtFs were gone.

"What'd you do, eat them?"

Rev shrugged. "Same old, same old."

Dylan raised his eyebrows.

"They said I was difficult. One called me a cow. Another, a cunt."

"Men!"

"What *I* said! Their insistence that I respect and affirm their delusion is nothing more, nor less, than male entitlement on display. That's when they went to get Security," she said sadly. "Said I was transphobic and violating their rights."

"Their right to what? To be able to sit in an airport terminal without being hassled?"

"What *I* said! Since when is that a right, right?"

"So ... when Security came ... "

"I said that I was transgender myself so how could I be not respecting their rights? I know, never mind that gap. I pointed out that I wasn't wearing make-up, that I wasn't wearing jewelry, that half the clothes I have on were purchased in the men's department ..."

"And the Security guy—it was a man, right?"

"Of course. Odd that men are the ones to assigned to protect us, when men are the ones we need protection against. Anyway, he was confused."

"No doubt."

"So *then* I said that I might be transexual too, seeing as I had a uterus but no breasts."

"And *then* you took your shirt off." He sighed. She'd had a bilateral mastectomy a few years back.

She nodded. "Evidence. It's important."

"And then he charged you with indecent exposure." They'd been here before. While on their blasphemy tour.

"Yes! And I said that indecent exposure is when one exposes female breasts—go figure—but since I didn't *have* any breasts ... "

"And he said that didn't matter. You were female and—"

"And I said that if what was indecent was a female *chest* and not necessarily female *breasts*, then when Lola—"

"Lola?"

"Yeah, didn't one of them say her name was Lola?"

"I don't think any of them gave us their names."

"Hm. Okay. Regardless, I said that when Lola got his, or her, breasts, it would be okay for him, or her, to go topless but not me?"

"And he had a cognitive meltdown."

"No, first Lola whipped off her shirt. His shirt. S/he's already got one breast. Said s/he could afford only one at a time."

"You're kidding."

Rev shook her head. "*Then* the Security guy had a cognitive meltdown. Told Lola and her friends to get on the plane and—"

"Put you on the no-fly list," Dylan sat down heavily. "And now we have to take the bus all the way to California."

"Canada doesn't have a no-fly list. Does it?"

"Well, a no-land list, then. And now we have to take the bus all the way to California," he repeated.

"No, we can take a plane."

Dylan turned his head and saw their plane take off.

"Just not that one."

inally, *finally*, they were able to board the plane. A plane. As they made their way toward their seats, fumes started giving Rev a headache. Shit. Oh well, she'd deal with that in a minute. She stowed her bag in the overhead bin. Dylan did the same. They took their seats, Dylan the window seat, Rev the aisle seat. Across from a woman. The woman who was the source of the fumes. But before Rev had a chance to open her mouth, the announcements began.

"Ladies and gentlemen, the Captain has turned on the Fasten Seat Belt sign … "

Two minutes later they were airborne, and the stewards started with the in-flight drinks.

"Would you please wipe off your perfume?" Rev said loudly to the woman.

"I beg your pardon?"

"Your perfume. It's already given me a headache."

The woman said nothing.

"Literally." Rev stared at her. "You may as well have punched me in the head." A few people turned. Started listening.

The woman smiled. As many women did. To pacify, to make the problem go away. To deny the existence of the problem.

"You think that's something to smile about? Punching me in the head?"

The smile faded.

"Good. Now please wipe off your perfume. With rubbing alcohol or non-scented soap or something."

"I have a right to wear whatever I want!" She'd caught up.

Rev sighed. "No. You don't. Your right to wear whatever you want stops when what you wear affects me. And as I've already explained, the chemicals you've doused yourself with have given me a headache. Next they will make me nauseous. I'm already prone to motion sickness, and I can't guarantee that the Gravol I took is up to the extra demand. I *can* guarantee that if I throw up, I'll intentionally spew in your direction."

She huffed. "I don't believe I have any unscented soap. Or rubbing alcohol." She turned away. Ending the conversation.

"So be it." Rev shrugged. Started to make slight gagging sounds.

Half a dozen miniature bottles of vodka, rum, and gin came flying through the air. Three hit the woman with not inconsequential force.

"Which is why," Rev said to Dylan, as if she was continuing the conversation that had ended several hours ago—because she was, because it had not, "I'd really be interested in studies—though they'd have to consist mainly of anecdotal, subjective evidence—of MtFs and FtMs, pre- and post-hormone treatment. Maybe we'd *find out* what it's like to be female and male, at least to the extent of biochemical influence."

"Well, we already know what additional testosterone does to men," Dylan said. "That should be a clue."

Rev nodded. Out of habit, her head swivelled toward the window, but even without the land in sight far, far below, the view triggered vertigo. She snapped her head back and focused on the seatback a few inches from her nose.

"I think what bothers me most about MtFs," she said a moment later, "is that they're so amazingly clueless about sexism. They lose their male privilege when they start identifying as women, but they think that happens because they're trans. So they all cry *transphobia!*

"But any unwelcome, unexpected, treatment—being ignored, being excluded, whatever—is probably happening because they're no longer identifying, identified, as male. They should be crying *sexism!*

"Besides which," she muttered, "said treatment isn't necessarily due to fear. Phobia."

"It would explain their suicide rates," Dylan had been googling. "Twice as many MTFs as FTMs commit suicide."

Rev nodded. "On top of everything else, they can't handle, are broadsided by, the sudden and almost complete disenfranchisement ..."

"I think that's probably true of most men," Dylan suggested. "When it happens. When they lose their hair. Then their jobs. Then their testosterone."

Rev stared at him. She'd never considered any of that to be disenfranchisement. Yes, she knew men were inordinately upset when they started losing their hair, and losing one's job was a blow to one's esteem, and a loss of status, especially for men, but ... she hadn't added the loss of testosterone into the mix—It explained a lot. About retired men. Their increased use of power tools, for starters.

"Sexism 101 should be mandatory in high school."

"Yeah."

"Though it's probably also happening," she suggested, "the unwelcome, presumably aggressive, treatment," she clarified, "because people— most people—conservative people—hate rebels in general. Don't rock the boat. Because they're inside. The boat.

"Especially," she added, "conservative people holding onto gender with everything they've got."

"But I thought we established that transpeople weren't rebels. They're accepting, reinforcing, gender norms."

"Hm. It's mostly *men* who assault them, right?" She was thinking that men were particularly fond of gender because it enabled their superior status.

"Yeah, but it's mostly men who assault."

"They want to be able to use women's restrooms," Dylan said a while later. Still googling. "You asked what they want. But you knew that one. Okay, they also—"

"*Why* do they want to be able to use the women's restrooms? Just because they're now women?"

"I imagine it's also because if they go into a men's restroom looking ... the way they do, the other men will give them trouble. Maybe rough them up a bit."

"Ah." Rev hadn't thought about that. Because "When I go into a women's restroom, even though half the clothes I wear are, or could be, men's clothes, and even though I don't wear make-up or jewelry, and even though I don't even have breasts anymore, the other women don't really give a damn. They certainly won't assault me."

"Yeah. Well. They also want to compete in women's sports," Dylan continued. "They want to be able to apply for women's scholarships. Maybe that one's a good idea."

She turned toward—then away. Window.

"Because," Dylan answered her implied question, "why should scholarships be categorized by sex? Or sports teams, for that matter?"

"I can agree with you about scholarships. I guess such scholarships used to compensate for the disadvantages women have experienced in academia."

"What disadvantages? Don't women get higher grades?"

"Yes, but for a long time—and probably still, to some extent, or again—they continued to be underrepresented in academia, probably because they weren't encouraged as much to go to university, let alone grad school. Scholarships provided that encouragement."

"Ah."

"Also, at least in my case, scholarships made up for the relatively lower pay for the kind of summer and part-time jobs women get. My brother's summer job paid for his tuition, books, and so on; mine didn't, so without a scholarship, I'd've had to work throughout the school year."

"Did not know that."

"Why do you think so many female law students take up pole dancing?"

Dylan had no answer. Just—no answer.

"As for sports teams ... I think I can agree with you there too. Sex-segregation of sports depends on the generalization that male and female bodies are different in athletically relevant ways. And it *is* a generalization. And it's just easier to use that generalization than to use complicated height, weight, strength, and flexibility categories. But the harm of using the generalization is far greater than the difficulty of using other criteria for classification."

"So MtFs should be allowed to compete in women's sports?"

"In theory, yes. But we'd have to develop ways to measure muscle mass and cardiovascular capacity and whatever else is relevant to fair competition. It's easy to measure weight for wrestling categories, but—"

"Even there, the sport is further segregated, by sex."

"True. Because even with equal weight, there's a difference in muscle mass."

"But that's the case even among men," Dylan pointed out. "Which is surely why one wins and the other loses. Partly why."

"It would be interesting to see athletic competition between people with identical body … attributes."

"No, wouldn't it be boring? They'd always tie."

"Well, no, wouldn't skill be the deciding factor then?"

They considered the matter.

"Until puberty, there aren't any significant athletic differences between male and female, right?" Rev asked. "So children's sports shouldn't be sex-segregated at all."

"It would be interesting to see what effect that would have," Dylan said. "Maybe if girls learned to be as physically aggressive, by playing with boys, who have been socialized differently, then when puberty *did* happen—"

"There would be fewer differences," Rev finished his thought. "The differences there are," she clarified, "wouldn't be magnified by that different socialization."

"And it should be 'tomgirl,'" Rev said a short while later. "'Bettyboy' should refer to males who adopt so-called feminine … things. Make the sex the noun part, the gender, the adjective part."

"Agreed."

"Better yet would be no gender shit at all."

"Agreed."

"And sex relevant only when it's relevant."
"Agreed. Wasn't that a tautology?"
"No. Maybe. Sort of."

"You know," Rev said, a long while later, after the salted peanuts, which necessitated water, which necessitated a trip to the single on-board restroom, as soon as it was unoccupied, which was, all in all, a rather stupid situation, "if we had more people with the courage to just do what they wanted to do, regardless of what others think they should do based on their indefensible notion of a sexual dichotomy based, in turn, on physical appearance, if we had more people who were willing to stand up to the consequent taunts and ostracization, maybe eventually the taunts and ostracization would disappear."

"Or maybe they'd worsen because people would feel *more* insecure, *more* overwhelmed by the—"

"By the what, though?"

"By the challenges to their worldview. What you said. Conservative people. Boat. Males must be men and females must be women. Males must be superordinate, females subordinate."

"On the one hand," Rev circled back, way back, "why *not* change sex? I mean, what's the big deal? It's a body modification. Like pierced ears, breast enlargement, and leg lengthening. Some modifications are more political than others, sure. Breast enlargement and leg lengthening reinforce sexism. But how is changing one's sex reinforcing sexism? I mean, if you *just* changed sex. Not gender. To go with it.

"On the other hand, the problem with men becoming women is that it allows men to invade women's spaces. Restrooms and—"

"But women invaded men's spaces long ago," Dylan pointed out. "The men's clubs had to start permitting women—"

"Yeah, but that's different because ... " Rev tried to figure out how it was different. "Because men's clubs are places of power, they're where important decision s get made, and women wanted some of that power. Women's places are places of protection.

"And when men are allowed in, they're no longer places of

protection." She'd read that MtFs even demanded that they be allowed to work at women's shelters. How ... *ignorant* was that?

"Also," she continued, "if men can become women, that erases the basis of our discrimination, and thus makes that discrimination invisible."

"You lost me there."

"If being a woman no longer means having a uterus, then the right to abortion is no longer a women's issue."

"But wouldn't that be a *good* thing? Aren't *women's* issues typically *marginalized*?"

"Yeah ... but I doubt the right to abortion would become, as a consequence, a mainstream issue, let alone a men's issue. It would probably become a non-issue."

"Or it would become even *more* marginalized, because then we'd have to say it's a *cis*-women's issue."

"See-women?"

"No, cis-women. It's what transpeople call those of us who were born with female parts. And they insist we call ourselves that too. Because if they're women, we have to be called something else."

"So doesn't that prove they're *not* women?"

"You'd think so."

"Also, doesn't that defeat the purpose? Won't they be upset then at not being considered *cis-women*?"

"You'd think," Rev shrugged. She was near giving up.

"So—I'm supposed to call myself a *cis*-man now?" he interrupted himself.

Rev nodded.

"So the ones who get to use the default terms, man and woman, are the ones who've gone through hell to change their sex? The rest of us, over 99% of us, have to use the new, 'exception' term?"

Rev nodded.

"They've also invented the word 'cis-gender,'" Dylan was googling again. "It means that someone's gender corresponds to their sex."

"Really?" She was surprised. For a second. "Ah. Of course. That's so bloody important, we have to have a word for it. Is it an insult?" she asked hopefully. "To call someone cis-gendered?"

She looked over at the page he'd opened. "What the hell is 'cis-privilege'? What privileges do female-born people have that female-made—let's go with that for the moment—*don't* have? Being able to use a woman-only public restroom? That's a *privilege*?"

"Apparently. Given what you said. About not getting beat up in them."

"Why are public restrooms sex-segregated in the first place?" She ignored the implication that not getting beaten up was a privilege. Just ... had to. "The washrooms in people's houses aren't sex-segregated."

"Men don't attack women in people's houses."

She stared at him.

"Yeah, scratch that."

"The restroom here on the plane isn't sex-segregated."

"Yeah, but there's only one. When you have a bunch of them, it's cheaper to build a group washroom with ten stalls than it is to build ten individual washrooms."

"So it's just a matter of economy?" Rev thought about that. As an explanation, it seemed ... incomplete. "Maybe women don't want men to see all the shit they do. Like putting on their make-up. I've heard that some wives get up early to put on their make-up so their husbands don't see them do it. I guess they think that if they never see them put it on, they won't think they wear it. They'll think they're naturally that beautiful." She snorted. Whether at the extent of men's cluelessness or at the implication that a woman wearing make-up was beautiful, it was hard to say.

"But that doesn't really make sense," she said, upon further consideration. "Nine times out of ten, women go in, do their business, wash their hands, then leave."

"They wash their hands?" Dylan grinned.

"Yeah," she grinned back, "*that* might be why we want segregated washrooms."

"Yes, well, you know, men and their pissing contests ... "

Rev stared at him. She knew men's restrooms were often pretty disgusting, because *real* men didn't clean up after themselves, that was what women were for, but—pissing contests? She didn't know whether or not to take him seriously. Literally. Decided not to ask.

"Getting back to cis-privilege," she said, "these men who decide to change their gender or sex, are they not allowed to drive? Or ride a bike? Are they prohibited from opening a bank account? Owning property? Voting?

"Do they have to cover their faces in the presence of people deemed actually human? Are they unable to leave their houses unless they're accompanied by a male relative? Do they have to wait until the men have eaten before they can eat?

"Do they get shot in the head for attending school? Do they get acid thrown in their face when they reject a man's sexual advances?

"Do they worry about getting pregnant when they're raped? Do they worry about not getting a job because they might get pregnant? Are any of them in prison because they had a miscarriage or a still birth?"

Dylan was speechless. He'd considered himself a reasonably educated man. But—

"And they say *we're* the privileged ones."

"Maybe the main reason women are upset with men becoming women is that deep down," she grimaced, "we know that MtFs will *continue* to have their male privilege, because they've had a lifetime of conditioning *as* a male, so they've got a confidence, even an arrogance, certainly a sense of entitlement, an expectation that doors will be opened for them—"

"Expect and you shall receive."

She nodded. "Well, if you're a man. Every time *I've* expected a door to be open—"

"You slam into it."

She nodded.

"So," Dylan was thinking, "it's actually privilege due to gender, due to social conditioning, more than a privilege due to sex."

"Yes, but being conditioned to have that confidence and entitlement is a privilege due to sex. Because only males get raised to be that way."

"Oh, right." Of course.

"So you're … jealous?" Dylan finished her initial train of thought.

"Yeah. I mean, come on, Bruce Jenner became Woman of the Year! It's not enough they beat us when it's an open category, but now they're going to beat us in the women-only categories too. How much more 'down' can we get?"

"So," Dylan thought that through, "men aren't upset with *women* becoming *men* because—"

"Because they're not paying attention," Rev cut him off at the pass. "Because, surprise, what women do isn't worth their attention.

"But if women can become men—let's suppose we can nail the arrogance, the sense of entitlement—a big suppose, granted—then the entire patriarchy could come tumbling down. Because then one of *us* might become *Man* of the Year. CEO. President."

Dylan nodded understanding.

"The ReGenderApp could make that happen," he said quietly.

"It could indeed." Just as quietly.

They landed in the early evening. Given the three-hour time difference, Dylan decided to make a quick call to Kit from the airport. Who knows how long it would take to get to the house. Yes, Loup was fine. Still fine. As fine as she had been at around noon.

When they opened the door—the house key was under the fake plop of shit, as promised—Moe greeted them enthusiastically, wagging his entire big, black, Lab body. Guests!!!

He looked at their bags, then glanced out at the taxi as if he would help bring in whatever other luggage they might have.

"No, this is all we've got," Dylan told him.

"Seriously?" Rev looked at him.

"What? I saw a YouTube video of some golden retrievers helping to bring in the groceries, and it's quite conceivable that Moe helped Mike bring in guests' luggage."

Rev held out her knapsack.

Moe took it by the strap and headed toward the stairs.

Dylan grinned at Rev, then followed Moe. Rev closed the door behind them, then followed Dylan.

"Guess this is our room!" Dylan dropped his knapsack onto the bed in the room into which Moe had led them. Rev's knapsack was on the floor beside the bed. Satisfied, Moe next led them to the bathroom.

"Okay, thanks!"

On to the bedroom at the end of the hall. Moe blocked the doorway.

"Guess this is his room," Rev said.

"Agreed."

Back downstairs, Moe led them into the kitchen, slowly passing by the fridge, oven, counter, cupboards. He paused at the coffee maker.

"Thanks, we'd love a cup of coffee." Dylan figured out how to use it and got things going. Moe wagged his tail.

Next, Moe lay his head on the kitchen table.

"House Rules," Rev picked up the booklet sitting under a pair of salt-and-pepper shakers.

"Thank you!" Dylan said to Moe.

Moe then led them to the patio door. Did he have to go out? Dylan opened it. Moe trotted out and circled a couple lounge chairs with a table set in between.

"Oh. Okay, thanks!" Dylan grinned at Rev again. Moe was the best! Well, no, Loup was the best. And Peanut! And Bob!

Moe came back inside and sat against one of the kitchen cupboards, beside his dishes. Both were connected to a large dispenser, which basically provided an endless supply of water and kibble. Well, five gallons of the former and who knew how many kilograms of the latter. Both were reasonably full. So Dylan was puzzled, until he noticed the cookie jar on the counter at just that spot. Aha! He gave Moe a doggy biscuit, then watched as he wandered off. Out, actually. Through his doggy door.

The House Rules confirmed what Moe had already told them. Their bedroom and bathroom was upstairs on the right; Moe's room was at the end of the hallway and off-limits; the kitchen was theirs to use; ditto, patio chairs. There were two bicycles in the garage they were also welcome to use. They could pocket the two extra keys, hanging by the fridge, while they were here, but the one that let them into the house was to stay where they'd found it. Lastly, Mike's sister had hired Spur, a teenager who lived a couple doors down, to come take Moe for a walk to the park once a day, keep his food and water dispensers filled, and check the house for anything that needed attention. She'd show up every day after school.

"We can tell her we'll do that while we're here," Dylan suggested.

"Or not. We don't want Moe transferring all his affection to you, because you'll be leaving."

"Good point."

"And just because Spur takes Moe for a walk in the afternoon, that doesn't mean he can't also have a walk in the morning or evening."

"Or both," Dylan grinned. "All three. You know."

"I do."

While they waited for their pizza to arrive, they set out to put away all the expensive stuff, as was Dylan's habit when housesitting, but then realized there was no expensive stuff. Moe wasn't interested in expensive stuff.

So they unpacked, showered, then took their coffee into the living room.

"So that's his couch." Moe was sprawled out on the couch. "And I'm guessing the Lazy-Boy is, was, Mike's. So we can probably sit in the other chairs." Tentatively, they sat. Yes.

Rev reached out for the remote. Moe growled. No, it was more of a grumble.

"Really? We have to watch sports the whole time we're here?"

"Guess that's why there's a tv in our bedroom." Dylan grinned at Moe. Who grinned back.

An hour later, post-pizza, Moe wanted to go for a walk. He'd gone to the door and returned to the living room with his retractable leash.

"See?" Rev said. Then smiled at Moe for proving her point.

"I do!" Dylan beamed and practically bounced off the couch. "Coming?"

"Absolutely. I need a walk. And fresh air. Do you think it will be safe at night?" she added.

"I think so. Though ... the sites I looked at did say that in San Francisco, the neighbourhoods can change dramatically from one street to the next. So maybe not. Let's just go around the block for now," he said.

"Sounds good. Oh, you were talking to Moe."

Partway around the block, they approached another couple walking a little spaniel. Moe had to stop and say hello. So Dylan and Rev did likewise.

A little further, another dog was out for a walk. This one looked like border collie mix. Moe had to stop and say hello. So Dylan and Rev did likewise.

And another. A big, floppy, something. This time, while Moe said hello, Dylan asked about parks and safety.

"Golden Gate is great, but only during the day," the man said. "Don't even think about going there at night." The woman nodded her agreement.

"Generally speaking, though, only the Tenderloin and Mission Districts are unsafe. There are some parts of the Haight that you'll want to avoid, but walking around the block here at night is okay."

"Okay, thanks," Dylan said. Belatedly realizing that Moe probably knew that. Wouldn't've asked to go for a walk at night otherwise.

"But we're all walking with pepper spray these days because of the coyotes," the woman added.

"Coyotes?"

"Yeah. Most sightings have been in Presidio, but there have been reports of coyotes coming right up to people with dogs on leashes."

"And doing what?" Dylan was puzzled.

"Attacking the dogs. For no reason."

Dylan didn't believe it. Loup would certainly never do such a thing. Not that she was a coyote.

"What time of year was it?"

"Spring, I think."

"Maybe they were walking too close to a den," Dylan suggested. "The pups would be born in spring, yeah?"

"Maybe."

"Was there any sort of warning? A growl, a nip?"

"Don't know, perhaps. You'd think so, wouldn't you." The couple started to move on. "Have a good evening!"

Three dogs later, they'd circled back and decided to call it a day. A long day.

Next morning—noon—*after*noon, given the recovery needed from their day of travel, Dylan was at the kitchen table with coffee and cold pizza. Rev was outside, lounging on one of the lounge chairs. It was warm. There were no bugs. They had the patio door wide open. Even the screen door part of it.

"I'm skyping Loup," Dylan called out to her. "Wanna come say hi?"

She came in, looked at the screen, and saw—Loup had a very big tongue. And she was apparently making sure she licked every inch of Kit's screen.

"So I guess she *can* distinguish images on a laptop screen."

"Yes … " Dylan was near tears. He had his cheek smooshed against his screen. "Good Loup, I love you too, I do, yes … "

"You'll want to buy some sort of screen protector for next time," Rev said to Kit, whom they could hear laughing. "Flaker, enough!" They caught a glimpse of Flaker licking Kit's cheek.

"It's the keyboard I'm more concerned about," Kit said. "Loup took off the S, D, F, E, R, C, and V. With her left paw. Hey! And the 3 and 6."

"Oh. Sorry about that," Dylan said. "I'll pay for the repair."

"No problem. I think they'll just pop back on. I'll rig something up for next time."

"So it's going okay?" Dylan asked. "She's being good?"

"Yes, the past *eighteen hours*," Kit emphasized with a grin, "have been uneventful."

"Okay, good. We talked to some people here and they say that coyotes are attacking dogs for no reason and—"

"No coyotes in this area, remember?"

Rev nudged Dylan with a 'See?'

"And in any case, I'm not sure they could climb over the fence."

Another nudge.

"Or even want to, once they saw Loup."

"Good point. Yeah, okay. Thanks. Just needed to hear that, I guess."

"No problem."

"Okay, bye then. Be good Loup! I'll be back!" Dylan closed his laptop.

"She's okay."

"She is, yes." Part of him wanted her to be distraught without him, but the other part, surely the stronger part, he hoped, was glad she was okay.

Rev sat down to have another slice of pizza. She'd finished the one she'd taken outside with her.

"So," Dylan said, "the orientation isn't until Monday, which gives us two days," he said proudly, noting his arithmetical deduction, "to do whatever. Are you up for a walkabout today? Or a bikeabout?"

"Hm. Not keen on pedalling all the ups and downs—San Francisco still has a lot of hills, right?"

"It does, yes," Dylan grinned. "I wonder if they have mopeds for rent. You know, for old people."

Rev decided a bikeabout would be just fine.

But first, they walked Moe again. Because he asked. Politely.

They stopped at the first bicycle repair shop they came to. Which was, fortunately, just ten minutes away. Because the creaking noise made by Rev's bike was driving her crazy. And the seat on Dylan's bike was too low.

"Be good to have them given a once over anyway," Dylan said. "Just to make sure the brakes are reliable."

"Agreed. Because, hills."

So a walkabout it was.

Dylan pulled out his to-get list. Cell phones. For both of them. With the features specified by the ReGender people. Shoes. Cheapest possible. Food and drink. Just the essentials, partly because there was only so much he was willing to carry and partly because San Francisco was overflowing with weird and wonderful cafes and restaurants.

Rev pulled out her to-get list. Cheesecake.

They were able to find everything on their lists within a half-hour's walk. It was nice. To be able to do that. For a moment, Rev missed living in a city.

They also found a used bookstore. And a great number of vintage stores.

But mostly, they found relics of the hippie era. Many had canes, some had walkers.

"Oh, oh," Dylan did Horshack—*Welcome Back Kotter* had had a big influence on both of them, "tie-dye t-shirts!" Dylan ran ahead to the store. "Remember tie-dying shirts?"

"We're not *that* old. We grew up in the 70s, remember? Not the 60s."

"Yeah, but … I thought I tie-dyed t-shirts … I did other stuff that they did in the 60s … "

"Which is probably why you think you tie-dyed t-shirts," she grinned. Having noticed that the store also sold cute little pipes …

Dylan bought a turquoise-green t-shirt. Rev opted for a red-orange one. Together, they were … visible. The store had bandanas too, of course. So Dylan bought half a dozen for Loup. Of course.

They carried on. And found cheesecake. In a café that delivered.

"Really?" Rev couldn't believe it. She could get cheesecake delivered. Right to her. Whenever she wanted. More or less. She looked at the many display cases, each one filled with cheesecake. Well, filled with a delightful variety of cheesecakes sitting on cake platters.

"Pretty much all the food places deliver now," the woman behind the counter said. "A lot of our older clientele have trouble with the hills," she explained.

"*We* made it!" She high-fived Dylan. And almost fell over.

"If you give me your address, I'll confirm that it's within our delivery area."

They couldn't remember their address.

"It's no more than half an hour's walk," Dylan said sheepishly.

"Then it's probably within our area," the woman, the young woman, assured them. "Why don't you take a menu home with you," she nodded to a neat pile at the end of the counter, "and call in your order, with your address, when you get back home."

"Well, it's not really home," Rev said. "I mean if it *were*, we'd know the address. Wouldn't we?" She turned to Dylan. They were getting so frickin' old.

"We would."

After they'd taken care of dessert, sort of, they stopped for dinner.

Dylan chose a Thai restaurant. It was small and crowded, but, oddly enough, not noisy. Not obnoxiously noisy. It was friendly noisy.

They made their way to an empty table at the back. A waiter appeared immediately, poured a couple glasses of water, and left a pair of menus. It didn't bother either of them that he hadn't said a word. Because really, what needed to be said?

Rev scanned the menu.

"Charcoal pancakes?"

"Oh, let's get some!" Dylan scanned the menu as well. "Monk Tacos. That sounds so ... inappropriate. Let's get one of those too."

"Do not get the Eel Taco. Please."

"Okay."

"Or the Garlic Frog."

"Okay."

She closed the menu. Before she lost her appetite.

Dylan got the Tom Yum Soup, because it sounded fun—tom yum— then decided to use that criterion for his other choices as well. Which explained, Rev assumed, the appearance of Pla Koong at their table.

"This place is way better than the Brown Sugar Factory," Rev heard a woman behind her say.

She had to ask. "The Brown Sugar Factory?" It sounded like the best bakery ever.

"Yeah, it's a restaurant over on Valencia." The woman was wearing beads. Lots and lots of beads. "You've never been?"

"No," Dylan said, "we just got here."

"It's not a bakery?" Rev was so disappointed.

"No, but if it's bakeries you're after," the woman with her said, smiling, "go to Schubert's. They have a Chocolate Truffle Torte to die for."

Rev rummaged in her knapsack for pen and paper ...

"Do you have an address?"

"Clement Street. Don't know the number. It's between Sixth and Seventh. They're open now." She grinned.

"Thanks!" Rev stuffed the paper into her pocket, then stood up.

"We haven't eaten yet."

"Oh. Right." She sat back down.

"Six-thirty," the woman said. Still grinning.

Rev looked at her watch. "Do they deliver?"

"They might."

They returned in the evening to find that Moe's friends had come over for the game. A boxer was sprawled out on the couch with him, and two little chihuahuas were snuggled in between.

"Maybe Spur let them in?" Rev suggested. They'd missed her again.

"Or maybe they came in through his doggy door."

"Yeah, but the yard is fenced."

They went out to investigate. And discovered that there were doggy doors in the fence, one connecting to the yard on the left, another to the yard on the right.

"Presumably, the yards on either side are fenced," Rev said.

"But perhaps they have doggy doors to the *next* yards," Dylan suggested. "So Moe doesn't get lonely when there's no one here!"

"Yeah, I wondered about that. You can leave a cat for days, but surely a dog—I mean even if he *does* have food, water, and outside access—"

"Maybe Spur hangs out more when there's no one housesitting."

"I would. If I was Spur. What teenager doesn't want a house of their own?"

It had been a while since they'd gotten silly. And of course they didn't bring a supply with them. But they had a supply now. So.

Rev preferred a rolled joint to a pipe, so Dylan unpacked his cigarette papers and got to work. Took a while because he wanted to try the pipe first. And got a bigger toke than he expected.

As soon as Rev took her first draw from the messily rolled joint, a husky-fox mix bounded into the room and set a squirrel onto the table.

"Is that like bringing a bottle of wine?" Rev asked Dylan.

Actually, it didn't quite set the squirrel onto the table as fling it into the air, catch it, shake the hell out of it, fling it into the air again, pounce on it when it landed on the floor, then roll on it.

"A bottle of wine isn't usually flung into the air. But we could try that with the next bottle we buy."

Rev took a second draw before handing the joint back to Dylan.

"Are dead animals allowed in the house?" Rev asked then, her rule-obsessed past rearing its ugly head.

"Actually, I'm not sure it's—"

"'No playing with your food'?"

"That would be a sad rule," Dylan turned his attention away from the squirrel to Rev, "and I don't get the impression Mike was a sad kind of guy."

"Do you think sad rules need to come from sad people? That's on the list, I'm sure of it."

"The House Rules list?"

"No, the list of fallacies."

"There's a list of fallacies?"

"Yes!"

"What else is on the list? Besides 'Sad rules need not come from sad people.'"

"That's not actually on the list, silly."

"But you said—"

"That's an example *of* one of the fallacies that's on the list."

"Oh. What's it an example of?" Nailed it. Words in the right order even. Unless you followed the no prepositions at the end of a sentence rule. Which he didn't. Certainly not when he was stoned.

"The genetic fallacy." Woh. Surprised even herself there.

Dylan was perplexed. "What does it have to do with genetics?"

"Nothing."

"Ah."

Rev sighed.

"Oh, wait," she recovered, "it has to do with origins! The origin, the *genesis*," she smiled broadly, "of an argument is irrelevant to the merit of the argument itself."

"But 'Sad rules have to come from sad people' isn't an argument. Is it?"

"No," she sighed again. "It's just a claim." She decided she needed another toke to figure out the difference between an argument and a claim. To *remember* the difference between an argument and a claim. Because surely she knew, right?

A few minutes later, a chestnut terrier mix pranced into the room with a bright green tennis ball in her mouth. Seeing Rev and Dylan, she wagged her tail in anticipation, then headed toward Dylan. Of course. Of the two of them, he was the go to person for dogs. But at the moment, he was investigating the squirrel. Making sure it was truly dead and not suffering a protracted and painful death. So the chestnut terrier chose Rev instead.

She accepted the ball and threw it down the hall.

The chestnut terrier flew after it and brought it back. Set it neatly into her open hand.

She threw it down the hall again.

The chestnut terrier flew after it and brought it back. Set it neatly into her open hand.

She threw it down the hall again.

The chestnut terrier flew after it and brought it back. Set it neatly into her open hand.

"Did you just spend an hour playing fetch with a dog?" Dylan asked. Ten minutes later.

"Yes. I'm making up for not having had a wasted youth."

"Ah. So you're having a wasted olth."

"A wasted what?"

"A wasted olth. Wouldn't that be the other end to a wasted youth?"

Rev considered a few other possibilities. 'Old agery' sounded a bit too much like buggery. 'Old fogeyness' was too foggy. Though that would certainly have been appropriate. She had to admit olth was the only single-syllable possibility that was also logically appropriate.

"Yes. I'm determined to have a wasted olth." She threw the ball again. It went through the window. Which, fortunately, was open. Because the little chestnut terrier flew after it.

A while later, the game was over and Moe changed the channel.

Wait, what? They just then noticed, really noticed, the black box sitting on the table. It had four large, raised buttons, one of which

Moe had just pawed. Dylan went over to check it out.

"This is so cool! I wonder if Mike made it! Look," he said to Rev, "it's just a large and simpler version of a regular remote. This button," he pressed the button to the left of the one Moe had pawed and the tv turned off—all of the dogs stared at him. Glared, actually. Okay, growled.—"is the power on and off." He quickly pressed it again.

"And the one beside it?"

"Hm." He was reluctant to incur again the wrath of his new friends. "I doubt he'd go through the trouble of a volume control. And Moe would have no need to see the on-screen guide."

"Because he wouldn't be able to read it?"

"Yeah, the text would be too small."

Dylan held his breath and pressed the button. The channel changed again. Dylan pressed it again. The channel changed again. Rev wondered how many more trials would be necessary for him to draw the correct conclusion. Three, apparently.

"And this one changes the channel. It must've been the one Moe pushed. I guess he can only change channels in one direction."

"Try pushing it with your other hand."

Dylan pushed it with his other hand. All of the dogs stared at him. "And the other two buttons?"

"Well, he wouldn't need DVD controls. There's a separate remote for that," he nodded to a human-sized remote sitting on top of the DVD player, sitting under the tv.

"So ... a direct line to Pizza Pizza? Maybe Moe has a standing order for a MeatLovers Pizza."

"Loup would love that!" Dylan started thinking right then and there about how to make that happen back at Rev's cabin. Programming the speed dial function on Rev's landline phone wouldn't be a problem, but he'd have to build something with larger buttons, like Mike had done. And then somehow wire it to the phone's connections.

In the meantime, Moe reached out with one of his paws and pressed the button on the left. On came the game. Which was over. He pressed the button on the right. On came the Puppy Bowl. All of the dogs cheered. In their own way.

"Puppies!" Dylan cried out. "Oh, look, they're so *cute!* " He *loved* puppies. He watched for a while as the puppies played and tumbled and teetered and tottered, without a teeter-totter—now *that* was interesting ...

"It's two pre-sets!" Dylan cried out half an hour later, with the enthusiasm of what's-his-name in the bathtub when he realized that the water level went up when he got in. "One for the sports channel and one for—the animal channel?"

"Is there an animal channel?"

"There are animals. Ergo, there's an animal channel."

Rev made a note to use that on one of her LSAT questions.

One of the puppies started squealing in distress. It was stuck in the corner! Rev empathized. Whenever she got stoned, she got stuck in corners. The boxer started whimpering in sympathy, and Moe barked. "Turn around, you little idiot!" Moe barked again. "Turn AROUND, you little idiot!"

The little puppy turned around. "FREE AT LAST! FREE AT LAST!" It ran out of the corner into the center of the room. "THANK GOD ALMIGHTY, I'M FREE AT LAST!" Rev cheered.

Fifteen delightful minutes later, the Puppy Bowl ended. Moe turned the tv off.

"What are they going to do now," Rev asked, with genuine—okay, pot-induced—curiosity, "play a game of poker?"

7

The orientation was held in SoMa—south of Market Street. They picked up their bikes from the repair shop and took a scenic route over. Not that they knew it, because of the fog.

"This is like biking through a cloud!" Dylan called back gleefully at one point. "Rev? Rev, where are you?"

They'd also taken the hilly route.

They signed in outside the conference meeting room and were given name tags. As they walked in, they saw that about a hundred people were there. Rev wanted to sit at the back. Dylan gravitated to the front. They met in the middle.

Three young men were seated at the table at the front of the room, a large screen behind them, showing the ReGender app logo. A stylized circle, arrow, and cross. They were using the symbols of sex. For gender.

At two o'clock sharp, one of the young men, of slight build, stepped up to the podium. He waited for silence. And got it. "Welcome," he smiled.

Rev wondered if it was a young woman using the app.

"I'm Dana Trett, that's Erin Trett," he nodded to another young man, "yeah, we're sibs, and that's Kim During," he nodded to the third person. "We developed the ReGender app."

"Was that Erin or Aaron?" Rev whispered to Dylan during the

applause. She'd noticed that all three names could go either way. Definitely three women using the app. It made perfect sense. Who else but a woman would even *think* of such an app? She was delighted.

"Each of you has, of course, already received details about the app," Dana looked out at the room, "but I'd like to start by reviewing some of the highlights. After all, you'll be testing it, living with it, over the course of the next several months.

"Understanding that ours is a very sexist world," s/he continued, "with privileges and penalties accorded arbitrarily to members of this or that sex, we thought we needed a better way to change things."

"Better than what?" someone called out.

"Better than the feminist movement," Erin/Aaron replied, "better than equal rights legislation, better than gender studies—all of which seem to have exacerbated the divide rather than eradicate it."

Rev nodded. Definitely three women.

"We're hoping that the app—" Dana stopped as Erin/Aaron shook his/her head, ever so slightly. "Well, I won't tell you what we're hoping the app will do. That will predispose you to—"

Erin/Aaron stood. "We want you to have as few preconceptions and expectations as possible. Aside from those formed by your own life experience. If you look around, you'll see that we have chosen—we've *tried* to choose—a cross-section of people to be part of this beta test. Our objective was to have a pool of people varied in age, appearance, education, occupation, and expressed gender preferences."

Rev raised her hand. Dylan lowered it. "He said *gender* preferences," he whispered.

"Oh, right. Okay."

"As you know," Dana resumed, "your task is to use the app over the course of five months in as many situations as you can, keeping detailed records of what happens. So we're depending on you to be observant, to be critical, and to be articulate in your descriptions. We'll be using your feedback to inform future versions, prior to release. In most cases, we'll wait until the end of the beta test to make changes, but in some cases, we might tweak the app immediately, which is why we're asking for weekly reports. You'll receive automatic updates as the beta test proceeds."

"Also," Erin/Aaron added, "we'll be making special requests as to where, when, and how to use the app. You're always free to refuse our requests, but we hope you won't."

"In a moment," Dana continued, "you'll be allowed to download the app and then we'll walk you through its navigation. Before we begin, are there any questions?"

"Does the app present a female version of ourselves," a red-haired man called out, "or can we create the female body we want from a … menu?"

Rev snorted with disgust at his word choice. "Bet he gets kicked out first week," she whispered to Dylan. "He'll probably use the app to get into the women's restroom, then jerk off thinking about the woman in the next stall pulling down her pants."

Erin/Aaron looked carefully at him. "At the moment, the former."

"'At the moment,'" Dylan whispered to Rev.

"Yeah, caught that."

"So we won't be able to change skin color?" Someone else spoke up.

"Or age?"

"'Fraid not."

"It would be cool if we could," Rev suggested. "Then we could expose not just sexism, but racism and ageism too. And if we could put Eminem's voice with James Bond's body, we could expose classism. Or culturism. Or whatever."

"True," Kim spoke up, "but that would make the app more expensive. As it is," she confessed, "this is by no means the first version … "

"More importantly," Erin/Aaron smiled, "putting Eminem's voice with James Bond's body would make it more likely that you'd be 'discovered'. If your hologram is too far off the mark—that is, too dissonant with your personal norm of presentation—you'll have to be that much better, with respect to what you do and say, in order to 'pass', so to speak.

"For this to work," s/he continued, "it has to be realistic. That's why, for example, when women use the app to appear as men, the app will automatically present a slightly taller version of you. In addition to a version with facial hair, an Adam's apple, and so on. And vice versa. More or less."

"The first version of the app transformed women into a male version of themselves," Kim spoke up, "but that meant she was still 5'4" or thereabouts. Reverse for the men. And that was such an obvious give-away. So obvious, I don't know why we didn't ... " s/he trailed off. "Anyway, we tweaked the proportion translation algorithm. Not only height but also shoulder and hip ratios. You'll actually be testing the fourth generation beta."

"That's why we're requiring all of you to attend gender training classes," Erin/Aaron resumed. "If you switch from male to female, but continue to walk and talk like a man, it's not going to work. And vice versa. The classes will make sure your behaviour matches your new appearance."

"Why is it so important that our gender matches our sex?"

Rev turned to try and locate the raspy voice.

"It's not," Erin/Aaron said, with a nod. "In a perfect world. In *this* world, the match optimizes the effect of the app."

"So I have to learn how to walk and talk like a woman?" The red-haired man laughed.

"What's funny about that?" Rev challenged him.

"Well," he looked at her with an 'Isn't it obvious?' expression on his face.

"Waiting."

He glared at her. Unable to say. What was funny about—

"The gender training classes will also increase your level of awareness of the sexism that we're hoping our app will render moot," Erin/Aaron continued. "You need to be aware of the prejudices in order to tell whether the app *is* in fact making a difference. If you don't realize that people respond differently to men than they do to women, you won't notice a difference when the app is on. Which rather defeats the purpose of our study."

"But," Rev raised her hand, like a woman, "even if we master all the mannerisms of the other gender, we're still going to have problems maintaining the ruse. I mean, when we apply for a job, we'll have to present ID at some point. We'll all have to change our names."

"'All' meaning men too," the raspy voice emphasized. "Because if only women do it, then gender-neutral names will be a give-away."

"Well," Rev said, "we could change to James and George. In honour of Tiptree and Eliot." She saw that most of the men were looking at her blankly. As were, sadly, most of the women.

"Yeah, and what about at the airport?" someone asked.

"Actually, facial-recognition programs present less of a problem for us than human gatekeepers," Kim replied. "A facial recognition program will recognize that it's the same person—because the bone structure stays the same, and do all of the other points such programs check for— but humans won't. The different sex throws them. Every time."

Someone else raised a hand. "So when you say 'talk like a woman'— the app won't change our voices?"

"It will change the pitch, but not the inflections," Kim answered.

"So if, for example," Erin/Aaron explained, "you change from female to male, but keep raising your voice at the end of a statement, well, that's a gendered way of talking. Women tend to do that a lot more than men. It'll seem 'off'. If you really want to pass as a man, you'll need to talk like a man—which goes beyond just having a lower voice."

"Any other questions?" Dana looked around the room.

"What happens when someone actually touches the hologram?" a woman with long braids asked. "I mean, do we have to be careful to keep our distance? To maintain the illusion?"

"Good question," Kim jumped in. "That's one thing we're interested in testing. Yes, people will be able to move through it. But it's positioned so close to your actual body that—"

"Hang on," a bearded man stood up to ask his question. "Is that safe? I mean, cell phones themselves give off dangerous electro-magnetic fields—will we be walking around all day *inside* an EMF? Can we look forward to brain cancer when this is done?"

"No. The app is completely safe. And, to return to your question," Kim nodded to the woman with braids, "although people will be able to pass their hands through it, because it's so close to your body, when they pass through the hologram, they'll be touching you. We're hypothesizing that one, that won't happen very often, and two, in most cases, it won't destroy the illusion.

"That said, if your hologram is wearing a wool coat and you've got a cotton shirt on, depending on how sensitive the other person is, how attentive they are, how long the contact is—yeah, they might realize something's amiss."

"If there are no other questions?" Dana paused. "All right then, let's take a break, and then we'll have you download the current version of the app."

Dylan and Rev had remembered to bring their smartphones. Were they good or what?

"Go to this website," Dana said as an address appeared on the screen, "and use the indicated code. It's good for five minutes. If you try to copy the app or send it to others—"

A shrill siren sounded. A security guard approached the guilty person and held out his hand. A blond-haired young man in a business suit handed over his phone, and was then escorted out of the room.

"—that will happen. Also, please be aware that the app will deactivate itself at the end of the testing period."

Rev glanced at Dylan. So much for Kit's request.

Dana walked them through the app, using a pre-uploaded photograph and voice sample first of a man, then of a woman.

"It's worth spending some time selecting the very best photograph and voice sample you can get," Kim cautioned. "And if you need help with that, let me know."

"But for now," Dana said, "use the photograph and voice sample we've provided and just … play around! If you have any questions, just raise your hand and one of us will come help."

A short while later, when it seemed that everyone knew what they were doing, the session came to a close.

"We've provided a light lunch, out in the foyer," Dana announced, "and you're all welcome to stay, mingle, et cetera. We suggest that later this afternoon, or this evening, you play a bit more with the app using your own photographs and voice samples. The gender training classes being tomorrow.

"So," s/he glanced at his colleagues in case they had anything more to add, then turned back, "thank you all for coming, and we're looking forward to the next few months!"

As everyone shuffled out into the foyer, Erin/Aaron approached Rev and Dylan.

"You're Rev? And Dylan?"

They nodded.

"Pleased to meet you," s/he reached out to shake their hands. It was a firm shake. An androgynous shake. And it happened too quickly for Rev to determine whether the hand she felt matched the hand she saw. "We were very happy to get your applications. Most of the applicants were considerably younger—"

"I wouldn't say *considerably*," Rev muttered.

"And so we look forward to, um, more mature insights from the two of you."

Dylan glanced at Rev.

"Especially as the two of you seem to be especially articulate. As you can understand, due to the nature of the product, our research methodology is necessarily flawed in that we're going to have to rely very heavily on what will be, after all, subjective report. But a philosopher and a historian! With respect to said subjective report, it doesn't get any better than that! So, well, I just wanted to say how very glad we are that both of you are in our beta test pool."

"Thank you!" Dylan said.

Kim approached.

"This is Rev and Dylan," Erin/Aaron said to Kim.

"I thought so! Welcome to our beta test pool," s/he reached out. "We're *so* glad to have you both!"

"And we're glad to be here!" Dylan shook her/his hand. Rev followed suit.

"I just wanted to tell you that we actually had the age thing in production, but we stopped when one of us pointed out that a lot of balding middle-aged men would appear as fifteen-year-old boys in order to have sex with fourteen-year-old girls."

"Of course they would," Rev said, mentally smacking her forehead. "Should've thought of that." She turned to Dylan. "What is *wrong* with you people?!"

"Hey!" he raised his hands in defence. "I didn't think of that either."

"But we are proceeding with a skin colour version," Kim said. "Might the two of you be available for another beta test? In future?"

"Yes!" Dylan said. "Maybe. Depends. On where and for how long," he added, thinking of being away from Loup.

"What he said," Rev seconded his response.

Dana also made his/her way over to them.

"Dylan and Rev, I presume?" s/he grinned.

"Yeah."

"Pleased to meet you." Another round of hand shaking. And Rev still couldn't tell.

"You know," she looked at the three of them, "these apps are going to change *everything*."

They nodded. "We hope so."

"If you ever develop an all-in-one app," Dylan agreed with Rev's assessment, "you could call it The MeritocracyApp."

"No one knows what 'meritocracy' means," Rev dismissed his idea. "How about The ChameleonApp?"

"Yeah, because everyone knows what 'chameleon' means."

The three of them looked ... amused.

"The RePresentationApp?"

"Too many syllables. The RePresentApp. No ... The AppearanceApp?"

"The AppApp!" Dylan shouted.

"I could turn myself into a wolf," Dylan said as they left the conference centre. "If they expanded the app's apps. The AppApp's apps." He grinned.

"Loup would—I wonder if the app masks our scent."

"Oh, good question!"

"Regardless, hunters don't smell before they shoot."

Dylan stared at her. "I'll keep that in mind."

"You know what would be a good idea?" Rev said a minute later. "If instead of house arrest or prison, rapists had to wear the app all the time. Set to 'woman'."

o," Dylan flopped onto the couch beside Moe when they got home—it was allowed, now, "shall we decide where we want to go?"

"No, first I have to order some cheesecake and a Chocolate Truffle Torte." She'd forgotten to do that the night before—how could she have forgotten? Oh yeah. They'd gotten silly. And stupid. On top of old.

"Of course you do," Dylan grinned.

While she found her phone (yeah, in her pocket), he found the cheesecake menu they'd brought home and the phone number for Schubert's Bakery. Five minutes later, slices of peanut butter cup cheesecake, oreo cheesecake, chocolate chip cookie dough cheesecake, german chocolate cheesecake, and lemon lime zingy zest cheesecake—Dylan's choice—were on their way. And a Chocolate Truffle Torte. A *whole* Chocolate Truffle Torte.

"We're here for a whole month," Rev explained. Right. *That* was why.

"Okay, so where do we want to go? After this month," he clarified.

They opened the document they'd received at the orientation session, and scrolled to the list of places to go.

"Okay, so for January, or at least for another two weeks, we're here. California. We've done the orientation, but we've still got the classes—"

Dylan's phone rang. At the very same time, Rev's phone rang.

"Hello?"

"Hello?"

"Hey, Dylan, Rev." They saw by caller ID that it was Erin.

"Aha! I knew it!" Rev exclaimed.

"Hey, Erin."

"Hey, *Erin.*"

"Yeah, I've gotta change my caller ID!" She laughed. "Anyway, I'm calling to say that we already have a special request for you, if you're interested."

Dylan glanced at Rev. "We are."

"We'd like you to go to the Pitchfest in LA while you're here."

"The Pitchfest?"

"Yeah, it's an annual three-day event during which reps from the film industry are available to hear pitches for films. Most new screenwriters can't access reps; it's a very closed industry. So the Pitchfest is a chance for them to present their screenplays. And we believe, well, the stats *show*, that there's a disproportionate number of male-written scripts that end up being optioned."

"Duh." Rev muttered.

"Duh indeed," Erin echoed, surely grinning. "See that's exactly the level of awareness we need if we're to determine whether the app makes any difference."

"When is it?" Dylan asked. "The Pitchfest."

"Last weekend of this month. So if you could stay in California ... "

"Sure, we can do that," Rev said.

"Great! I'll send you the details."

"So," Dylan said once they'd all hung up, "January, we're here. February? Where haven't we been yet," he turned his attention back to the list. "Well," he qualified, "where haven't *you* been?" Of the two of them, Rev was by far the less travelled."

"Oregon."

"You want to go to Oregon?"

"Sure. I mean, it makes sense to just sort of crawl up the west coast. Oregon is supposed to be cool, in an indie radical sort of way, yeah? Portland, Seattle ... "

"Portland more than Seattle, I think. Okay, so February we make our way up the west coast, spend some time in Oregon, then Vancouver, yeah?"

"Definitely. We could rent bikes and tour Saltspring Island."

"*Bike* bikes or bikes?"

"*Bike* bikes for that, though if we spend all of February there, I might look into renting a motorcycle while I'm there. I miss it."

She'd *loved* the short ride on Sarah's Harley. Despite the way it ended.

"Okay, so we're renting a car to go from here to there?" Dylan asked.

"I'd much rather do that than fly."

"Me too. And then March—up to Alaska to see the aurora borealis?"

"Sounds good," Rev said. "Is Alaska the best place? For seeing the aurora borealis?"

"Well, no, I think Iceland is the best place."

"Is Iceland on the list?"

"Iceland isn't in Canada or the States."

"So that's a no?"

"April?"

"April we could go home," Rev said. "Spend a few weeks there after thaw before bugs. Go kayaking. See Loup. Test the app on the local rednecks and the kept women. Whose worldview is completely composed of small town shit plus mainstream tv shit. Which is a really contradictory composite, now that I think about it."

"And then leave her again?" He'd zoned out after 'See Loup'. "That might make it worse. To see her, then leave her again."

"Good point."

Dylan was thinking about Loup. Rev was thinking about Dylan.

"But April's too soon for the east coast, isn't it?" Rev asked. "I mean won't it still be all ice bergs?"

"There aren't any more ice bergs, silly!" He grinned when he said it, but.

"Oh yeah." Truthfully, they'd both wondered about forest fires and rising sea levels and other apocalyptic disasters happening while they were there in California. It was one reason Dylan hadn't looked for a house right on the coast. Didn't want to mudslide into oblivion. Or worse.

"Pity San Francisco will be flooded out of existence," Dylan said.

Rev nodded. It was one of the most environmentally responsible cities in the country.

"Well," Dylan returned to their decision-making, "we could fly from Alaska, or wherever, to somewhere else—somewhere in the lower States—for April. And then do the east coast in May."

"Yeah ... "

"Why don't we just sit on that decision for a while? We've got January, February, and March figured out." Used to be Dylan didn't figure out more than the next day of his life. At one time. If that. Unlike Rev, who'd had her entire life planned out when she was in high school. So all things considered, both of them were taking a walk on the wild side.

Dylan rolled a joint, and they spent the next hour or so experimenting with the app. Taking photographs of themselves and recording voice samples, figuring out which ones worked best with the app. Then they explored some of the app's options.

Dylan stood in the middle of the room, faced Rev, then turned on the app. To a default he'd tweaked a bit.

"How do I look?"

Rev grimaced. "Okay, first, turn the pitch down a bit. You sound like a six-year-old."

"But—"

"I know. Most women do speak in a higher voice than is actually natural, but."

Dylan adjusted the voice settings.

"Better?"

"Better. Still female."

"And ... ?"

Rev considered Dylanna's appearance.

"You've got so much hair!"

"Yeah, I was going to go with the ponytail, but thought this made my face look more feminine."

"It makes your face look … something," Rev considered. "Try it with a different pair of glasses."

Dylan obliged.

"Closer, but … "

He tried yet another pair of glasses.

"Better?"

"Yes. But I'd tone down the make-up a bit. You look a bit Barbie."

"Aren't I supposed to look a bit Barbie?"

"Well, if that's the kind of woman you want to be … "

"I don't think it's about … " He walked to the mirror hanging in the hallway. "I do, don't I. Look a bit Barbie. And it doesn't match my age."

"Nothing about looking feminine will match your age."

He considered that, then took a few moments to figure out how to tweak skin tone. Skin quality. Something.

"Okay," he turned to her. "Better?"

"Perfect. A female version of you!"

"I feel like a Romulan ship."

"But you're not invisible."

"In a way, I am. The real me is."

"Is the male version of you the real you?"

Dylan just sort of stared at her. He didn't have an answer. Anymore.

"Your turn." He sat down.

Rev stood up, then turned on the app to the default she'd been tweaking.

"Well?"

"It's good."

"But?"

"I expected someone taller," he laughed.

"Yeah, well, any taller and I won't be able to pull it off."

"True."

"And how about this one?"

"Oh, wow, a female version of you! Sor—No, not sorry. But it's as much not-you as the male version."

"It is, isn't it? Not-me." Rev was looking in the mirror that was hanging on the wall in the hallway. "I look like a clown."

"You do, a bit. Hey, have you ever been mistaken for a man? I mean, as you are? Were?"

"A couple times. Once from behind while I was walking. Apparently like a football player. And once by a kid at a camp. I was working on the maintenance crew and had shorts on. It was the hairy legs. The kid didn't believe me when I told him his mother had hairy legs too, she just shaved the hair off."

"See, I've never been mistaken for a woman."

"I think that just shows that in our society, as it is, it's easier for women to cross over than it is for men. I mean, no make-up, short hair, and jeans can be enough. And that's perfectly acceptable. Much more acceptable than you putting on make-up, growing your hair long enough for a pony tail, and wearing a dress."

"True."

"You've been called a fag. Which indicates that your behavior or attitude is sometimes feminine. So that sort of attests to your androgyny."

"Yeah. But you've probably been called a dyke more often."

"Probably. But again, just being unmarried is enough for a woman to be thought a lesbian. An unmarried man is just considered a bachelor. Not a fag."

"That is weird, isn't it."

They played around a bit longer until they each had at least three plausible versions of themselves. Casual, business, and formal. Not that they—not that Rev, at least—intended to use the last one.

"So, are we going to name our alteregos?" she asked.

"Yes! We should! I'm going to be—"

"Dylanna. Not Twinkletoes or La Princessa or anything else you won't be able to say out loud when you introduce yourself."

"Good point," he sighed. "Who are you going to be?"

"Revv." Dylan stared at her. "What?"

While they were deciding what to do with the rest of the day—with what was left of the rest of the day—Moe's friends came over again. First, the boxer arrived and climbed onto the couch beside Moe. Then the little chestnut terrier came running into the house and went straight to Rev, a bundle of hope and excitement. Rev grinned and held out her hand for the bright green tennis ball it had in its mouth. Two throws later, the little husky-fox showed up. (The chihuahuas must have had a previous engagement.)

"Okay, body parts are surely not allowed in the house," Rev said, as it pranced past her, trailing ... something.

Dylan waved his hand at her.

"Detached body parts," she clarified. "Body parts of *dead* animals."

He waved his hand at her again. This time it held a hot dog. The hot dog he'd made for Moe. Per House Rules. Moe got one hot dog a day when he had guests. Though, now that he thought of it, Dylan wasn't sure whether that referred to human guests or canine guests. No matter. He went into the kitchen to make hot dogs for—

"We really should find out their names," he said as he returned with a plate of three more hot dogs.

"This one's Mel," he reported, checking her tag as he gave her one of the hot dogs.

"And this one's Fetchnut," Rev checked the chestnut terrier's tag. She threw the ball again. It wasn't interested in a hot dog. Of course it wasn't.

"What about the blood-guts-and-gore one?" she asked.

"Priscilla." He'd managed to trade the forementioned blood-guts-and-gore for a hot dog and at the same time checked her tag.

A shared joint later, they considered biking across the Golden Gate Bridge. Upon further consideration, and googling, they decided against the idea. It would be windy, cold, and, deal-breakers as far as Rev was concerned, they'd be high up and riding alongside six lanes of nonstop traffic. During rush hour.

So they decided to bike just as far as the Golden Gate Park and watch the sunset from the beach.

"It's *not* like biking through a cloud," Rev noted at one point. "It's more like biking toward a rainbow."

"But it's all white. Well, grey."

"Yeah, but only *ahead* of us. Once we get there, the grey's gone."

"Well, it's not gone. We just don't see it. Just because you don't see something doesn't mean it doesn't exist."

Rev thought about that. "It does when it's a rainbow. Because rainbow is *defined* in visual terms. The colours."

"But that doesn't apply to cloud. Does it?"

"Doesn't it?"

"No, isn't a cloud defined by a certain density of water vapour, which simply *appears* as a cloud? So the certain density continues to exist as we approach. It's just that we don't see it once we get to it *because* we're so close to it."

Rev considered that. For a long while.

"Usually we don't see stuff because we're so far from it. I wonder what else don't we see because we're so close?"

Hoping that maybe the fog would dissipate and they'd get to see a sunset after all, they decided to stop and spend some time at the famously tranquil, apparently, Japanese Tea Garden. Which, Rev noted, would have been far more tranquil if the people hadn't been there. Clearly the fog in her brain had dissipated.

Then, since it looked like the fog wasn't going to dissipate, ever, they decided to check out the planetarium. It was closed.

"So, what, we just head back?" Rev asked, a little wistful, because there were so many people, everywhere, but also a little disappointed, because they'd biked all that way ...

"No, hang on, there's got to be something ... " Dylan rummaged in his knapsack and pulled out his list of things to do in San Francisco.

"What's that?"

"My list of things to do in San Francisco."

"When did you make a list of things to do in San Francisco?"

"November."

"Before we even got here?"

"Before we even got accepted," he confessed.

"Wow, talk about expecting doors to open."

"No, it wasn't that, it's—I like travelling, remember? I'm always doing this. I've got tons of these lists."

"Yeah? You have a list of things to do in France?"

"Of course."

Okay, that was an easy one. Rev thought for a minute. "Ice—No, you knew the aurora borealis would be the best there." She thought for another moment. Or two. Ireland, for sure, and while he was at it, Scotland and England. And not only France, but Italy and Spain. And China and Japan. And probably Australia ... Hell, he probably even had a list for Nunavit.

"North Korea!" she shouted with victory.

He simply stared at her.

"You have a list of things to do in North Korea? *What* things?!"

"Well, I have a long list of question to ask Kim Jong Un."

"Before or after he executes you?"

"Well, before, preferably."

"But—" Rev didn't want Dylan to get executed. She realized, then and there, she didn't even want him to—

Dylan read her face. And smiled.

"I'll write him a letter instead. Anonymously. Without a return address. While we're here so it has a California postmark."

In the meantime, he'd been perusing his list. "Let's go have some toast."

"Toast."

"Yes. Toast."

"We're in San Francisco, and you've got 'have some toast' on your list of things to do?"

"Well, not just *any* toast. Toast at the Trouble Coffee and Coconut Club. We could also go to The Mill or some other toast café. But Trouble is closer."

"Toast."

"Yeah. It's a thing here. It's over an inch thick and could be made out of figs and walnuts. And it comes with all sorts of weird and wonderful things on it. Almond butter, avocado ... "

They started walking their bikes toward Judah Street.

"Can I help write that letter?"

"Can I stop you?"

"This is cool," Rev said as they approached the café. Instead of tables and chairs, there were trunks and branches of trees. Pre-tables and pre-chairs.

Rev ordered the cinnamon sugar toast; Dylan, the peanut butter and lavender honey toast.

"It's an odd combination," Rev noted as they waited for their order to be prepared. "Coffee, coconut, and toast."

"Yes, but it makes perfect sense. The owner, who has quite a history—schizophrenia, bipolarity, drugs—put coconuts on the menu because they helped her strike up conversations with strangers. She did an experiment once: she stood on a street corner holding a sandwich and saying hello to people; no one would talk to her; same thing holding a coconut; people would engage."

"Go figure."

"Anyway, that explains the coconuts. She put toast on the menu because it reminded her of home, which she often didn't have."

"And the coffee?"

"She figured it was one thing she was good at. Making coffee."

"Here you go!" the tattooed woman called out sliding a couple trays onto the counter.

They took their trays outside and sat on a tree branch.

"I like it," Rev said once she had a bite. "Crusty on the outside, soft on the inside."

Dylan grinned. At her.

"What does lavender taste like?"

Dylan offered her a bite of his toast, while he took a bite of hers.

"I'm tasting mostly honey and peanut butter."

"Me too," he said, a little disappointed.

A few bites later, Dylan said, "So what do you think we'd see if we were really close to toast? If we were *inside* toast."

Rev considered the question. "I think it's not just a matter of relative distance, but also of relative size. Because we'd have to be really small to get inside toast. And so things would look—"

"That movie! The guy shrinks and travels through blood vessels and gets attacked by antibodies!"

"Yeah ... I don't imagine that being inside toast would be nearly as exciting."

They'd also gotten coconuts, of course. Once she'd finished her toast, best eaten while warm, Rev stared at her coconut for quite a while.

"What?" Dylan finally had to ask.

"How do they do this?" She stared at the squat polygon of coconut, the top sliced off, a straw in it to drink the milk or water or whatever, and a spoon to dig out the remaining whatever. "Whenever I buy a coconut, I drive a nail into each of the three soft spots, drain the milk, then smash the thing with my hammer to crack the shell, then spend an hour picking shards of shell off the coconut. By the time I'm done, I have bits of coconut. Not a squat polygon of coconut."

Dylan nodded sagely. "Understandable. Given your method."

9

ood morning, my name is Tania, and this is Kevin." Tania smiled, and Kevin nodded to the room. It was actually a theatre. Appropriately enough. The one hundred beta testers had been divided into five groups of twenty, ten women and ten men, and each group had, apparently, its own pair of gender training instructors. One woman and one man.

Tania and Kevin told the assembled participants a bit about themselves, then explained that each session over the next couple weeks would last only half the day. "But we'd like you to spend the afternoons practising what you learn in the mornings. You may find it harder than you think to act like someone of the other sex slash gender."

Dylan and Rev exchanged a glance at that phrasing.

"We'd like to start by having each of the women make a list of ten things you do that identify you as a woman. The men will make a list of ten things that identify them as a man."

Rev pulled out the pad of paper she'd brought and a pen. Most of the people around her seemed to wait expectantly to be given something to write on. And something to write with. Rev snorted with disgust. They were as bad as her classes had been. Full of unprepared students. Or maybe everyone thought they'd remember everything worth remembering. Had they anticipated it would be that little?

"Isn't it about time you moved into the 21st century?" a young man beside her said with derision as he started writing with a stylus on the tablet he'd brought.

She grabbed his tablet and shook it.

"What the hell are you doing?"

When she looked at it, the words were still there.

"Never mind. And fuck off."

She started her list. *1. I tell men to fuck off.*

"But I do that too," Dylan said, having read what she'd written.

"Yeah, but I do it more." *A lot,* she added. "And, at the same time, I object to using a word that means sexual intercourse in order to express anger."

Dylan conceded. And turned back to his own list.

"All set?" Tania called out a few minutes later. "Laura, let's start with you."

Someone already had a list of ten? Rev had a list of three.

"Well," Laura smiled, "I take an hour to get ready in the morning!"

The man sitting beside her, presumably her husband, smiled with good humour. No one bought it.

"I like to go shopping. I buy a lot of shoes. I'm a caring person. I smile a lot … "

Rev heard what she was saying, but it wasn't helpful. She was still stuck for a fourth thing she did that marked her as a woman.

"I open doors for other people." It was Sam's turn. Laura's husband. "I watch sports a lot. I like beer."

"Who *are* these people?" Rev muttered, having given up on her list.

"They did say," Dylan replied sotto voce, "they were aiming for a cross-section of people for the beta test. Maybe Laura and Sam are the token Cleavers."

"Thank you, Sam. Rev, would you like to go next?"

"No."

Tania stared at her.

"I'm not done yet."

"Well, maybe we can help you out. What have you got so far?"

"I tell men to fuck off a lot. I don't expect to be paid much. I don't negotiate for more money. Oh," she started writing as she spoke, "I know where the nearest abortion clinic is. Well," she confessed, "I used to know."

"Okay ... Can anyone help her out? With adding to her list?"

"Don't you wear jewelry?"

"No. Back in high school, I wore clip-on earrings once, but they hurt my ears so much, I took them off halfway through homeroom. I did wear an ID bracelet—they were fashionable then—but guys did that too." Dylan nodded confirmation.

"My aunt gave me a charm bracelet," Rev continued, "but whenever I wore it, I couldn't lay my arm flat on the desk in order to write. Unless I wanted to end up with miniature drum, violin, and flute indentations on my wrist. I wore a choker—they were also fashionable back then—but as soon as I understood their history— they're derivatives of the collar used to shackle slaves—I stopped."

Everyone was silent.

"Make-up?" There was something in the woman's voice that suggested genuine curiosity. And a dare.

Rev shook her head. "Rubbed a dab of my mother's lipstick on each cheek one day, thought that was how you got the rosy cheek look, but hated the feel of it. I already wore Chapstick on my lips, but again, guys do that too," Dylan nodded again, "and there was no way I was going to attempt eyeliner or mascara. Probably lose an eye." Again, Dylan nodded.

"Dylan?"

"Yes?"

"Would you like to tell us what you do that identifies you as a man?"

"I expect to be paid more than women. I negotiate for more money. And I take credit for women's ideas," he grinned.

Everyone stared.

"Tough crowd," he muttered.

"We don't have to teach the men how to put on make-up—" they'd moved on to the next item on their agenda.

"Or Rev," Sam interjected.

"Or jewelry—"

Dylan looked up. He'd been looking on Etsy for a new earring. He was looking forward to wearing one again. Or two, he thought.

Rev looked over at his open laptop. He had his shopping cart open.

"I think you're missing the point," she whispered. "When women wear earrings, they match."

"Because the app will present you with make-up and jewelry," Tania continued, "and that doesn't necessitate a change in how you act, how you move. But we do need to pay attention to the different clothes men and women typically wear. Men, if you put something in your pocket when the app is on, you'll give yourselves away, because women's clothing typically doesn't *have* pockets. For example."

"So you're saying we have to carry a purse when we use the app?" Sam asked. With disgust. No way was *he* going to carry a purse.

"You don't *have* to do anything. But unless you tweak the settings, the app will show you with one, so it'll be easier to match your behaviour with the app if you actually *have* one."

"We can do that?" someone asked. "Tweak the settings?"

Dylan and Rev looked at each other and smiled. Just a little smugly.

"Yes. The app will give you a default—and there are several you can choose from—but you always have the option of tweaking the features."

"Cool."

"But keep in mind that the more you tweak, the more you risk defeating the purpose of the app," she looked pointedly at Sam.

"Another thing for you men to keep in mind is that women's skirts often limit stride. We're going to spend a big chunk of time on walking, after we master sitting and standing, but as another example of needing to be aware of what your app is wearing, you'll have to take smaller steps if your app is wearing a skirt."

"You won't be able to sit with your legs apart either," a woman piped up.

"Well, you, men, shouldn't in any case. Even if your app-you has pants on. It just isn't ... "

"Lady-like?" Rev had her legs apart. Of course she did. It was far more comfortable than keeping them squeezed together.

"On that note," Kevin stepped forward, "let's start with sitting. As most of you know, or should know, men and women tend to sit differently. Men make themselves big. They take up a lot of space. That means they sit with their legs spread and their elbows out. Men even invade other people's space. So they spread their legs *beyond* the boundaries of their *own* chairs and rest their arms on *other* people's chair backs. Okay, women, let's see what you've got."

Kevin walked around the room, giving pointers to the women as they attempted to sit the way men do. It was ridiculously hard for many women. To take up so much space. To be so invasive of other people's space.

"Yes," Kevin said loudly to Rev as he passed by, "leaning forward with your elbows on your knees apart. Good one." She hadn't started yet.

"Now try leaning back and putting your arms on the chair backs, on either side," Kevin said to her.

She did that. But then her feet left the floor.

Kevin frowned. "Yeah, I guess that only works if you're a bit taller."

"Or the chairs are smaller. Built for women."

Dylan looked on with interest.

"You're right! So our furniture is built for men?"

Rev grimaced. "*Everything's* built for men. Well, except the pink tools in the hardware store."

"Actually," someone spoke up, "those tools are just a different colour. Would've been smart to have sized them for the female hand while they were at it. But ... duh."

"And when your feet dangle like that," Dylan pointed out to Rev, "it makes you look like a child. Think it's intentional? I mean, there's no reason chairs couldn't come in at least two sizes. Institutions could easily order a fifty-fifty mix."

"But then women would be sitting lower than men," Rev said. "That would look even worse. At least when your legs don't reach the floor, that's not always visible."

"Here." Tania pulled an oversized chair from the corner of the room. Must've been left over from a *Jack and the Beanstalk* performance. "Come sit in this to get the feeling."

Dylan obliged. His legs dangled. And it was awkward, a strain, to put his arms along the back. Oh wow.

"And Rev, sit in this." She brought forward a slightly smaller-than-average chair. *Goldilocks?*

Made to fit! She looked at Dylan. "This is how comfortable you've been all your life? How well you've felt you—fit?"

He nodded. Around the room, women sort of stared at men. Many insisted on trying the slightly smaller chair. They then *glared* at the men.

"Another good one," Kevin resumed walking around the space. A woman a few down from Rev had crossed her legs, ankle on knee. Rev had tried that, but had failed. Didn't have the hip flexibility.

"Also," Kevin tossed out a bit more advice, "adjust your package. A lot."

"Seriously?" Dylan objected. In defence of mature men everywhere. He'd accepted the invading bit, because many men *did* that, even though he himself didn't, but—

"Depending on the kind of man you want to be," Kevin conceded.

"Okay, men, your turn," Tania took over. "Make yourselves small. Take up as little space as possible." She started walking around the room. "Use only half the chair if possible. Keep your elbows in. Crossing your arms is iffy," she said to someone who'd gone that route, "it looks a little aggressive. You can, however, cross them over your purse. In a protective manner. No, don't put your arms on the backs of the chair," she said to another man, who obviously hadn't been paying attention. "Try putting your hands in your lap instead,"

"They're really going for the stereotypes, aren't they?" Rev muttered to Dylan.

"They are, yes. But that's what gender is, isn't it? At its worst?"

"Hm."

"So we could aim for what they tell us to do, fall short, and still be okay."

"Or we could just be our androgynous selves and let the app do the rest."

"You may cross your legs," Tania was back at the front of the room, "and in fact, that's preferable. But whatever you do, keep 'em together." She sat down, primly, with her legs neatly crossed.

"I can't," a man said from across the room.

"Oh come on," Tania chided, "your balls aren't *that* big!" Many of the women snickered. A few applauded.

"British men sit with their legs crossed this way all the time!" she continued. "Are you suggesting that an entire nation of men have small genitalia?"

Sam nodded. He refused to cross his legs. Sat with his ankles crossed. But with his knees apart. Well apart.

"No, it's not that," the man finally got one leg over the other but had to hold it there with his hand. Otherwise it kept slipping off.

"He's telling the truth," Rev spoke up. "I can't cross my legs that way either unless I do what he's doing. Or at least I couldn't until a few years ago." When I started losing muscle mass, she didn't say out loud.

"I think it's a matter of how thick your thighs are," she suggested, "combined with how inflexible your hips are, and well, maybe how inflexible you are in general—my muscles have always had a tendency to cramp. I couldn't walk for two days after my first marathon—"

"Me neither!" the man said. "Everything just … seized up."

Rev nodded. She remembered very well turning into cement. And crawling on the floor for half an hour after she made the mistake of getting to her knees to undo her shoes.

"And look," she continued, "he doesn't have long legs to begin with. I think it's easier for women with long, thin legs to cross their legs than it is for those of us with short, thick legs." A few women were nodding. "Which is why it's so stupid. That rule. That expectation."

"Hear, hear!" It was the woman with the raspy voice again. Rev looked for her again, again in vain.

Tania and Kevin declared a break, during which coffee was available in the foyer. Everyone stood. Then stretched. Self-consciously.

"Everyone back?" Kevin looked around the space. "Okay, we're moving on to standing. When men stand, they distribute their weight evenly on both legs," he demonstrated. "Women tend to put more weight on one leg." Tania demonstrated.

"But that means we'll be off balance," Sam pointed out.

"And easy to knock over," Rev assured him.

"Also, no surprise, men stand with their legs further apart than women do."

"Even though our hips are wider."

Tania gave Rev an odd look. Then nodded.

"All right, everyone up," Kevin said. "Let's see … "

He and Tania walked around the room, giving pointers, making small corrections.

"Okay," Tania said from the center of the room when they'd made one circuit. "I'd like everyone to stand on one leg. Good. Now look around."

All of the men, and Rev, had lifted one of their legs up in front of them. All of the women, and Dylan, had flicked a leg up behind them. Dylan was even trying to stand up on tippy toe.

"What the fuck are you doing?" Rev asked him.

"Trying to master the pose so many actresses have when a man kisses them."

"You look ridiculous."

"So do all those women. I mean seriously, what is it with that? They kiss and one of their legs flicks up behind them. It's like what happens when you scratch a dog in just the right place and their back leg starts jerking around … "

After a few more standing exercises—standing at a counter, standing in line, standing with something in your arms—the group was dismissed. They'd tackle walking the next day.

They decided to stop in at the City Lights Bookstore on their way home. It was on their to-do-while-in-SF list. Dylan's do-to-while-in-SF list. Rev pointedly didn't make a list. Wild side and all that.

"Should we try this with our apps on?" Dylan asked.

"Sure. We can do standing-at-a-bookshelf," she said dryly. "As a member of the other sex slash gender," she added.

"I'll go to the Women's Studies section and see what happens. No, wait. I should do it first with the app off. See if I get any looks. Then with the app on."

They discovered the City Lights Bookstore didn't have a Women's Studies section. It had a Gender Studies section though.

Dylan stood, in a very manly way, in front of the feminist research sub-section. No one paid any attention to him.

He waited until for sure no one was paying any attention to him, then turned on the app, stuck out a hip, lifted one of his legs, and almost fell over. Still, no one paid any attention to him.

"You know, it was probably enough to establish no reaction to your being there as you."

"You're right. The app is needed only when—*When* is the app needed?"

"When you go to the vintage auto section."

"Right. Or *you* could just go the vintage auto section. As you. And see what happens."

They discovered the City Lights Bookstore didn't have a vintage auto section.

So they just browsed. Dylan bought a copy of *The Essential Ginsberg.* And *God's Lunatics.* Which would give new meaning to the phrase 'blinded by the light'.

Rev wandered into a section titled Evidence. Didn't know whether to be intrigued or dismayed. That there *was* a separate section called Evidence. She supposed it was intended to make up for the Religion section, but it seemed to her to take evidence out of the mainstream and put it in a neat, little box. A neat, little *separate* box. Like the one Women's Issues was in.

When they entered the house, late afternoon, they heard the blues. Not sports. Alarmed, thinking someone was in the house, they crept carefully toward the living room. Moe was lying on the couch, belly up, groovin'. Only then did they notice the other box of paw-sized touch buttons sitting beside the stereo.

"Cool. Do you think Spur changes the CD every now and then?"

"She'd better not. Not if Moe is anything like me." And that was a sentence Rev never thought she'd say. But it was true. She could listen to the same piece of music over and over for hours. If she liked it. If she didn't, the piece didn't make it past the first few bars.

After some pizza—so many options for delivery!—and a few different kinds of cheesecake, they spent the evening making notes for their book about the gender training class. Dylan had convinced the editor to bring Rev on board as co-author, fifty-fifty.

"Hey, what about your ecotourism-is-an-oxymoron book?"

"Thought we'd work on that one *after* this one. You know, when we're back home."

"We?"

"Hey, did you know that the fog in San Francisco has already decreased by about 30% because of global warming?" Dylan asked. He'd finished with his notes.

"Nope."

"And," Dylan sighed, "if we want to see the fog roll in—"

"That's on your list?"

He nodded. "—we have to be here in the summer."

A little later, when Kit was likely to be home, Dylan called Loup. Well, he called Kit and asked her to put Loup on—asked her to get Loup.

"Hey Loup, how are you?"

Loup wagged her tail and licked the screen. Well, the screen protector.

"Hey, listen to this," Dylan pressed 'play' for Moe's blues CD. Loup left the room. Apparently.

"Seriously?"

"Maybe she's a rock-and-roll wolf," Rev suggested.

"Actually," Kit said, "she likes Vivaldi."

"What? How do you know?" Dylan asked the obvious.

"Because whenever I play some Vivaldi, she comes into the room and lays down. Not too keen on Beethoven, but Bach will do."

"That's—I don't—You think she can really tell the difference?"

"Yes. But I'm as surprised as you, because—"

"And she just lays there? She doesn't sing, howl, along?"

Kit stared at him. "Have you ever tried to sing along to Vivaldi?"

"Can't say as I have, no," Dylan made a note to himself right then and there to try. Next chance he had.

"Dogs tend to howl along to wind instruments," Rev said, googling. "Though a long note on the violin would do."

"But Vivaldi doesn't have long notes," Kit replied. "It's all quite busy, quite complex."

"It is," Dylan agreed. Wondering if that was why Loup liked it. But why would she like busy, complex music? She wasn't a city dog. Her life was, for the most part, calm and simple. 'Course, maybe that was why.

"Hey, you should listen to *Howl*," Rev said after he'd said bye (and "I'll be back") to Loup.

"I already have. One of the reasons I bought the Ginsberg."

"No, not that *Howl*. There's this guy, Kirk Nurock, trained at Julliard by the way, who composed and conducted a piece for twenty voices and three canines. At Carnegie Hall."

"Called *Howl*," Dylan said, with delight, reading over Rev's shoulder.

Rev skimmed right past mention of *Sonata for Piano and Dog* and pointed to *Expedition*: an arrangement for Jazz Trio and Siberian Husky.

"iTunes!" Dylan cried out.

Rev was already there ... but, sadly, *Expedition* wasn't there. Or anywhere else Dylan looked before he went to bed.

10

ood morning," Kevin said enthusiastically to the class the next morning. Almost everyone was still in the group.

"Today we're going to focus on walking. As Tania mentioned yesterday, and as most of you already know, men take longer strides. They have a higher center of gravity, so they lead with their chest. Women take smaller steps, they have a lower center of gravity, so they lead with their hips."

"Do not," Rev muttered.

"Men very often take the stairs two at a time—"

"In a pathetic attempt to exude fitness," Rev muttered.

"Women are more likely to hang on to the handrail."

"No, they—" Rev stopped. Kevin was right. She couldn't remember ever seeing a man hang on to the railing. 'Course, men didn't wear high heels. While walking up or down stairs.

"Anything else?" Kevin tossed it out to the class.

"Men can't walk and talk at the same time."

"Can she join another group?"

Once the preliminaries were over, everyone got up and started walking around. Dylan looked like Data with a few circuits blown as he tried to co-ordinate what he thought his hips were supposed to be doing with what he thought the rest of him was supposed to be doing.

"Smaller steps," Tania said to Dylan, as she and Kevin circulated around the room, again making corrections and giving pointers. "Don't forget you may have on a short, tight skirt."

Dylan made his steps even smaller.

"Smaller still."

"But it will take me forever to get anywhere!" Dylan protested.

Rev nodded.

"*And* I'll look like a child! These are baby-steps!"

Rev nodded. As did another woman. They exchanged a smile.

"Don't turn your feet out like that," Tania said to another man. He stared at her. He'd never *ever* paid attention to the turn of his feet before. Whether they were turned out or in—who the hell cared?

Rev nodded. Along with two more women. Knowing smiles were again exchanged.

"No, don't hunch over like that."

"What?" Another man was stunned by the attention needed to— to whether or not he leaned forward a little bit?

"And don't swing your arms."

Seriously?

"Pretend you're walking along a straight, single line," Tania said to another man. "Instead of along two parallel lines."

The man looked at her as if she was crazy.

Rev nodded. Along with several women. Several smiling women.

"Here," she handed the man a book that had been left on a nearby chair. "Try walking with this on your head. It'll give you a clue."

Every woman in the room applauded.

"I wonder if we'll cover running tomorrow," Dylan said to Rev during a break. He thought he'd mastered walking. Small steps. Minimal arm movement. Easy, since he had a purse over each arm and was clutching them to his sides.

"Don't be silly. Women don't run."

Dylan stared at her.

"Unless they're athletes," she added. "In which case they're dykes. Not real women."

He stared at her.

"Speaking of which, where'd you get the purses?"

"One of the props boxes." Dylan nodded to several large chests against the side wall.

Rev walked over—lengthening her stride halfway there, then changing her mind and shortening it again, because she didn't want to pull a hamstring—then rummaged around. She found a pair of football shoulder pads. She put them on.

"You know," she said to Dylan, who had finally arrived at her side, "this is sort of what wearing a men's suitcoat feels like."

"Now, men," Tania smiled, such a devilish smile, "your app-you will probably be wearing heels." She pulled a pair of heels from one of the props boxes. Size eleven. Pretty scuffed up. "So although *you* don't actually have to wear them, you're going to have to walk *as if* you *were* wearing them. So ... ?"

Dylan raised his hand. Sure, he'd be the first one to try. Tania handed them over. He sat down to put them on. Like he was about to lace up a pair of hockey skates.

"No, most women put them on while standing. Either they slip into them one foot at a time, or they stand on one foot—"

Dylan lifted his foot to put the left shoe on.

"No, don't bend your knee and lift your foot," Tania said. "Flick your foot up behind you, remember? Then reach back—"

Dylan tried that. Fell over.

Rev laughed so hard, she too fell over.

Tania passed out the rest of the man-sized high heels.

A minute later, you could *feel* the frustration pheromones, the air was so saturated with them.

Dylan managed to take a few steps. But then he stood in one place for a moment, teetering. "Could you women be any more—"

"You women?" Rev said, archly.

"No. Right. Not you. Not all women."

He reached out and put his hand on Rev's shoulder for balance before he attempted another step. She was, of course, standing with her feet apart. And was oh so stable.

He ventured a few more steps. And fell over again.

"Bloody hell! I'm going to really hurt myself wearing these!"

Rev nodded.

"And I certainly won't be able to break into a run."

Rev nodded.

"How the *hell* do you walk in these things?" Half an hour had passed. Dylan was still hobbling along, wobbling along ...

"I don't."

"You've never worn high heels?"

Rev shook her head. "My dress shoes had low thick heels. Mostly I wore desert boots and then when Adidas were invented ... "

"Your mother let you wear Adidas with your—you never wore dresses?"

"Actually, I did. The grade school I went to insisted on skirts and dresses. I actually didn't mind too much. Back then. What I hated though was wearing leotards, tights, panty hose. I wore knee socks instead, but in winter, my thighs got so cold they'd turn red. Fortunately, in grade ten, the school changed its policy and allowed girls to wear pants."

Dylan stared at her. It had never occurred to him that skirts and knee socks wouldn't be *warm* enough.

"But to answer your question, my mother considered saddle shoes and penny loafers acceptable footwear for school. For when I was wearing skirts and dresses."

"Saddle shoes and penny loafers." Dylan was lost in the 1950s for a moment.

"And now?" he asked. "When you have to dress up to ... go to a ... funeral?" Because she sure as hell wouldn't go to a wedding.

"I don't go to funerals. No point. But to answer your other question, when I'm in a dress, I feel like I'm in drag."

"Me too!"

"Legs closer together," Tania said as she passed Dylan, who was standing still. Not falling over.

"I can stand on stilts or I can stand with my legs close together. I can't do both."

Tania just smiled.

On their way home, they went shopping. First they went to a store Tania had mentioned, and Dylan bought a pair of red sequined high heels. With a pretty little bow on the back of each heel.

Then, "I want to buy a kazoo."

"Okay."

"It'll be cheaper than a clarinet or saxophone."

"And easier to play. Though that might not matter," Rev added, realizing then why Dylan was going to get a kazoo.

"They've hypothesized that wolves howl to assemble the pack and to reinforce the pack identity. When a wolf joins a group howl, or jam session," Dylan amended with a grin, "they intentionally don't howl on the same note as the other wolves. In fact," he quoted what he'd read, "'a wolf seems to revel in the discordant sound it makes.'"

"But Loup doesn't howl along to Vivaldi."

"No, apparently classical music has a calming effect on dogs. Heavy metal makes them agitated."

"Duh."

"I want her to revel."

"Of course you do."

"When I'm back."

Rev thought Loup would revel when Dylan was back, kazoo or not. Even so, she decided to get one too.

At first Dylan was horrified, since she was a notoriously bad singer. Enthusiastic, but hopelessly tone-deaf. But then he realized that would be perfect.

As soon as they got home, Dylan put on his new shoes and started puttering around the house. He lasted an hour. Which was fifty-nine minutes and thirty seconds longer than Rev had lasted when she had first put on a pair of high heels.

"I think the trick is to not put any weight on the heel. Try just walking around on your tippy toes. With the shoes on."

Dylan tried that. "Better," he said. "But my Achilles tendons are sore already."

Rev nodded. "And within a year, you'll have bunions, blisters, ingrown toenails, and pinched nerves, not to mention chronic back, hip, and knee pain. Oh, and permanently shortened Achilles tendons."

Dylan decided never to have his app wear heels. If he couldn't walk in them for real, he certainly wouldn't be able to pretend enough to maintain the illusion.

"So you're going to return them?"

"I don't think I can, now that I've worn them."

"You could send them to Loup."

"I'd have to scrape all the sequins off first."

"EBay!" they said together. Surely there was *someone* out there who wanted to buy a worn-once pair of red high heels. In size eleven. With sequins. And pretty bows on the back.

They ordered out for dinner again—this time, arepas, cachapas, tajadas, and yuca fries from a Venezuelan place—and had dessert while they waited.

They made notes about the day, then thought about what to do next.

"You know, I'm tired," Rev confessed.

"Yeah, the last couple days *have* been a little exhausting!"

Moe stared at them.

"Oh, but we're not *that* tired!" Dylan said to him. "Are we?" he looked at Rev.

"No. We *might* be that tired if we had to put on coats and scarves and hats and gloves and boots … But we can just open the door and walk out!" She demonstrated.

"Well, maybe we should put on a jacket," she walked back in.

"And shoes." Dylan laced up his track shoes with *such* delight.

They went for a lovely long walk. In January. In San Francisco.

And then they went to bed.

Because they were so old.

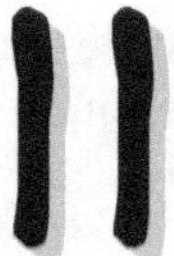

"Are we dancing today?" Dylan asked eagerly. It was day three of their gender training classes. Everyone was back in the theatre, some looking more ready than others. No one was looking more ready than Dylan.

"No wait," he said then, "men don't dance."

Rev grinned. She knew very well that Dylan danced. He *loved* dancing.

"No wait," Dylan said again, "I'll turn on my app! *Then* I can dance!"

Rev thought of Sam having to dance 'like a woman' and grinned.

"No," Kevin said, "no dancing today, but we would like you all to expand your physical movement repertoire. Men, first."

"Of course."

Kevin ignored her.

There were a few actual couples in their group, like Sam and Laura, as well as a few same-sex couples, but most were friends, usually in same-sex clusters. So Kevin and Tania put everyone into male-female pairs.

"All right, everyone. Men, turn on your apps, then start moving. Reach for something, something high, something low, carry something … Women, watch them, make suggestions, help them out."

"Because that's what women do. They help out."

Kevin glared at her. "We'll be reversing things in a moment."

"And then the men can tell us what we're doing wrong. What we should do instead. Because that's what *men* do."

Some of the other women grinned.

"But 'If I can't dance, I don't want to be part of your revolution,'" Dylan pouted. Then turned to Rev. "Did I do that right?" He stuck out his lower lip again.

"How the hell should I know?"

The exercise was amazingly productive. Most people knew when their partner wasn't doing it right, but it took a while to figure out what, exactly, was the problem. The analysis was enlightening.

During their break, in the mood for something cold (in January!), they got a couple cans of Pepsi from the machine. When Dylan finished his, he crushed the can. Well, dented the can. He tried harder. Then added his other hand to the task, squeezing the can as hard as he could. Finally, he just put it onto the floor and stomped on it.

Rev stared at him.

"That's what men do," he said. "Whenever they're finished with something, they destroy it."

"Why?" she asked a long moment later. Deciding not to tell him that *she* could crush a can with one hand.

"Don't know. *I* don't."

She agreed. "No, you don't."

And then after another long moment, "Why not?"

He thought about it. "Well it's not because I've thought about it," he said.

"That's—not encouraging."

"It isn't, no."

The after-break session was just as productive. Just as enlightening.

On their way home, Dylan stopped at a discount store to buy a new pair of shoes—running shoes—so he could send Loup his current worn-a-bit pair. Then they stopped at a post office so he could do just that.

Moe wasn't in the house when they got home, but a quick glance out the back door snuffed out their momentary anxiety. The dogs were in the yard romping about. Diving onto the grass and rolling about. Weird. No matter.

Ten minutes later, Moe came into the house.

"Eew!" Rev was the closest. "What the hell?"

He smelled of fish.

"Priscilla must've brought sushi for everyone."

"Out!" She shepherded Moe out the door, trying not to touch him, then closed it behind him. Hoped no one came at it at a run. "We need to give him a bath."

"We should probably give them *all* a bath."

"Yeah. Too bad we can't just throw them into the lake." Rev missed her cabin. On a lake. In a forest.

"I think I saw one of those kiddie pools in the garage. We could fill it with water—there must be an outdoor faucet and a hose somewhere, yeah? We can put bubble bath in it!"

They found the pool, the faucet, and the hose. No bubble bath.

"Back in a minute," Dylan said, and took off on the bike he'd been using.

Rev found a pair of gloves in the garage, then proceeded to pick up all of the fish bits, her search guided by the dogs, and put them in a plastic bag. Once she figured she'd found them all—that is, when the dogs lost interest in what she was doing—she tied the bag with a double knot, put it into the outdoor garbage bin, and secured the lid.

Dylan returned soon after, triumphant with a big bottle of bubble bath.

"The upside of living in a city!" Back home, he would've had to drive all the way into town. And even then ...

They filled the pool—pausing momentarily to wonder about water rationing in California and whether it was environmentally responsible to use water for this purpose, but Dylan pointed out that he'd seen not one but two people washing their probably-not-fish-stinky cars on his way to and from the store—then added a generous amount of bubble bath.

Moe loved it. 'Course, he was a lab. They had a fondness for lying in every puddle they came across. Mel had to be coaxed. By Moe. And the beach ball Dylan had found, and inflated. Soon, Moe and Mel were having a great time batting it about. Dylan soaped their shoulders and backs with the bar of soap he'd also purchased.

Fetchnut went into the pool only when it became absolutely necessary. To fetch her ball. Rev grinned. Was she smart or what? Her. Not Fetchnut.

And Priscilla—apparently neither huskies nor foxes like the water. Unfortunately, she was the one who stunk the most. She wasn't aggressive, they weren't afraid of getting bit, but she was agile and quick and she thoroughly enjoyed being chased around the yard. Eventually, she scooted out through the doggy door on the left side of the yard. She could've done that right at the start, but then she would've missed the fun of the chase.

Almost immediately, Rev and Dylan heard a shriek. Then a no-nonsense "OUT! NOW!"

"We've got a bubble bath going on over here!" Dylan shouted out.

"Be there in a minute!" The woman called back. Laughing.

Sure enough, a minute later, a middle-aged woman holding Priscilla firmly against her chest came in through the gate at the side of the house. She was wearing shorts, a tshirt, and flip flops.

"Thanks. Sorry about this," she took in the scene. "It was her fault, wasn't it? She brought the dead fish?"

"Yeah. But no worries. We're having fun."

Moe burped bubbles.

The woman laughed again, flipped her flip flops off, and got into the pool. With Priscilla. She held her down without drowning her and started bathing her, gratefully accepting the bar of soap Dylan handed her. A few minutes later, she stood up, Priscilla still in her arms—

"You picked up all the fish bits?"

"I think so," Rev said.

"Okay, away you go!" She let her loose.

Priscilla tore around the yard like a crazy dog, body surfing to get herself dry. It didn't actually work, since the yard was pretty much soaked, what with Moe, and Mel, and Fetchnut having already done that. No matter. It was fun.

Moe burped bubbles again.

"Speaking of which," Dylan said, "would you something to drink? We don't have any beer, but we've got three different kinds of juice." They'd also stopped at a grocery store on their way home.

"Sure," the woman said. "Surprise me."

Dylan went into the house, and Rev got a few lawn chairs from the garage.

"Thanks," the woman said when Dylan handed her a glass, "I'm Cheryl, by the way."

"Dylan."

"Rev."

"Nice to meet you!" The three of them settled into the chairs.

"So, we were wondering ... " Dylan said, "is Priscilla part husky, part fox?"

"It would explain a lot," Cheryl agreed, "but I really don't know what she is. She's a rescue dog. She just walked into my house one day and rescued me."

"It can happen like that," Dylan nodded. Rev smiled.

"I was in a really bad place. My baby daughter had just died, and my husband had left, said he couldn't deal with his own grief *and* mine, and most of the friends I'd had from college had left when I became pregnant, they weren't even married yet, so things just ... And all my new friends were really just acquaintances, you know, new moms I'd met at the park, or wherever, so it was—I just couldn't bear to be around them, each with their own little baby, and so—too much information?" She broke off suddenly and grinned. Sort of.

"Not at all," Dylan assured her.

"And so when Priscilla—We'd named our baby girl Priscilla and— It was probably stupid to name the dog—But I just needed so bad for her not to be gone ... "

"I doubt you get the two of them mixed up," Rev said. Seeing as Priscilla, the dog, had a chipmunk in her mouth.

"DROP IT!" Cheryl commanded.

Priscilla dropped it.

"Wow. That's impressive," Dylan said. "Good for you!"

"Thanks," the woman smiled. "It was hard, teaching her stuff, but it was exactly what I needed. As well as the warm, little body to hold."

"Good girl!" Cheryl called out. Priscilla bounded over at the sound of the praise, jumped up into Cheryl's lap, and curled into the sweetest little doggy ball.

"A rescue dog indeed," Dylan smiled at the two of them.

Speaking of which, that evening …

"Loup's still doing well?" he asked. Though he could see that she was.

"She is. She and Flaker spend most of their time outside, happy and safe. We go for a walk in the forest every afternoon when I get home. I take my rifle with me."

"You have a rifle? You weren't thinking of offing some of the little juvenile delinquents, were you?"

"I was, yes, but no, I'd never do that. The rifle is to scare off whatever might come after us. I don't trust Loup not to engage with—whatever. So I thought if that happens, I'd just shoot a couple rounds into the air and the whatever would take off."

"Loup would take off too."

"Yeah. But I'm hoping they'd take off in different directions. Loup, toward your place. Or mine."

"Yeah. I think you're right. Good plan. Thanks. If that ever happens, if she *does* take off, you know to check not only Rev's screened-in porch, but also Loup's little den in the shed? That's where she hides out during thunder storms." The very day Loup had followed Dylan out of the forest, Dylan had made a perfectly comfortable wolf den for her in Rev's shed. Just in case she needed a place to stay. He'd actually spent an hour making a nice little cave of crates and flattened cardboard boxes; then he put food and water dishes inside, and one of his shoes; then he hung a blanket over the entrance. Froot Loup moved into Rev's porch. It had a couch. And, since he'd brought it with him, one of Dylan's shoes. Perfect.

"Okay, good to know."

"Thank you for taking such good care of her," Dylan said, then told Loup that she was such a good little wolf. And that he'd be back.

12

Today we're going to talk about talking," Tania opened the session on Friday, day four. "As you know, the app will change the pitch and timbre of your voice, to match the vocal cords and larynx of the other sex, but it won't change your inflections or, of course, your words."

"But we all speak English, don't we?" Sam looked around. "Ergo, men and women use the same words!" He was getting a little fed up with all this gender crap.

"Actually we don't," Tania replied. "Use the same words. At the very least, there are some words that men use with greater frequency than women, and vice versa. For example, women use the word 'like' more often than men. And you'll never hear a man describe something as 'cute'."

Rev looked pointedly at Dylan. Who shrugged.

"Except maybe his girlfriend. Or infant daughter," Kevin added.

"Which they often mix up," Rev added.

"Can she *please* join another group?"

"In addition to the vocabulary differences," Tania continued, after a run-down of the main vocabulary differences, "there are syntax differences. Men issue commands; women issue requests. Men use declaratives; women use interrogatives."

Rev was making notes. It was all old news to her, of course, but she thought it best to have all these things in a list she could consult before she apped over to the dark side. Somehow the verbal stuff seemed more slippery than the physical stuff.

"And, this isn't really a syntax difference, but compared to men, women explain too much. Men don't feel the need to explain themselves."

Rev's pen stopped moving. Okay, this is new, she thought, with interest. She'd never noticed that difference. And if she had, she would have attributed her tendency to explain to having been a teacher or to being a philosopher. But Tania's explanation seemed much better. She was impressed. Clearly, she was going to enjoy today's session much more than yesterday's.

"They also apologize more than men do. I swear women apologize for simply being alive. It's like they think they're not entitled to ... anything. So they're always apologizing for taking, for having ... "

Yes, exactly!

"Women especially apologize for wanting money. That's why they so seldom ask for a raise. But there's no shame in wanting financial success!"

Indeed.

"And then there are inflection differences. Women tend to raise their voices at the ends of sentences."

"Expressing uncertainty—" one of the men nodded.

"Or seeking agreement," Tania added. Rev smiled. And again, was impressed. Tania was up to date on the research.

"Women, you'll have to shear away all the politeness, all the 'Would you pleases' and 'If you don't minds'. Use more demanding diction, like 'I need you to ... ' Men, you'll have to start adding those—"

"Are you saying that men aren't polite?" Sam interrupted.

"And you'll have to stop interrupting the other person." Tania glared at him.

Rev grinned.

"Men interrupt far more often than women do," Tania continued, "and women are interrupted far more often than men are. Because of that, because women are *used to being* interrupted, they speak more quickly than men and with shorter sentences. They have to rush to make their point."

Yes! So true!

"Women stop speaking as soon as they're interrupted. Men start competing with the interruptor."

That was *exactly* what they did!

"Men, on the other hand, go on and on … "

"They're allowed to," Rev couldn't help interjecting.

"They hog the conversational space as well as the physical space," the raspy voice added.

Tania nodded, then continued. "And they speak slowly. That is, they insert lengthy pauses of weight and gravity. Not only is that a way hogging the space, as you say, but it's one of the ways they maintain their so-called natural authority. Of course," she added, "if it *were* natural, they wouldn't have to work so hard to maintain it."

Rev nodded. As did, no doubt, the raspy-voiced woman. And several other women in the room.

"Despite talking more," Tania continued, "men are less articulate."

"Go figure."

"They have a greater tendency to mumble. And, or perhaps because, though the app will take care of this, they don't move their lips as much when they speak. Nor do they open their mouths as wide."

Sam snickered.

Rev quickly turned on her app, turned to Sam, and said, aggressively, "Just shut up and listen!"

"Good," Tania said.

"Good? She can't talk to me like that!"

"Sure she can. Men talk like that to women all the time."

"Well, not all the time," Dylan interjected. Tried to interject. Was ignored. His app was turned on too.

"And what am I supposed to do about it?" Sam demanded. He knew what he'd do about it if—

"Nothing. If your app is on."

He crossed his arms across his chest. And spread his legs a little wider. Without realizing it.

Tania waited a moment, then continued. "And while we're on the face, men don't open their eyes as widely. They tend to squint."

"Pretending to have a thought."

"Men speak more in a monotone," Tania carried on with her list. "Women are far more expressive, there's more variation in pitch.

"And, of course, men speak more loudly than women.

"Lastly, women use their hands a lot when they talk. To communicate."

"Do I use my hands a lot to communicate?" Rev asked Dylan.

Dylan thought about it.

"You use your middle finger a lot. Does that count?"

"Any questions before we start putting all that into play?" Tania asked after the break.

No questions.

"Okay," Tania looked out over the class. "Who'd like to go first? Let's say you're in a store, shopping. Dylan?"

Dylanna stood then approached Tania. "Excuse me," she gently touched her sleeve, "could I get a little help, please?"

"Oh that's good. Real good," Tania was impressed. "You used the polite 'Excuse me' *and* you asked for help *and* you said 'please' *and* you used the word 'little'. The gentle touch was icing on the cake. Women touch other people far more often than men do. Nicely done."

Dylanna beamed.

"Yes, good!" Tania said. "Men typically don't smile in response to praise."

"Men typically don't smile period," Rev grimaced.

Dylanna curtsied. To Tania.

"Okay, that's pushing it."

Dylan grinned.

"Rev?" Tania invited Rev to try.

Revv stood up, walked right past Tania, bumping her a little on the way, then stopped, planted his feet wide apart, put his hands on his hips, and bellowed. "Where the hell are the—twisty nails?"

They decided to get silly when they got home. They'd both had enough of talking. And thinking about what they said.

They forgot that when they got silly, they talked a lot. But at least they didn't think about what they said. At least not before they said it.

They also listened to Moe's blues. After a minute, or maybe it was an hour, they decided to play along with their kazoos.

Moe left the room. Left the house, actually. The property, in fact.

On Saturday, they went to the Palace of Fine Arts, which was quiet and peaceful, relatively speaking, and then they walked along Baker Beach at sunset. It was very nice.

Until they came within hearing distance of a bunch of guys …

"Oh don't be such a girl about it!" one of them chided.

"Hey!" Revv said sharply. "Don't use what I am as an insult!"

"But you're a—guy!"

"Oh yeah." She'd had her app on.

Dylanna stepped up. "Don't use what I am as an insult!"

"What?"

"You said 'Don't be such a girl!' in the same tone of voice as 'Don't be such an idiot!' Girls aren't idiots. All things female aren't to be despised."

"What?"

They glanced at each other, agreed that further interaction would be pointless, and so carried on their way, surreptitiously turning off their apps.

"You know what your problem is, lady?" one of them called out.

Dylan sucked in his breath. And held it.

"Yeah," Revv turned. And took half a dozen steps back. "Having to share a world with pompous assholes who feel entitled to tell me what my problems are."

And then she hauled back and decked him one.

"Did I do that right?" she asked Dylan as she rushed back to him. They hadn't covered assault in their gender class yet.

"How should I know, I've never hit anyone."

"Really?"

"Really."

"Oh."

But the highlight of the weekend was going to the Red Victorian, which was resurrecting the work of Sami Sunchild, environmental artist and social activist who, in the 70s, hosted "World Peace Conversations" every Sunday morning.

"'As part of a movement to restore the lost art of conversation,'" Dylan had read from the website, "'Peaceful World Conversation brings people together to talk about topics that matter in their own lives and in the world as a whole.'"

"Cool," Rev said. "It sounds a bit like a philosophy cafe, which were popular for a while in the 90s, then fizzled out."

"So, shall we go?"

"Yes!"

"It's in the morning."

"Oh. Still. Yes."

So, Sunday morning, they got up—a necessary prerequisite—got ready, turned on their apps, and went to the Red Victorian. To converse with like-minded people about significant issues.

"Welcome to The Lost Art of Conversation," said a tie-dyed woman. Literally. She was 60s tie-dye meet 00s tattoo. "We'll start, as always, by going around the room for quick introductions."

"Dylan-na O'Toole," Dylan-na stuttered when it was his turn. "Part historian, part travel writer."

"Revv. Philosopher. Writer," she added. Insisted.

There were a few lawyers, a few professors, a psychologist, a physicist ... For a moment, Rev considered moving to San Francisco. To be surrounded by kin rather than no-necks who called her a cunt and kept women who treated her like a child because she wasn't married-with-kids …

"Now, as for a topic—"

"How about automated systems and their influence on human agency."

Dylan stared at her. Him. Rev stared at herself. Himself. She'd interrupted. Without apology. Not to mention, with something intelligent. In the morning.

"Oh, that sounds like a good one. Would you like to start us off?"

And she wasn't reprimanded for it. By anyone.

"Sure. I lost my wallet last year—it fell out of my pocket when I was testing mattresses at Bay Street Mattress—and so when I went to BetterBuy—next on my list—to return a flatscreen tv I'd purchased and then decided I didn't like—I was told they couldn't process a refund."

She kept waiting to be interrupted. That explained, in part, why one incomplete sentence followed another. She kept tagging them on. Realizing she still had the floor. If someone had told her she'd have a full five minutes, she would've, might've, formed *complete* sentences.

Though, she realized, she was doing a lot of explaining. She'd explained why she lost her wallet, why she went to BetterBuy, why she was returning the tv …

"It had to be on the same credit card the purchase was made on," Michael anticipated.

"Yes!" Revv said. "Which I didn't have! Because, lost wallet. So I said, 'Okay, I've got another credit card'—I keep a back-up in my car that I use only for gas—'put the refund on this card.' No, it has to be the same card," she, he, nodded to Michael. "'Okay,' I said, 'so give me cash back.' No, they can't do that. They can give me credit though. Toward future purchases. 'I don't want credit,' I said. At this point, I had no intention of buying anything from BetterBuy ever again. 'Why can't you give me cash?' I asked. And the manager said—yes, by now I was dealing with the manager—the manager said, 'The system doesn't allow it.'"

Revv paused. For effect. No one jumped into the silence.

And there *was* silence. People had become quiet as soon as she'd, he'd, started talking. They were paying attention. It was like they thought that what she, he, was saying was important!

"'Well,' I said, 'work around the system! Does the system serve you or do you serve the system?'"

She paused again. Someone applauded. She was stunned. No one had *ever* applauded the brilliant things she'd said. And she'd said many brilliant things in her lifetime.

"'*You're* the human,' I said. 'Why can't you just give me cash?' 'It's not that easy,' the manager said, smiling at my ignorance. The prick. 'Of course it's that easy,' I replied."

She kept going. She, he, was *allowed* to keep going.

"'Open the till, reach in with your hand, take out two hundred dollars and forty-nine cents, and give it to me.' *But the system seemed to have deprived him of such agency.*"

Several people nodded.

"I once insisted that someone from the water company make a correction manually," James said, "because, same thing, the system wouldn't allow it, and the customer service person said, 'What do you mean?' *What do you mean?*" he repeated, then laughed with incomprehension.

Revv nodded. "Have you seen *Idiocracy?*"

Dylanna jumped in. "A big part of the problem is—"

"—the system in the first place," Maurice took over.

Dylanna was—surprised. Then insulted. Then angry.

Maurice continued. "The automated systems are designed by computer studies graduates at the bottom of their class."

"The ones unable to imagine exceptions to their few rules," Revv added.

Together the men would figure this out.

"And, or, who are no doubt themselves simply following some protocol that—" Dylanna tried again.

"—doesn't leave any room for exceptions." Maurice took over again.

"Or even all the less likely possibilities," Revv added, "the infrequent situations."

"Yes!" Maurice agreed with her. With him. Whole-heartedly. "Because, having to issue a refund when a credit card has been lost or stolen isn't all that unimaginable!"

"But even so," Revv said, "only a real person could just open the till and give me my money back. Which means," she said, with great reluctance, "that humans are more capable, more competent—"

"More intelligent?" Dylanna teased.

Revv ignored him. Her. Because she was a he.

"—than AI systems. *Some* AI systems. *Most* AI systems."

More nods.

So she, he, expanded her analysis. "Another effect of all these complicated automated processes is that people expect you to watch them work. Figuratively. I remember back in the late 90s, when I was teaching at a university, I had to call someone to book a room for seminars. Mondays and Wednesdays, 7pm, for six weeks, starting two weeks hence. The call should have taken the time it took for me to just say that. Thirty seconds max.

"But the woman replied very slowly, 'Mondays and Wednesdays … ' and then there was silence. So I repeated the rest, thinking she'd forgotten what I'd said.

"More silence. Then, 'Okay, 7pm … '

"More prompting. By this point, I was wondering whether she was paying attention. Wondering, truthfully, whether she was mentally delayed.

"'And you'd like the reservation for six weeks?'

"'Yes!' I practically shouted. 'Mondays and Wednesdays, 7pm, six weeks, starting in two weeks. It's not that difficult!'

"Well, she thought I'd been rude, reported me to my department head, who called me into his office, and reprimanded me for my behaviour."

"She'd been making the reservations as you spoke," Jennifer spoke up, "inputting it into the system, waiting for it to respond … "

"Yes!" Revv said. "I didn't know that! I expected her to just make a note of it, then put it into the system on her *own* time. Why did I have to stay on the phone while she did her job?"

Several people nodded.

"Same thing happened to me the other day with the phone company," Revv continued. "After I explained my first problem, that I'd been billed incorrectly, the woman went into the system, made the correction, which of course took a lot longer than that, then actually asked if she could put me on hold while she made notes about our conversation, after which she'd transfer me to the appropriate person for the second part of my call, which was to change my plan. When she came back online, she asked, per script, if I had any other questions.

"I said 'Yeah. Why did I have to wait while you made your notes? Why couldn't you have transferred me *before* you made your notes?'"

"She was following protocol," Maurice anticipated the explanation. "No doubt, she was *instructed* to input information about the call before transferring in case there was some other information she needed from you."

Revv nodded.

"And when you called the phone company," James added, "you no doubt had to spend several minutes making choices among non-exhaustive options, sometimes even non-exclusive options, and then when you finally get a real person, she acts like a robot!"

"But if they don't follow the script, they're fired," a woman, Jill, explained. Briefly. Quickly.

"Yes, but geez loueez, the script!" Revv exclaimed. "You have to give your name, your address, your date of birth, your account number, your mother's maiden name, your neighbour's cat's name, and the name of the sixth planet from the sun before they'll say 'And how can I help you today?' Then it turns out you've gotten the wrong department," she nodded to James, "because, non-exhaustive and non-exclusive, so she transfers you, and you have to start all over with your name, your address, your date of birth ... "

"It's beyond Kafka, isn't it?" James said. "I mean, at one point you just give up. Is two hours of time and hassle worth the fifty dollar correction on your bill?"

"You know, that wasn't much of a conversation," Dylan said angrily as they started walking home. Rev had been thinking that the app had passed its first test with flying colours. Using it would give women airtime. Lots of airtime. They would be heard, and, my god, applauded.

"Agreed." She gave him a moment. "And yet it was exactly like every conversation I've ever been part of except that this time—"

"Yeah."

"But," he wasn't done yet, "when I started to make the point about relative intelligence, you *ignored* me!"

"*I* didn't ignore you. *Revv* did."

"Seriously?" He stopped and turned to her. "Is that the kind of man you want to be?"

"No, I—" She stopped too. And saw that he was really upset. Well, good. But. "No. But—"

They spent a long time making notes that evening. For their book *and* for the app people.

"I think we should call them," Dylan said at one point. "Dana, Erin, and Kim. Ask them exactly what we're supposed to be testing."

"Okay."

14

Okay, let's put it all together," Kevin said bright and early, at nine o'clock, Monday morning. "We're going to spend this week in various role play situations. We'll assign a scenario to two, three, or more of you, and as you act it out, the rest of you will watch carefully and offer feedback.

"For example, suppose the two of you," Kevin looked out at the mixed couples in the theatre, "are shopping for towels, or silverware, or something."

Rev and Dylan looked at each other. Blankly.

"And you're in, say, Pottery Barn. Tell me how you'd be acting, Rev. What would you be doing?"

"Never been in Pottery Barn."

"It doesn't have to be Pottery Barn. Any kitchen store."

Dylan snorted.

"Um, never been in a kitchen store?" It was a question because Rev wasn't actually sure what a kitchen store was.

"Okay ... let's say you're buying a new pair of shoes."

"Actually," Rev corrected, "Dylan—"

He lost patience. "What I'm trying to get at is how women behave when they're shopping. I just—You need to—"

"EBay." Rev said.

"No, don't scootch over like that when someone sits down beside you." It was a riding-the-bus scenario.

"But he's too close."

"Yeah, but men stand their ground."

"And women—Sam, you would never sit down that close to a man. In fact, if that was the only empty seat, you'd probably stand."

"Why?"

All of the women rolled their eyes.

"No, women look at their nails like this—" Tania held her hand with the palm down and then spread her fingers. "Men do it with their palms up, and they curl their fingers." She demonstrated.

"And the rest of us have better things to do than look at our nails." That was Rev.

"Don't smile."

"Smile more."

"Walk a little behind her," Kevin said, "perhaps with your hand on her arm."

"He's not blind," Revv said as the two of them pretended to cross the road.

"Car's coming!"

Revv broke into a run and realized immediately that that was wrong.

"Stand your ground!"

"But I'll get hit!"

"No, the car will slow down. You'll force it to slow down by not scurrying out of its way like that."

"I didn't scurry," Rev muttered. "And what if it *doesn't* slow down?"

Tania shrugged. "Better dead than a wuss." She grinned at Rev.

"Don't apologize."

"Apologize more."

"Okay, next up, Jim and Sarah. You're booking a room for the night at a motel."

Rev turned to Dylan and said quietly, "Will that be by the hour or by the night?"

"Seriously? You've been asked that? When you're a woman alone walking into a motel?"

Rev nodded.

"Oh. I get asked 'Business or pleasure.'"

Rev nodded.

"Remember, the golden rule for women is 'Don't offend.'"

Dylan snorted.

"You don't … ," Laura tried to put her finger on the problem. "You don't look like you might not know what you're doing." Yes. That was it.

"Because I *don't* not know what I'm doing!" Sam shouted at her.

Dylanna and Revv were up again. Security was having trouble getting a streetperson to leave the lobby.

"Hi, I can help you—what?"

Rev had winced.

"You implied the guy's incompetent," she explained to him. Her.

Tania nodded.

"But—" Dylan was perplexed. "I meant to be helpful." He turned to Tania. "Women are ever helpful, right?"

"Yeah, but … " Rev thought for a minute about how to explain the subtleties of negotiating the power imbalance, between a man and a woman, especially since she was apparently so bad at it.

"Imagine if a ten-year-old said that to you. 'Hi, I can help you.'"

Dylan smiled.

"Yes! See! There was just a touch of amusement in that smile.

"And," she added, even though she knew it would confuse the issue a little, "if I were on the receiving end of it, I'd find it patronizing, that smile."

"Because you're not ten."

"Precisely." She returned to the issue. His issue. "But most men think of most women that way. 'Women and children.' We're subordinates. *We* require *their* help."

"So ... " he put it together, "I have to go through life pretending that I'm—acting like a ten-year-old?"

"In order not to challenge, not to anger—yeah. Well, *Dylanna* does. Dylan doesn't." Her resentment was palpable. How could it not be?

"Always stand your ground." This time it was Tania who used the phrase. "Even when you're wrong."

"That's not being a man," Dylan objected. "That's being immature."

Tania shrugged. "Same thing."

"You need to act like you're in charge!" Kevin said to Revv. The scenario was a staff meeting at the office.

"But I'm not."

"You need to assume that people will pay attention to you!"

"But they won't."

"They will. If you're a man."

Rev thought about that. And he was right. He was absolutely right.

"Assume they'll accept your authority," Kevin continued, "assume they'll do what you tell them to do. And they will."

"That might work for men, but ... " Women who act like they're in charge are called bitches.

"With the app on, you *are* a man."

"Oh. Right."

"And men," Tania added, "you have to *stop* assuming that you're in charge, that people will pay attention to you, listen to you, defer to you."

"Women, you have to 'own' your mannerisms!" Kevin sounded frustrated. "You—all of you—you have to be more convincing."

Right. Easier said. Women had to convince themselves they were important before they could convince others. And that would not be achieved in a week. Or five months. Or even five years.

Which was exactly what Tania said when she wrapped up the second day. "We understand that this orientation isn't nearly long enough. It would take months, perhaps years, to appear as the other sex, the other gender. In fact, tomorrow we're going to have some drag queens here. Men who have been trying to perform femininity for as long as they have will surely have some insights to share, some tips to give.

"The women might have the physical bit a little easier, partly because it's more acceptable in our society for women to cross over, at least occasionally, and partly because moving like a man is, perhaps, more natural. But you'll still have a lifetime of relatively low self-esteem, of not feeling important or powerful, to overcome.

"And men, you're finding the physical *and* the inter-personal stuff a challenge. We get that.

"But keep working at it," she encouraged them all. "Keep in mind that if you don't master the other-gender skills, if you don't accept the other-gender socialization, the app will be 'given away' so to speak."

Wednesday, the promised drag queens showed up. There were ten of them.

"No drag kings?"

Everyone stared at Rev. Who looked at Tania and Kevin. "By having drag queens and not drag kings, you're providing more information and assistance to the men among us. What about the women? Are we invisible? Not as important? You're reinforcing exactly what you're asking us to leave behind."

"There aren't many drag king shows," one of the queens said.

"It's not very entertaining," another one added.

"Says who?" a raspy voice challenged.

"And why exactly do you think *you're* so fucking entertaining?" Rev added. "Who is entertained by seeing a bunch of men make fun of the things women have to do to get a little respect?"

The women cheered.

"Get drag kings for tomorrow!" Revv barked the order at Kevin.

"Did I do that right?" she whispered to Dylan as she sat back down.

"We'll see." Dylanna gently patted her hand. "Did I do *that* right?"

"How the fuck should I know?!"

Thursday, two drag kings showed up. They ... sauntered into the room.

Yes! Rev suddenly realized that she had to learn to saunter.

But she didn't want to learn to saunter. She didn't want to learn arrogance. Indifference.

On Friday, Dana, Erin/Aaron, and Kim showed up. To watch. To see.

"Dinner party," Tania called out a new scenario. They were doing whole-group role plays. "Tweak your apps if you need to."

"Sam, honey, don't wear that shirt," Laura said. "It makes you look tall. Choose something plaid. Or at least with horizontal stripes."

"Right!" Tania said. "And ladies, women, choose something with vertical stripes. To make your app-you look taller than its max."

Kim made a note. Hire a fashion designer to advise on additions to the app wardrobe defaults. S/he'd send out the update as soon as it was available.

"Ready?" Tania asked. "Okay, begin."

During the break, Dylan and Rev approached Dana and Erin/Aaron. Kim was talking with Laura and Sam.

"Do you have a minute?" Dylan asked. They hadn't actually gotten around to calling them with their questions.

"Sure, what's on your mind?"

"Well, we were wondering," Dylan opened, "what exactly are you wanting us to test? What's the purpose of the beta test?"

"We want to know whether the app enables a person to be perceived as a member of the opposite sex," Erin/Aaron said, "and, therefore, to be treated accordingly."

"So gender is irrelevant. Genderized behaviour," Dylan clarified. "So these gender classes—they're really emphasizing the stereo-types, you know that, right?"

"Yes. But some of the stereotypes are pretty subtle. The different ways men and women talk, for example."

"Agreed. But most of the stuff we're learning here, it's just supplemental? To the app?"

"Maybe. We don't know how much people use appearance and how much they use behaviour. When they assign sex."

"But probably not," Dana spoke up. "It's doubtful that people assign sex *solely* on the basis of appearance."

"True," Dylan agreed.

"So if our behaviour clearly *contradicts* our appearance," Rev suggested, "the app will probably fail. But if our behaviour neither contradicts nor supports—"

"We understand that you're not particularly feminine, Rev, and you, Dylan, are not a He-Man," Erin/Aaron said. "No offence."

"None taken."

"So if you two turn on the app and continue to act the way you normally do, you both might pass. And we'd definitely like to know that. Because that would mean the app will work even better than we've thought."

"Or it might just mean that the app will be more successful with androgynous people."

"Yes," Erin/Aaron said, "given the difficulty that people like Sam and Laura will have acting like ... Samantha and Laurence."

They both nodded.

"Then again," Dana spoke up, "we may be surprised. What if the app works just as well with Sam and Laura as it does with you two? What if appearance, physical appearance, *is* ... all?"

"I suspect the app, or rather the relative role of physical appearance, might be context-sensitive," Dylan suggested after a moment.

"You may well be right," Erin/Aaron replied, nodding her/his head, and thinking ...

"So in some cases, acting in a stereotypical feminine way might help me be perceived as a woman. And vice versa for Rev."

Both Erin/Aaron and Dana nodded.

"Whereas in other cases, it might not make any difference."

"And if we don't do it well," Rev pointed out, "acting in a

genderized way might actually undermine the app."

Again, they nodded.

"Okay," Dylan said to Rev when they went into the foyer for coffee, "so when we have the app on, we're going to continue to act like we normally do? None of this feminine or masculine shit?"

"Agreed. Unless a little bit of it seems necessary to draw out the desired response. Meaning response to us *as* female and male."

"Agreed."

The rest of the session continued with whole-group role plays. Most were, truthfully, not very convincing. But then, Rev thought to herself, most of the drag queens and kings hadn't been very convincing either. Dana, Erin/Aaron, and Kim continued to watch and make notes.

"All right," Tania said to the group an hour later, "that's our time. Congratulations! You've made it to the end of gender training!" Kevin started clapping. Everyone joined in. So they were clapping for themselves. Idiots. Rev's arms were crossed on her chest.

"But before you go," Tania said, "I have one more thing I'd like you to do. Or more to the point, one more thing I'd like you to understand. What you wear affects not just how you move, but how you feel. And as a result, how you move. How you act."

She walked over to one of the props boxes and opened it. "I'd like all the men to put on a tiara."

"Oh come on!" That was Sam.

"You'll find a nice selection here." She wafted her hand over the box in the best game show host fashion. "Ladies, choose yourself a football helmet."

A few moments later, Rev was facing Dylan. "You know," she said with some surprise, "she's right. I feel ... stronger. I feel—invincible." In truth, she felt like hitting something. Or someone one.

Dylan nodded. His tiara fell off. It broke when it hit the floor. He burst into tears.

"Oh, you're good."

Dana, Erin/Aaron, and Kim said a few final words of praise and encouragement, reminded everyone that the three of them were available by phone and email at any point during the next five months and that reports were due at the end of each week, and then officially concluded the orientation for the app's beta testers. Everyone packed up their stuff and shuffled toward the exit.

"Rev?" Dylan said to her as they too headed out the door.
    "Yeah?"
    "That helmet doesn't belong to you."

You know," Rev said, "if the two of us just walk around, each with the app on, that's not going to be very helpful." It was Saturday and they were just walking around, each with their app on. "We'll see the same things happening that we do when we walk around without the app. People will treat the man of us differently than the woman of us."

"But won't we notice the difference more if it happens to us? Because the man of us is now the woman of us and the woman of us is … " He lost it. They'd gotten silly the night before.

"Maybe." It seemed a safe response.

"So," Dylan found it, "if we really want to do it right, we should each be doing each thing we do twice. Once with the app, then without."

"Well that's not going to be any fun. Doing everything twice." Though half the time, she had to do everything twice anyway. No, that couldn't be …

Because the other half the time, she'd done the same thing considerably *more* than twice. And had expected a different outcome every bloody time.

"Plus," she added, "whether we're together as a mixed pair or a same sex pair will surely influence the results."

"It will. And it will be interesting to compare the two. I'd like to see what happens to me when I'm with you as a man. And you're a man."

"Yeah, that's good. And I should be with you as a woman. When you're a woman."

So they both turned their apps off.

"No, this isn't right."

That night—it was a pretty wasted day—when he called Loup, Kit had some news.

"We went for a long walk in the forest, it was so pretty, what with the snow falling softly in thick flakes—"

"I *love* it when it's like that!" Rev said. "Did you take a picture?"

Kit got up and aimed her laptop out the window.

"Oh, that's so pretty! Dylan, let's go home!"

Dylan stared at her.

"Kit, point the laptop to your driveway."

Kit obliged. The plow had just gone by. Again.

"Yeah, let's stay here a bit longer."

"Anyway, Loup took off and wouldn't come back when I called a short while later. But she kept barking. It was an urgent bark, but not an emergency bark. If you know what I mean."

"I do."

"Anyway, when I finally caught up to her, I saw that she was sitting right in front of a snare trap. Baited with a fresh deer leg. Just a few metres from the path!"

"*In front* of the snare?" Dylan wanted to be sure. They'd worked very hard last year to teach her that. To teach her to not get caught *in* the snare.

"Yeah."

He smiled. Loup shoved her face in front of Kit's. She was clearly proud to have been *in front* of the snare. Or happy to hear Dylan's voice and see his face.

"So I praised her, told her what a good dog she was—I keep forgetting she's a wolf—but she refused to budge."

"Yeah, she was—"

"I finally realized that she was waiting for me to unset the snare. Which I did. Bastard!" Kit was referring to the guy who set the snares. "There were three more right there that I also unset. Next time I'm going to take a pair of wire cutters with me."

The orientation and gender training was over, and the Pitchfest wasn't until the following week, so they decided to make their third week in California a miscellaneous week. They considered trying to get a couple temp jobs, but with only a week ... Instead, they decided to just go for interviews. They'd wait until they were in Vancouver to get jobs.

"Okay, so let's think this through." It was Sunday. They'd gotten silly again. Or were still silly. Hard to tell, really. "We each go to OfficeTemp as our app-us."

"No, then we may as well just go as our us-us. Because one man and one woman would be going. Either way."

"Right. So why are we using the app?"

"Because we're testing it."

"Oh right." Rev considered that. "And what are we testing it for?"

"To see if it works. To see *how* it works. When it works? Oh, oh, *why* it works!"

Dylan suspected they were confused. He took another draw from their joint. Then tried again.

"Each of us goes as their app-them *and* as their them-them."

"We can do that? We can be two people at once? With the app?"

Dylan had trouble being one person at once.

"No," Rev answered her own question, "I don't think it can change the linear progression of time." She grinned. She'd used two big words in a row. "You go as you-you, and *then* you go as app-you. And me as me-me, then me as app-me."

"Me-me and you-you," Dylan giggled. "Mimi and Yuyu."

She knew she shouldn't have used those words, but what other words could she have used? Interesting that there were no synonyms for such critical concepts. Me. You. And they were such simple words. For such complex concepts. That was weird. Shouldn't complex concepts have complex words?

"And that's preferable to—what we said before—because ... " Dylan had no idea what they said before. Nor did Rev. 'Course, even when she wasn't stoned, she couldn't remember what she said from one moment to the next.

They waited a minute. Then two minutes.

"I've got it!" Dylan shouted. Moe looked over in alarm. "Because it'll be more likely to only change one variable. Change only one variable. Change one variable only." He grinned. "They all mean the same thing!"

"How can that be?" Rev asked in wonder. "'We smoke a joint' means something totally different from 'We a smoke joint.'"

"Does it?"

They thought about that for a minute. Then two minutes.

"In both cases," Dylan said, "you'd otherwise be doing the same thing, saying the same thing."

Rev stared at him.

"If we compared Mimi and Yuyu, instead of comparing me-me and app-me, and you-you and app-you, we'd be introducing so many other changes, we wouldn't be able to say for sure whether any differences were due to the app. To the change in sex."

"Yes! Brilliant! And gender. Or gender. And gender."

They spent Monday looking through the classifieds for jobs to apply for.

"I'm so glad I'm writing for the LSAT," Rev said. She didn't want to apply for *any* of the jobs she saw.

"*I'm* so glad we're getting a per diem for this." Dylan felt the same. About the jobs they saw.

"And Kyle still sends us a share of the profits from his Great Hands business." They didn't *have* to apply for any of the jobs they saw, right?

"And we're still getting royalties from our blasphemy tour book and our licensing parents book." Right.

"Maybe we should just work on our RegenderApp book instead."

What they ended up doing instead was go on one of the 'hop on, hop off' cable car tours of San Francisco. Though, after Rev's first attempt, it became a 'step on, step off' cable car tour of San Francisco. Still.

The best part was stepping off and then walking a few blocks to the mosaic stairs on 16th between Moraga and Noriega.

"We need more art in cities," Rev commented as she climbed the steps a second time.

Tuesday, they took Moe to the Buena Vista Park. Although much smaller, it was way better than the Golden Gate Park. With its secluded trails and oak groves, it was as close to forest as they were going to get. *And* it was a just a short walk away.

AND, they discovered, it was a veritable dog park. Moe had a *blast!* They walked every single trail and spent an hour in the off-leash area. On the one hand, it made Dylan sad, because it made him miss Loup all the more, but on the other hand, it made him happy. Because Moe!

Dylan apologized profusely to Moe for not having discovered, investigated, the park sooner. He hadn't realized San Francisco was one of the most dog-friendly cities in the world.

When they returned, he made an addition the House Rules.

Wednesday, they went rock climbing. Well, Rev watched Dylan go rock climbing. She wasn't good with heights.

They put in their reports that the app didn't work well for rock climbing. The slight dissonance regarding limb length was too apparent.

Thursday, they did a one-day beginner surfing clinic. Turned out Rev was good with surf boards. In water.

"Woo-hoo!!"

They put in their reports that the app didn't work in water.

Friday, they browsed the classifieds again, intending again to try the job interview thing. After a few minutes, Dylan pointed out a listing for a Project Manager. Rev got up to look over his shoulder.

"I'm not qualified."

"What? Of course, you're qualified! You've been a teacher!"

"Yeah ... but never a project manager."

"But as a teacher, you've juggled half a dozen projects at a time and managed thirty people."

Rev just—sat down. She'd never thought of it that way before. And Dylan had. *That's* how men get jobs they're not qualified for. Or how women *don't* get jobs they *are* qualified for.

She scanned the listing. They wanted a dynamic, high-energy, self-starter for a fast-paced, deadline-oriented environment. They wanted a player capable of providing cutting-edge insights.

"See, right there." She pointed. "Women don't consider themselves players. Men do. The ad is 'selecting' for men."

"But Revv's a player."

She thought about that. "He could be," she conceded and looked at the ad again. They wanted someone who was ambitious, dedicated, and driven, a strong thinker with creative vision, capable of excelling at all things at all times. "He could be just such 'a cocky little bugger'."

Dylan looked at her, puzzled.

"Monty Python. *Big Red Book*."

"Ah."

"But see," she explained, "only men can *be* cocky little buggers. Only a man could lie to himself and to the interviewers to think, to say, that he was all that!"

Dylan stared at her.

"A woman wouldn't apply. She wouldn't waste their time."

"But—We don't—" He was a little speechless. "That's just—"

Rev looked at him. Waiting.

"Job descriptions are just so you can figure out if you want the job or not."

"You mean—You—" Now she was a little speechless. "Men don't take any of this seriously? You don't read these as requirements? Necessary qualifications?"

"Not really. I mean, yeah, you have to be in the ballpark, but ... " he trailed off.

Rev sat down heavily. Men assumed they were qualified. They assumed that if they wanted something, they could just go ahead and take it. Or at least try to get it. Whether they deserved it didn't enter the picture. Of course it wouldn't. Not when you figure you deserve everything, not when you think you're entitled to everything. She had a vague feeling that she'd had this realization before, that she and Dylan had had this discussion before, but the insight was so shocking, she'd have to have it several times before it really stuck.

So they both called about the job. Put the phone on speaker. Dylanna was discouraged from applying. The manager didn't think she was right for the job.

"Seriously?" Dylan disconnected in disbelief. "He doesn't know anything about me!"

"He knows you're a woman," Rev pointed out. "Or thought you were, given the app's voice."

Revv was invited to come in for an interview that very afternoon.

"I think another thing is that women see responsibility where men see power," Rev continued her analysis of why women wouldn't apply for so many of the jobs men applied for. "Women see burdens where men see benefits."

"And why is that, do you think?"

"Well, one, women haven't *had* a lot of power—so they're not used to looking for it, seeing it, using it.

"Two, women *have* had a lot of responsibility—so *that's* what they're used to noticing."

"Are you implying that men *haven't* had a lot of responsibility? They run the government, big business—"

"Ironic, isn't it.

"I mean," she continued, "girls get jobs as babysitters: that's a lot of responsibility—what if the house catches fire, what if the baby starts choking? Boys get jobs throwing a newspaper onto someone's porch.

"And then later, women become camp counsellors and recreation leaders, while men work on maintenance crews. Women are entrusted with the physical, social, emotional, and artistic development of children, while men are entrusted with the shrubbery.

"So yeah," she concluded, "definitely ironic."

Fresh battery in the phone. Check. App on. Check. Record function on. Check. Revv stepped into the room with his hand outstretched.

"Hello, Revv, is it?"

"Yes, thanks for the opportunity to interview," she said during the handshake, in order to distract him. It seemed to work. The handshake didn't give her away.

"Thank *you* for coming in so quickly. Have a seat."

Revv sat. Carefully. Thoughtfully.

"So, I see you're not married. Got a girlfriend?"

She thought about that. Yes, meant she wasn't gay.

"I do, but I'm not sure how serious it is." That meant she was a player.

"But family is in the cards?"

She picked up on the tone. "Oh sure, at some point." She was amazed at how casually she said it. Having kids. As a casual commitment. Wow.

She knew that if she'd been a woman, confessing to wanting a family in the future would have ended the interview right then and there.

But he was a man. So having kids, and a wife, added status. More than that, family men were reliable. They'd keep their head down, to keep their job.

"So tell me a bit about your past job experiences."

Shit. They should have prepared more. If she told him about working at the shelter, about teaching, as a woman ...

"Well, I was a high school teacher for a while. Math. And Phys-Ed."

He nodded approval.

"I enjoyed managing all the tasks one has to, as a teacher—" 'Enjoy' was wrong, but 'manage' was right, and 'tasks' was right ... "And I liked the responsibility—" Yes, that was good ... "But, I confess the babysitting aspect of it didn't appeal to me." Ooh, nailed it with that one.

He nodded again.

"Although it certainly fine-tuned my ability to think on my feet, so to speak." Was s/he good or what?

"And what are your thoughts about the Project Manager position here at Sure-Tech?"

My thoughts? About the position? It's a job. It'll pay well.

"Well, it's a great opportunity, of course, and—"

He stared at her. Waiting.

She became disconcerted. It was the Red Victorian thing again.

"What I mean to say is … " Revv tried pausing. With gravity.

He kept waiting! As a woman, she'd never have gotten away with that! You pause, you're done.

"It'll give me the opportunity to utilize my skill set to my own advantage and to the advantage of the company."

What a load of shit. He'd never buy that.

The man nodded as he stood, a broad smile on his face and his hand outstretched for another shake.

16

On Saturday, they discovered the Yerba Buena Center for the Arts—"The Center for the Art of Doing Something About It."

"Imagine if centers like this were as common as ... banks," Rev said.

"Or hospitals."

"Schools! Or," Rev added, "imagine if the expectation was that once you'd finished with school, you'd attend one of these centers, once a week or something."

"Most people become too busy with work and kids."

"Yeah."

They wondered a bit more about how such centers could be integrated into the mainstream.

"What if we elected representatives to work at such centers," Dylan suggested, "as we now elect representatives to work in the government?"

"But isn't the government supposed to be for Doing Something About It?"

They also went again with Moe to the Buena Vista Park to wander along the trails, among the trees—actually, they'd been doing that every day since they'd discovered it—as much for themselves as for Moe.

Then in the evening, they prepared—Rev helped Dylan revise—a Los Angeles to-do list. The Pitchfest would happen at the end of the week, on the Friday, Saturday, and Sunday, and accommodations were included. Dylan found accommodations for Monday to Thursday, and he rented a car for the drive.

"Or we could rent a motorcycle. Put you on the back and our stuff in the ... things."

"I'd love that! But you'd have to focus so much on driving—" He opened a YouTube video that highlighted the twisting cliff-hugging road, with its narrow shoulders and sharp drop-offs.

"Okay, yeah, car."

And good thing she'd kept the football helmet.

Sunday, one last day with Moe. In the Park. And then at home with all his friends. Dylan skyped Loup to see if she wanted to join the party. But she wasn't home. Probably having her own party with Flaker. In the Forest.

Monday, they made the trip. Part way. The scenic route along Highway 1 was so amazing ... they went slowly, often stopping. Dylan wanted to see Cannery Row in Monterey. And the jellyfish at the aquarium. Rev wanted to hike to the McWay Waterfalls in Big Sur.

Rev took the wheel for the higher up stretches, so Dylan could have the window seat. Because she would not have looked out ... and down.

"We should have made the trip south-to-north," she commented at one point. "We'd be a bit further from instant death by cliff."

"And a bit further from Los Angeles."

Tuesday, they finished the trip. After stopping to see the opulent Hearst Castle and the corpulent sea lions. Not as much contrast as one might think.

"So, shall we write our pitches?" Rev asked once they'd unpacked and gotten settled in. It was Thursday. Wednesday had been full of—had been full.

"No."

"No?"

"The first day—tomorrow," Dylan said, mostly to hear it confirmed by Rev, "has a workshop on how to prepare a pitch. I thought I'd wait until after then." He'd also discovered that Dana had already registered them. Not only for the Pitchfest, but also for that workshop.

"Oh. Okay. But maybe you should write a screenplay. So you can, you know, pitch it."

"Or I could use one of yours."

Dylan guessed correctly, clued by her use of the second person, that Rev had already written a screenplay. Perhaps several. All unproduced of course. None even optioned. Because no one knew about them. Except all the producers she'd sent them to who had returned them unread. As was policy. Plus almost all of the agents she'd sent them to, who had also returned them unread. Most took on screenwriters by referral only. The three who had read them, so they said, rejected them. For reasons, as far as Rev could see, which were totally unrelated to the screenplays themselves.

"Sending you access to my screenplay folder ... now," Rev tapped a few keys on her laptop.

So Friday night, they worked on their pitches.

"Okay, to review," Dylan was excited, "a pitch should be succinct, emotional, and powerful. It should convey the artistic, entertainment, and commercial value. We should open with how we came up with the idea."

Rev snorted.

"And we should end with 'Would you like me to send the script?'"

"And in between, we should ... ?"

"Introduce the protagonist," Dylan read off the list provided, "explain why we will empathize with him—"

"And right there is why there are no female heroes."

"Yeah," Dylan sighed. A couple weeks ago, he wouldn't've noticed that. "So we'll both pitch female heroes. See what happens."

"But then we won't know if rejection is due to our sex or our screenplay."

"You assume we're going to be rejected."

"Well, yeah."

Dylan sighed. A couple weeks ago, he wouldn't've understood why.

"Okay, but wouldn't it be interesting if Revv got invited to send a script with a female hero, but Rev didn't? The same script?"

'Interesting' wasn't the word Rev would use.

"Okay, what else is on your handy-dandy how-to-write-a-pitch list?" Rev hadn't taken notes. She'd already been-there done-that. Her submitted screenplays had been accompanied by query letters that had included pitches.

Dylan returned to the forementioned handy-dandy list. "Describe the event that will get the plot moving. Describe the primary conflict. Describe the goal."

"All in three sentences."

"All in three sentences."

"Okay, ready to practice?" Dylan asked. A couple hours had passed.

"Sure. Shoot. What a stupid ... euphemism? Begin. Proceed. Speak."

"Okay. *Sweet Sixteen* is a sci-fi movie in which at age sixteen, people have to prove they deserve to be alive."

"That's one sentence."

"I know. But what else should I say? I've got plot trigger, primary conflict, and goal. Implied."

"How about adding 'Will Sheila, our protagonist, succeed?'"

"Oh, that's good." Dylan made the addition, then looked at his list. The handy-dandy one. "I've got nothing about artistic, entertainment, or commercial value. Or why we'll empathize with Sheila."

"And again, right there. No matter what you say, women will somehow be able to empathize with men, but men will remain unable, *completely* unable, to empathize with women. As a matter of honour."

"Even if we describe her in a non-sexed way? If we say she's an ordinary teenager just trying to make it through high school?"

"You'd think that would work, but boys, men, will still consider it a chick flick."

"They would, yes." Dylan stared for a bit at his screen. "What have you got?"

Rev read the pitch she'd written years ago for one of her screenplays. "It's ten years from now and about time. LJ lives in a new U. S. of A., in which *this* is the Three Strikes Law: first crime, rehab; second crime, prison; third crime, you're simply kicked out—permanently exiled to a remote area, to fend for yourself without the benefits of society. At least LJ used to live in that new U S. of A.—he's just committed his third crime. *Exile* presents an important message about the social contract wrapped in an adventure survival story."

"That's more than three sentences."

"Yeah." She counted. "It's four sentences."

"Do you think a horn will blow after your third sentence and you'll be dragged out of your chair with a big hook?"

"Probably."

"All set?" They were about to make their way to the conference centre at which the Pitchfest was held.

"Yes!"

Dylan looked at her.

"Have you ever wondered whether people respond to you the way they do not because you're a woman but because of the way you ... dress?" Dylanna had been wearing business suits. Low heels. A bit of make-up. A bit of jewelry.

"You mean not because of my sex but because of my gender? My lack of? My refusal to perform femininity?"

"Yeah."

"Good question."

"You could test that with the app."

"I could!" She was certainly not going to test that with her self.

The conference centre was crowded with people, the hope so palpable it hurt. As Dylan and Rev made their way to the registration table, to get their tags and Pitchfest booklets, they saw Santa Claus. Must be pitching a Christmas movie. They also saw that most of the people in attendance were considerably younger than them. Of course. By the time they were their age, they'd have been established. Or driving a taxi.

They also discovered that most of the agents were young as well. That would explain Hollywood's heavy emphasis on dick flicks and chick flicks, Rev thought.

It would also explain what she thought was about to happen. To both of them. To all four of them. Unless they tweaked the age of their apps. Which they weren't allowed to do.

'Course, had that been allowed, they would've had to change their pitches as well. Their screenplays. Their lives. The world. Well, Hollywood at least. Okay, the world.

"So," they compared notes, as they waited in line for round two—the Pitchfest was organized like a speed dating event, "anything happen of interest?"

"Yeah. When Revv said 'Stuff happens'—I got tired—the agents just smiled. But when Rev said it, she was told not to do that and given instructions as to what to do instead. Explain the plot, describe the events."

"So ... it's good to be corrected, right? Given advice? No, that's bad, if it happens just because you're a woman. As if women need to be instructed. Need to be given advice."

"At the workshop we went to, they said *don't* tell the whole story."

"Which suggests that the advice was gratuitous? Given just *because* you're a woman?"

"Or it could just suggest that not everyone agrees with the people who gave the workshop." She shrugged. They couldn't possibly know. "You?"

"They gave suggestions to Dylan about how to change the script to make it more marketable. They didn't bother with Dylanna."

"See?"

"Yeah ... but isn't giving suggestions about how to change the script also giving instruction, giving advice? So in this case, it's the man who gets the instruction, the advice, not the woman."

"Yeah ... But it feels different. Did it feel different to you?"

"Well, yeah," he confessed. "When I was Dylan, the advice felt like they were giving me a leg up. When I was Dylanna, its absence felt like I wasn't worth it."

"And when I was Rev, the advice felt patronizing. When I was Revv, its absence felt like they just thought I knew what I was doing."

"So is that us internalizing the sexism of our lives or is it them being sexist?"

"What?"

Dylanna had left to get some coffee. Dylan returned. With the strangest look on his face.

"Some guy asked if I wanted to suck his cock." He shook his head with disbelief. "He didn't even know me!"

Rev raised her eyebrows at him.

"Yeah, I know ... it just—" He shrugged helplessly, unable to put what he felt in words.

But Rev knew. Of course, she did. It was the context that made the 'invitation' so disconcerting. So incredibly deflating. To be reminded that one was just a sexual service. When one was trying to be a screenwriter.

After round three, they discussed whether it mattered whether the agent was male or female.

"I don't think so," Rev said. "Both look at me like I'm some sort of talking monkey."

"They expect women to pitch relationship movies. Not lessons about the social contract. How did they look at Revv?"

"With respect."

Dylan nodded. "They must get so few pitches for movies of substance."

"What about you? *Sweet Sixteen* is, would be, a movie of substance."

"Well, I couldn't put my finger on it, but now that you've described it, I think they looked at Dylanna the same way. Like she was some sort of talking monkey."

"And Dylan?"

He didn't want to say.

She *knew* it! "You were asked to send the script."

He nodded. Forlornly.

"By more than one agent."

He nodded again. Even more forlornly.

"It's *my fucking script!!!*"

"I know. And if anything comes of it, anything at all, we'll tell them that. But now we need to figure out why Revv wasn't asked to send a script."

He was right. She tried to calm down. And think. It could be the script. Maybe they should have switched part way through. Though—

"Do you think it's because Revv's short?"

"Maybe. Give him a beard," Dylan suggested, grinning. "And glasses."

"Well?" Round four had ended.

"Two agents asked Revv to send the script," she said tersely. Tightly. Ready to explode.

"But—that's good news! Isn't it? *Exile* might get optioned after all!"

"Yeah, but—"

Next morning, late, while they were having coffee and pizza, and still a little silly, as they had to use up their supply before they crossed the border, Rev's phone rang. She looked at Dylan. He looked at her. Was it for Rev or Revv? Should she turn on the app? It would modulate her voice.

"How do I turn off caller ID?"

"I don't know. I mean, I don't think you can when it's ringing."

It was still ringing.

"Okay, so if we stopped it from ringing," she stared at the phone, "somehow, then turned it off, the caller ID, not the phone, because we need the phone to be on in order to turn the ID off—fascinating … Isn't it?"

"It is. Something has to be on in order to be turned off." Dylan was pleased with himself.

"Oh, but," Rev remembered where she was, where she had been, and so was pleased with herself as well, "they'd call back, right? It would ring again?"

Dylan shrugged helplessly. Not because he was still a little stoned, but because he had processed that the call could be Rev's once-in-a-lifetime break—

He picked up the phone and answered it. "Rev/v's phone.   Just a minute, please."

He put his hand over the phone, grinning. He'd solved the problem! "He asked for—shit!"

"Ask who it is. No, tell them I'll call them back. Ask who it is. And get a number."

"May I ask who's calling? Sh—I'll have Rev/v return your call. Doug Pearson at … " Rev wrote down the name and number.

"Well?" Dylan handed her phone back to her. "Who's Doug Pearson?"

"I don't know!" she said in frustration. The name didn't ring a bell, so she went to get the Pitchfest booklet. In the meantime, Dylan turned off the caller ID on both their phones. Then turned it back on. They'd wanted to turn off the ID of the callee, not the caller. Okay, less stoned now …

"There's no Doug Pearson listed. Might it be someone's assistant?"

Dylan started googling.

"It's a San Francisco number, and—"

"The Project Manager guy! Hm … "

She turned on the app, composed herself, himself, and returned the call.

"Doug Pearson, please. Hello, it's Revv—I see. Yes. Yes. Thank you."

She disconnected and set down the phone.

Dylan waited.

"I got the job." She looked at him with disbelief. And, of course, anger. All those years of being told that there were no openings or that there were only internships or temporary positions, and now— she was not only offered an interview, but a job, and not only a job, but a management level job.

Well, not her, exactly—Revv.

17

They decided not to head north by the same route, so they headed inland. They reached Fresno by the end of their first day, arriving at the converted farmhouse Dylan had found on AirBnB.

While there, they spent some time in Yosemite Park. The rock formations were unlike anything they'd seen. Not quite mountains, but not quite just rocks either. The day they happened to be there, the rock and trees were frosted with ice and snow, and the water was gleaming silver ...

And the waterfalls! They hiked until they could hike no more.

Which meant they were hiking in late afternoon and the effect of the light as the sun got lower and lower was absolutely stunning.

There wasn't much else they wanted to do in or around Fresno, so in the evening, after they made their notes of the day for the app people (they had nothing much to report in this respect), Rev worked on some LSAT questions and Dylan worked on their book.

After he skyped Loup. She was fine. But she was running out of shoes. Dylan made a note.

"I think having our apps on while we're together minimizes its effect," Dylan looked up from his laptop a few minutes later. "People still see a heterosexual couple."

"True," Rev looked up from her writing pad. "Although they're seeing 'tall woman with a short man'—"

"*That's* why the stares! I thought my make-up was a mess or something."

Rev stared at him. "Seriously?"

Their next stop was Sacramento. They went to *Ghandi: The Musical.* Because.

Eager to be where they would stay for a while, they motored on, through Redding, along the mountains, through the mountains, past Eugene, and into Portland.

Dylan had wanted to stay in a "cute little tree house" he'd found, but it didn't have internet access. Rev wanted to stay in the "calm and cozy beach cottage" he'd also found, but it was two hours north of Portland.

"We could keep going, to Olympia. To the calm and cozy beach cottage."

"No, that'll be too long a drive. I'm already ready," she grinned, "to stop for the day."

So they decided on the "whimsical private studio in a garden oasis" which looked quite woodsy inside and was within walking distance of shops and stores, theatres and restaurants. And a volcano.

They settled into the house, ordered out for pizza and Pepsi, then settled into the comfortable chairs by the window. They were tired. After all, they'd been sitting in a car for days.

"Coffee?" Dylan asked, thinking there was probably some in the kitchenette. Then answered, "No, we'll be up all night."

"Yeah, even the Pepsi is risky."

"And the pizza."

"We're so old."

They had no notes to make, so they just googled and talked a bit about their plans for the week.

After Dylan skyped Loup. Of course. Dylan told her about the Ghandi musical. Did a few of the dance steps for her. Loup wasn't interested.

"Peanut would be."

"He would, yes!" Dylan grinned, remembering their time on the blasphemy tour with the lovable Newfoundland dog—and his delightfully silly, but impressive, dance to "Sweet Pea."

"Loup would be interested if it were a pas-de-deux with a dead rabbit."

"Or, better, a live one."

After a moment, Rev said, "We're so old we don't even need to get stoned."

"An upside."

Next day, they went to an art museum. It was raining, so they decided to take the bus. Unfortunately, everyone else in Portland had made the same decision.

As they were standing in the not-quite-but-almost-packed bus, hanging on to the overhead straps—

"This is another thing," Revv started to say, intending to comment about the height of the straps which made it more difficult for most women to hang on—

"Hey, you're nowhere near my wallet, budddy" Dylanna said loudly. Glaring at the man beside him who had his hand—

"He wasn't going for your wallet," Revv said, as the man shuffled away.

"But—oh." Dylan made a note to make a note that evening.

Five minutes later, she felt another hand on his body and delivered a sharp elbow.

"Bitch!"

"Oh, *I'm* the problem?" Dylan was amazed.

Rev was not.

"Yeah, you're the problem! Can't you take a compliment?"

The man moved on. Before Dylanna could respond. She/He had his mouth open though. S/he'd gotten that far.

Five minutes later, s/he boomed at yet another man, "Does this bus *look* like a petting zoo?"

The women on board applauded. At least, the ones who had both hands free.

"No one offered me a seat," Dylanna said once they'd disembarked and were heading up the steps to the museum.

"No, that doesn't happen anymore," Revv said. "Actually, I don't think it ever did. At least, not to me. Maybe back in the 1950s ... which was before I was born," s/he added. Because.

"Well, you probably never looked like you needed to sit down."

Rev wasn't sure that was the reason.

"I wonder if I can tweak my app to present me as pregnant. It would—"

"They didn't teach us how to walk and sit while pregnant. Not that I need to know," s/he added. Then suddenly realized she'd interrupted him. In an interruptive way, not in an interjective, additive, way.

"God damn it!"

"Yeah." Dylan had realized. She'd interrupted him. Or rather, he'd interrupted her. Still. "Zimbardo."

"Yeah. And Rosenthal."

They paid their admission and received their guide booklets without anything noteworthy happening.

"Why would a blind person come to a museum?" Rev wondered out loud, having already opened her booklet to start reading. Service dogs were allowed. "The sculptures can't be touched, can they?"

A moment later, she laughed. "And what would a special program for those with dementia be like? *Fifty first dates? Groundhog Day?*"

"Maybe the point is to quarantine the happy wanderers from the other patrons?"

"Do you think they're happy?" she asked as they entered the first room. She'd often wondered about losing her mind. Well, her memory. "And if they are, wouldn't they keep forgetting they are?"

Dylan turned to stare at her.

"You should know I have a living will," she said before he reprimanded her for her sick sense of humour. "If my mind totally goes, have me euthanized. No point in my body being a burden to anyone."

"Yeah, me too."

"Okay. Good to know."

"It is, yes. What if your body totally goes? Wait, should we be having this discussion now? Here?"

"Same thing. If it *totally* goes. If I'm totally unable to communicate 'I want to live,' then you can safely assume I want to die."

"That's actually a good way of—putting it. Me too," he added after a moment.

As they continued to move through the rooms, through the 17th, 18th, and 19th century exhibits, Rev, Revv, noted that Dylan, Dylanna, was getting slower and slower.

"Time travel slowing you down?"

He/she grinned at her. "No, I'm just noticing that whenever there's a woman in one of these paintings, she's half-naked."

She/he nodded. Years ago, Rev had had a similar moment, a recognition that almost the entire history of art was the history of porn and portraiture. Not beauty. Not insight. The whole 'nudes' thing? Just titillation. And all those posed dignitaries? Just pre-photography.

"And *I'm* always the real center of attention," Revv said. It felt … good. To have her importance so consistently reflected back at her.

The last room was a delightful surprise, containing a piece of installation art in which a dense wave of tiny figures came at you from the corner of the room. The perspective was handled in such a way, it made you utter 'Too many people!' And they just kept coming and coming.

"You know what would make a good piece of installation art?" Rev asked. "A room built for women. Remember the chair exercise during orientation? It'd be interesting to be in a whole room where not just the chairs, but everything was sized for women. Counters would be, what, six inches lower? And cupboards! I'd be able to reach everything without stretching, without straining. The ceiling would be lower. Making the room cozier. And the steps—"

"You'd fall down," Dylan said. "After a lifetime of expecting a seven inch rise instead of what, a six inch rise?"

"Yeah, but it would be a new falling down," she said.

"It should also have a car," she added. "Built for women. One in which I could actually see where the hood ends."

"You can't see where the hood ends?" Dylan stared at her. "How do you know when to stop behind the car in front of you? How do you park without hitting the other cars?"

"I have to guess. It's always a risk."

"I didn't know that. But yeah, since my eyes are a good seven or eight inches higher than yours, when I'm in the driver's seat, I *can* see where the hood ends."

"And driving over bridges—I can *never* see the water. I always see the damn rail. Speaking of which, the installation should also have a porch deck, built so when I'm sitting in a lounge chair, I see *over* the rail, not straight *at* the rail." Which was why she'd torn away her porch deck railing. And violated the building code in the process.

It was still raining when they left the museum, but it was more of a drizzle than a pour. So they decided to walk. They found a shoe store and a post office.

Good thing they were hungry, because they also came upon several of Portland's famous food carts. An hour later, after Chinese crepes, a delightful selection of handmade dumplings with weird and wonderful fillings, served from the aptly named 'Dump Truck', and some crème brûlée donuts from the further-away donut shop, they carried on their way.

But stopped at a gadget store. Dylan loved gadget stores. Which was poignant since he had to travel light. In an alternate universe, Dylan had a huge garage full of gadgets.

"Here," Dylan said when they finally exited the store. He handed Rev a pair of cardboard frame glasses with some sort of film. "Put them on."

"Cool!" Rev smiled at him. The rain became rainbow. They were refracting glasses.

"Have you seen Hiro Yamagata's works?" he asked a few blocks later, as she was still delightedly walking through rainbows.

"No. What does he do?"

"Google when you get home."

They made a detour back to the post office so Dylan could mail his other gadget purchases to himself. A herd of remote-controlled toys, each covered in fur. Fake fur presumably. Which might, of course, make a difference …

"Woh! Just … woh!" Rev had found Yamagata's "Quantum Field" and his *Holographic Cube Building*. Lasers turned mirrored skyscrapers into shining, shimmering, multi-coloured wonderfuls …

"You know," she turned to Dylan, "it would take so little to make our world just a bit more beautiful! Can you imagine every skyscraper in every city being like this?" She explored some of his other works.

"I bet he could make one look like a sun-sparkling lake or a moon-glimmering lake … "

"Or the Veil Nebula … "

Rev googled.

"Oh yeah, that'd be cool too … "

Day after that, they spent the whole afternoon in Forest Park, billed as 'The only city wilderness park in the U.S.'

"Pity we don't have Moe with us," Dylan said near the beginning of the five-mile hike. "Or Peanut. Or Bob."

"Not to mention Loup," she stared at him. How could he not mention Loup first?

"Actually, I was thinking she'd hate this. She'd know it's make-believe wilderness."

"But it's—yeah. Not the same. Still. It's pretty damn good for being in a city."

"Are you picking up the same vibes I am?" Dylan asked Rev after a couple of miles. "When we're both men, we're a gay couple, a pair of harmless, old fags."

Rev nodded. Men and women, solo and not, just sort of ignored them. Passed them by.

"Though I wonder," she said, "if a small group, of males, came upon a couple of old fags somewhere else … "

"Quite right," Dylan agreed. "Here, we might be in a sort of special social context."

Rev nodded. "Though … Central Park … "

"Portland versus New York?"

"Maybe."

"And when we're both women," Dylan continued, "we're just a couple of good friends, away from hubby for the day."

"Sad that only women are allowed to be friends without being lovers. Good friends, *real* friends, not just acquaintances."

"It is, yes."

"I was going to say 'just' friends but."

Dylan nodded. Friends, *real* friends, was nowhere near 'just'.

"I think it'd be different if we were both men in our twenties or thirties," Rev said a while later. "Instead of forties."

"Fifties. But yes. Ditto for being both women in our twenties or thirties?"

"Oh yeah."

After, they went to the Salt and Straw for some ice cream. Dylanna chose the Pear and Blue Cheese ice cream. Revv went for the Arbequina Olive Oil ice cream. Apparently, while real men don't eat yogurt, but they can eat olive oil ice cream when the alternatives are Pear and Blue Cheese, Rose City Centennial, Petunia's Peach Crumble Bars, and Cinnamon Snickerdoodle. She'd considered whether the Bone Marrow and Smoked Cherries would have been a more appropriate choice, but—cherries. Smoked though ...

"We can't tweak the app for age," Dylan said that night when they were back in the whimsical studio, "but what if we uploaded pictures of ourselves from when we were in our twenties?"

"Good idea!" Sigh. "No, can't. I don't have any," she explained. Not only were digital cameras not yet invented, which meant Rev didn't take a lot of pictures, but back then, she didn't have any friends. Who would have taken pictures of her. Because she certainly wouldn't have taken any pictures of herself.

"I do."

"Do what?"

"Have pictures of us from back then."

"You do?"

"Yeah. Remember our graduation party?"

"Oh yeah!" she said brightly. They'd ended up under the table drinking tequila. To celebrate becoming certified, legitimized teachers.

"I also have some from the Hallowe'en party we went to."

"But those—well, *you'd* be in costume." Rev had *always* had trouble presenting herself as anything but what she was. Which, come to think of it, made this whole Revv thing even more … amazing. Anomalous, at least.

Dylan opened his laptop and a few seconds later, turned it to face her. She looked. Dismay crossed her face.

"What?"

"I'm wearing the same clothes. Jeans, tshirt, track shoes."

He waited. Then said, "Did you really think you'd start wearing a turquoise polyester pantsuit when you got old—er?"

"No," she burst out laughing at the thought, "but I don't want to look like … "

"Like what?"

"Like one of those people stuck in the past. I had an aunt who didn't move beyond the 50s. In the 70s, she still looked like … Ethel. From *I Love Lucy.*"

"But you're *not* stuck in the past. Cabin, not basement apartment. LSAT-writer, not high school teacher. And just a few years ago, you bought kamut flour, remember? You'd never've done that in your twenties."

He had a point. She was a jaguar trying to turn into a monkey late in life. Dylan was a playful amoeba. Always had been, always will be. Which meant that *he* was … no, in many ways, he'd moved on as well.

"I still eat cold pizza for breakfast."

"Because it's the perfect food. Just like jeans, a tshirt, and track shoes," he pointed to his own attire, "is the perfect clothing. Why mess with perfection?" he asked the obvious.

"Yeah … " She got up off the couch. Staggered, didn't quite fall down.

"And there's that. More evidence that you're not living in the past," he grinned.

"But I still *feel* twenty. Kind of."

"You still feel *passionate*. Thank god. Well, not god, but … the Great Big Purple Platypus."

So just for the hell of it, they went for a walk as two young women.
"Wanna party?" A small pack of young men was soon following them.
"No thanks," Dylanna replied. Smiling.
"Aw, come on!"
"We'd rather just go home," she said again.
"But we wanna party, come on, it'll be fun!"
"I said no!" She said yet again.
"What's your problem, bitch!"
Dylanna turned to face the young men, reaching into his pocket to turn off the app.
"You know," one of them called out, "bitches shouldn't be walking the streets at night. Maybe we should teach you a lesson."
"Run away! Run away!" Dylan changed his mind.

And when they went for a walk as two young men?
"You know, we don't like faggots 'round here … "

"The problem is numerical," Rev said. Later, when they were making notes about their experiences. The second experience had surprised her. The first had not. "Two is a couple. Three is a group, a gang, a tribe, a herd."
"But they didn't assume, in the first case, that we were a couple."
"They might have. It just wouldn't have mattered."
"Ah."

"I wonder if the balding middle-aged men will think of this work-around."
Dylan looked at her, confused.
"You know … to appear as fifteen-year-old boys, in order—"
"Oh right. But surely, once they get close—"
"Might be too late."
"Yeah." Dylan sighed. "We should tell them. Dana et al. Confess."
"Yeah." But Rev wondered how they could prevent it. Damn it!

Next day, they rented bikes and did the eleven-mile Waterfront Loop, which was a lovely scenic route almost completely on bike paths. They stopped at a Mexican food cart for some burritos. Then at the Cultured Caveman food cart.

"Didn't cave women eat food?"Dylanna asked the man running the cart.

Rev waited for the answer that she knew would not be forthcoming.

"What?"

"Didn't cave women eat food?" Dylanna asked again. Politely.

The man didn't answer. Didn't get it.

"Your food cart is called the Cultured Cave*man*. That implies that it doesn't provide food for cave *women.* Cultured or not."

"What?"

"I'll have an order of Bacon Almond Dates," Revv said, pushing Dylanna aside. The Mini Meatballs with Heart and Liver sounded just a little too gruesome. "Actually," given that, "make it an Almond Butter and Blueberry Jam Wrap instead."

"That's from the kids' menu," he said to Revv with disdain.

"So?" Revv glared at him. Actually, maybe it was Rev who glared at him.

"No, actually, make it a Chocolate Pot de Crème instead." Okay, that was Rev.

The man stared at her. Right. Men aren't supposed to change their minds. Nor are they supposed to eat chocolate.

Then he stared at Dylanna, waiting for her order.

"The Ethiopian Cabbage? That's no-cal, right? Next to eating no food at all. I'll be a size zero in no time!" She beamed at Revv.

Day after that, they went to the huge Powell's book store. There was actually a map of the store at the entrance.

Three hours later, they went Papa Hadyn's for dessert.

"I'm starting to appreciate living in a city," Revv said, a bag of books tucked beside her, a piece of Raspberry Gateau sitting in front of her. She'd picked it out from the dessert case because it looked so densely chocolate. The menu said it was made out of a fallen chocolate soufflé.

"It is nice," Dylan said. "Having so much within walking distance. Not just books and food, but art and theatre and music and all sorts of weird and wonderful things." He'd missed it.

"That's just sad," Rev said, staring at the painted salmon swimming through the corner of a brick building.

"Well, it is a seafood restaurant," Dylan said.

"By definition, sad."

"It's on Salmon Street."

"That doesn't salvage the sad."

"It doesn't, no."

"So we have one day left before we head up to Vancouver," Dylan said that night, googling for something to do. They'd finished their stash. "How about we go to the vacuum cleaner museum?"

Rev stared at him. Pity they'd finished their stash.

"Okay, how about we go to a dance club instead? You as a short man, me as a hot babe. Our young usses."

"Okay, but first we have to practice dancing."

"But we already know how to dance. At least, *I* know how to dance."

"Shut up," she smiled. Then added, "As a hot babe?"

"Oh right." He thought about that. "Do I *have* to dance? Don't I just have to stand there?"

She thought about that. "Yeah."

"But it'll be more fun if I dance." Dylan stood up and started moving his hips in a circle. He looked like he was doing the hula hoop.

"Am I doing it right?"

"Don't think so."

Rev got up and started stepping from side to side.

"What are you doing?"

"Dancing like a man."

Dylan was horrified. "*I* do *not* dance like that!"

"I know. But most men do."

"Oh right."

He watched her for a few moments. "You're good."

"Could you tell?" Dylanna shouted, joining Revv at the small table they'd claimed, having stayed on the floor with all the women for an up-tempo, sexy number. The men had left the floor, en masse, as soon as it had come on. Go figure.

"Yes," she shouted back. "You were the tallest woman on the floor. Plus no one fell off her shoes three times in the first minute of the song." He'd resurrected his sequined red shoes for the night, as there had been no takers on EBay.

Dylan thought about that. "I suspect the app'll work better for women than for men."

Rev nodded. Who but the most clueless of men—and Lola—will want to present as a woman?

"How did Ginger Rogers do it?" he asked once the volume decreased a bit. He was sitting with his legs comfortably apart.

"And backwards yet."

"Oh for fuck's sake," Dylan said to the crowd of men edging ever nearer. "What do you think is up there that you want to see so badly?"

As soon as another slow song came on, one of the men asked Dylanna to dance.

"No thank you."

Then another man approached and asked her to dance.

"No thanks. I'm with him," Dylanna nodded to Revv. Suddenly understanding something. Something appalling.

Yet another man approached Dylanna and asked her to dance.

"No!"

The next man had been reading *Cosmo*. He'd read that women liked strong, take-charge men. So he just grabbed Dylanna. Underestimated the weight attached to the arm. And the resistance. Which made him look like a fool. Dylanna's fault, of course. "Fucking cunt," he said as he tried to recover.

And then yet another man approached Dylanna and asked her to dance.

S/He ignored him. And had another insight about women's behaviour.

Then the first guy approached again and asked Dylanna to dance.

"No, just leave me the fuck alone!"

"Bitch!" he muttered as he walked away.

"That wasn't very lady-like," Rev said. Once she got over her amazement. Because no one had *ever* asked *her* to dance. Not that she ever went to clubs like this. But even at the one-star versions. No one. If there was some guy she wanted to dance with, she asked him. And if she just wanted to dance, she just got up on the floor and danced.

"It's like they're a pack of lobotomized feral dogs stuck in fuck mode," Dylan said. Yes, *he* had on occasion asked a woman to dance, but only after eye contact that suggested a 'yes'. When had men become so nuance-impaired? Or was it that a 'yes' had become irrelevant?

"Your turn."

Revv nodded, reluctantly, and got up. He approached a woman and asked her to dance.

"Go away, you little troll."

He approached another woman. "Excuse me, would you like to dance?"

The woman looked at him. She looked *down* at him.

"With you?" she inquired sweetly. Then laughed. All of her friends joined in, rubbing salt into the wound that could have ended in a report on the six o'clock news about a rabbi, a priest, and some guy with an AK-47 walking into a dance club ...

Instead, "Bitch!" Revv muttered as he walked away.

At the last minute, they decided to stay in Victoria instead of Vancouver. They'd both already been to Vancouver, and they wanted to spend some time on the islands which they figured would be more easily accessible from Victoria, *and* Dylan found an ocean front house with a 3k walk along the beach and sunsets to die for.

The plan was to get two-week jobs while they were there, to test the app in a work setting. They arrived on a Tuesday, got themselves settled, then went for a walk on the beach.

After Dylan skyped Loup. Well, Kit.

"Hey, how's it going in sunny California?" Kit asked.

"We're in Victoria now. Still west coast though, so—"

"Warm! No snow!" Rev shouted from across the room.

Kit grinned. She turned away then and called Loup. "I've got my laptop connected to my tv screen today."

Loup appeared, saw Dylan in the tv, then took off.

"Loup—" Dylan was crestfallen. "Where'd she go?" he asked dismally.

Kit turned away again. "I'm not sure … She—"

"Why THANK YOU Loup!" Dylan was laughing. Curious, Rev went into the room. An overly dead rabbit filled the screen. "What a good little wolf you are!"

"Tell me you have the keyboard protector rigged up."

"I do," Kit was laughing.

"Loup would like this," Dylan said, thoroughly enjoying the long walk, after the long, long drive.

"She would. No rabbits though."

"True … Seagulls though."

They both smiled, imagining Loup running, racing, taking flight as she tried to catch one.

First thing Wednesday, afternoon, they turned on their apps on and went to the OfficeTemp office, slightly revised resumes in hand.

"Hello, I'm Dylan-na O'Toole," he gave the receptionist a copy of his resume that said exactly that. And a bit more.

"Christopher Reveille. But everyone calls me Revv," he smiled. Charmingly. Or not.

They both got one day, next day, jobs as telemarketers.

"They called me 'chipper'," Rev said on their way home.

Dylan just stared at her.

"I know, right? I think we set the cheerfulness bar higher for women. Rev would have to be a Little Miss Frickin' Sunshine to be considered chipper."

"But Revv can be just your usual surly self."

"Exactly." She grinned.

"And I imagine it goes in the other direction for other stuff. All Rev has to do is show a little speak-up-for-yourself-ness to be called 'aggressive'. I'll bet Revv will have to act like one of those enforcer guys." They'd actually watched a bit of a hockey game the night before. "Fresh off the rink."

She made a note to herself.

"No. Don't."

"It's a beta *test*. We have to *test* our hypotheses."

"Promise you'll wear your football helmet when you test that hypothesis."

She considered that. "I think the mixing up hockey and football thing would confuse people."

"Right. *That's* what would confuse them."

"That's why I've always advocated blind interviewing," Rev continued a moment later. "You can take as much care as you like, sticking to the same list of questions, but if your assessment of the answers is skewed, by their gender expectations, what's the point?"

"There's no reason they can't identify cover letters and resumes with numbers before they get to the assessors," Dylan agreed, in principle, "but what about when they call your references? They'd give your sex away. You know what I mean," he added.

"Yeah ... I don't have any references."

Dylan grinned.

"And the interview itself would be a give-away."

"Until now."

At the end of the day, next day, there was no difference in sales. Both of them had sold nada.

But ...

"Do you think it's easier to be rude to men?" Revv asked when the tenth person in a row hung up on her. Without even a cursory 'No thanks, I'm not interested.'

"Possibly. Men don't have feelings, remember?"

"Yeah, but men are more feared than women. Men generally get more deference than women. For that reason. Don't they?"

And ...

"He asked me what I was wearing!" Dylanna said with disbelief.

"Yeah, because it's real easy to mistake a telemarketing call for phone sex."

That evening, the reconsidered their plan.

"Do you think OfficeTemp is sort of built for women?" Dylan asked. "Being both temporary and officey?"

"Maybe. So we should go to an agency that's sort of built for men? *Is* there an agency that places men in temporary positions?"

They googled.

"Employers Overload."

"Is that Employer's Overload or Employers' Overload?" Rev asked. Out of perverse curiosity.

"Employers Overload."

She snorted.

So Friday, they went to Employers Overload. Dylanna got a temporary job doing data entry. At $11.40 per hour. Revv was placed as a temporary forklift operator. At $16.60 per hour.

"But you have no experience—"

"I think they assumed that since I can drive a motorcycle, driving a forklift would be a piece of cake." She knew, she just *knew*, they wouldn't've made that assumption if she'd been a woman. They would have doubted that she *could* drive a motorcycle, or considered it a fluke, or been distracted by biker chick images.

At the end of the first day ...

"No one ever gives me what I need," Dylan, Dylanna, said. "The primary data packet. The secondary data packet. The revised guidelines for entry. I have to ask for it. Which makes me seem incompetent."

Rev nodded.

"But if I don't ask for it, I *will* be incompetent, doing a job without the stuff I need."

Rev nodded.

At the end of the second day ...

"They keep treating me like I'm an assistant! A general, all-purpose assistant! All day, guys kept coming to me with extra little jobs to do. Not data entry jobs."

Rev nodded.

"And most of them were younger than me! *Considerably* younger."

Rev nodded.

At the end of the third day ...

"Josh got a stapler."

Rev waited.

"I made a request for a stapler my first day. It wasn't among the office supplies in my desk. And today, I see that Josh, who just got hired, today, has a stapler. I've been waiting three frickin' days."

"Yeah, men seem to prioritize requests from other men. Informal requests. You just asked, right? You didn't fill out a form?"

"So ... 'Bros before hos'?" It wasn't a code Dylan lived by. "And all women are hos. Except married women. Right?" He was getting the hang of this.

"Right. And although married women may seem to get request priority, it's only because they're affiliated with men. So it's still bros before—women."

"But the supplies manager is a woman."

"Yeah, women seem to prioritize requests from men too."

At the end of the fourth day ...

"I know it's been only four days, but I'm never asked to do anything of importance."

Yeah.

"So I just went ahead and took a look at some of the department's policies and procedures today, and made a few recommendations. Met with my supervisor."

A sharp intake of breath from Rev.

"And he was—everyone—they're always so angry with me. At me."

Yeah. It wasn't *what* Dylanna said that made his supervisor angry. It was *that* Dylanna said ... something. She was supposed to be nice, quiet, and invisible. *Anything* she said would be cause for anger. Rev's whole life flashed before her eyes.

"He actually reprimanded me for it! What?" He saw her expression.

"You're just a data entry clerk." Besides.

"Exactly. Which is why I have to show them that I can do more, that I was meant for bigger things."

But you're not meant for bigger things.

"You have to develop a reputation!" Dylan was on a roll.

But the only reputation Dylanna could have, could ever have, was that of a bitch or slut. A reputation for good work would never precede her. She could never rest on laurels of competence. If a woman wanted respect, she had to earn it each and every time. Prove herself each and every time. Over and over. No wonder we're so angry, so tired.

"You have to be assertive, show initiative. What?" he asked again. Rev had sighed.

Men look for opportunities to showcase their leadership; women talk about team work. Men ask for challenging assignments; women never ask for more than they can handle.

Dylanna, a *woman,* acting as a man—how dare she! The resentment would fuel even more aggression.

"Go for it," Rev said. It would provide good material for their reports and for their book.

Part way through the fifth day …

"Hey," Dylan was so happy, he'd called her, "guess what? Despite what happened yesterday, or maybe because of it, I was assigned a project today!"

"Really?" She was surprised.

But then, that night …

"I thought I knew," Dylan said. "You *know* me, I'm not your average asshole. But today—again—and I keep being *surprised*. All the guys after work went for a drink, and I wasn't invited. At lunch, they all go down to the cafeteria together. Without me. They huddle around the water cooler, and when I approach, conversation stops. It actually *stops*."

Rev nodded.

"I feel so … out of the loop."

Rev nodded.

He looked at her then. Really looked at her. "You've been out of the loop your whole life."

"Haven't *you*? As you say, you're not the average asshole. If I were a married-with-kids made-up-woman, I'd probably be in the loop. Quite a different loop, admittedly, but still."

"No," he thought about it. "I guess non-masculine men are more men than non-feminine women are women?"

"Maybe." She was unconvinced. Because it seemed women could cross the gender line more easily than men. But maybe they just crossed into a no-person's land.

Dylan was spent the entire weekend working on his project.

And then on the following Monday …
"Bloody hell! Fucking George! He's such a fucking idiot!"
Rev waited.
Apparently some important details weren't attached to the project assignment. So Dylan had done it all wrong. A whole weekend of hard work—for nothing.
Yeah.
Rev made a note to buy Dylanna a copy of Courtney's *Golden Handcuffs.* In the meantime, that evening, they watched *North Country.*
Dylan was shocked. "Has that ever happened to you? That kind of … sabotage? Or even something like what happened to me?"
"Probably," she said. Then elaborated. "I'm too stupid to know. Takes one to know one, and I'm not … strategic. That's why I didn't go into politics to change the world, remember? I'm very … literal. So I take what people say at face value. I *believe* them," she cringed.
Dylan nodded. And it was exactly what he loved about her. What you saw was what you got. She said what she meant and meant what she said. She wouldn't've stood a chance in politics.
Would definitely *not* have changed the world.

And on Tuesday …
"We had a planning meeting today, but somehow I was left off the email list. I guess they hadn't updated it since I'd been hired."
Yeah, that was the explanation.
"Anyway, once I found out, and showed up—What?"
Women wait to be asked, to be included.
"I apologized," he continued. Apologetically. He still had Dylanna on. "For being late. Anyway, then they assumed I'd take notes."
And?

"I told them Josh should take notes. Said I had seniority," he grinned.

Rev laughed.

"Later he called me a bitch."

Yeah.

"But—it wasn't just anger, it wasn't just insult, it was … " Dylan was still trying to put his finger on it, "there was such a righteous indignation, it was as if I'd cheated, as if I hadn't played fair—"

"Yeah."

"How 'yeah'?"

"Men *can* win when they're against other men, but the rule is that they *always* win they're against a woman. Whatever else, they can expect to have victory there. It's guaranteed. You one-upped him, you deprived him of that, you cheated him of that, you broke the rules."

Dylan looked at her as if she was nuts.

"But then … "

Wednesday …

He kept trying, harder and harder.

"Nothing I ever do is good enough."

Yeah.

When men fail, they attribute it to something external. The course wasn't taught well; the material wasn't interesting. When women fail, they attribute it to something internal. I wasn't smart enough; I didn't try hard enough.

"But I—"

She waited, then asked, "What?"

Silence.

"I just cut myself off," he said. Appalled. "I've already become so used to *being* cut off. By men interrupting me."

"Yeah."

"I have to start using longer sentences."

Won't help.

"It's not that what you do isn't good enough," she returned to the initial conversation. "It's that it's irrelevant."

Dylan processed that. And was horrified. "You say it so … casually."

Casually? No.

She powered up her laptop and quickly found the post she was looking for. She read it again, smiling.

"What?"

"A post on 'I Blame the Patriarchy'. The best blog ever." She turned her laptop toward him.

"No dudes allowed," Rev cautioned. "Only partly because they've pretty much taken over everything else."

Dylan nodded. Then read. Out loud. "'Another effective technique before the Great Backlash was corporate conscious raising, that is, sexism sensitivity training for executives by actual feminists. The trainers set the men three small tests upon which they were graded. By the end of the second test, the men were demanding to know the criterion, because their scores didn't change. Some began cooperating instead of competing ('cause women like that stuff, right?), but still they did no better or worse. At last the bathing trunks were pulled out for the swimsuit competition. The men categorically refused to go on with the exercise, and still, STILL had to be told that they were being judged on appearance, not performance, the whole time.'"

"That's not funny," Dylan said.

"No, it's not." But try not realizing it until you were forty. That is, after *twenty years* of thinking what you did *did* matter. And then realizing that your life was, had always been, would always be, lose-lose. If you weren't good enough, you weren't good enough. If you *were* good enough, it didn't matter.

"So if performance, achievement—if it's all irrelevant, how do you ever get ahead?"

The answer was obvious.

After a while, Dylan spoke. "You know, most men wouldn't survive being women in—a patriarchy."

She was silent for a moment.

"What makes you think most women survive?"

A long time later, Dylan said "I guess it depends on our definition of 'survive'. At the very least, men would be killing their oppressors."

"Oh please. They wouldn't have the chance. They'd have been brainwashed from birth to think violence is wrong. So much so that even in self-defence they'd hold back."

Thursday ...

"Someone called me unladylike today," Dylan said that evening when Rev got home. "I hate the way they feel entitled to tell me what my problems are, to tell me whether I measure up to their standards, to tell me whether I please them or not."

"What'd you say?"

"Thank you." He grinned. As did she.

And yet, "I need to tweak my app's wardrobe again," he said. Dylan had been tweaking his app almost every night. Agonizing over what it, he, she, looked like. Rev—nada. She, he, was always good to go with whatever.

"Why?"

"Because someone else called me a hottie."

"And you weren't flattered?"

Dylan stared at her. He wasn't, no.

"Sexual innuendos undermine," he said. Although surely Rev already knew this. "They reduce one to sexual body parts and functions." He already knew this too, but now he ... he'd *felt* it. Though he probably didn't quite realize that it subjugated women as a class, not just him/her as an individual.

"So what did you do? When you were called a hottie."

"I told the guy to fuck off."

"And ... ?"

"It didn't seem to register. He was confused. Didn't know what he'd done wrong."

"And did you explain it to him?"

"No," he sighed. "I was just so ... tired."

After just two weeks.

He tossed his phone onto the couch beside him. Wardrobe untweaked.

Only two weeks for him to move through anger to apathy.

It's not like Dylan was unaware of sexism, systemic misogyny, etc.

Still the app had been an eye-opener.

"I was also called sentimental," he said a while later.

"By the same guy? One of the same two guys?" she corrected.

"No, a different guy." And then Dylan looked at her. "So many guys call me things ... Do women call guys things?"

"Yeah. But not as often to their face."

We're not entitled to do so.

"But you? Sentimental?" It didn't really make sense. Dylan was well acquainted with his emotions, but unless dogs, or wolves, were involved, 'sentimental' was not a word she'd—"Ah."

"What, 'Ah'."

"Ethics in a woman is called sentiment. In a man," she added, "it's called integrity."

Friday ...

She found him sprawled on the couch, beer in hand. He hardly ever drank beer. He'd been fired.

"'It's not working out,'" they said. "'You're just not a good fit,'" they said. "What the hell does that mean?"

It means you're a woman.

Revv, on the other hand, was having the time of her life. On the first day, he organized some impromptu forklift racing at lunch. Lots of fun.

On the second day, he discovered a lunch-time basketball game. No one shoved him off the court when he joined in. No one even tried to stare him down. In fact, they passed him the ball. Often.

On the third day, when he finally wandered into the cafeteria, the men at the corner table waved him over.

"Pull up a chair, Revv!" someone said. Someone he didn't even know. "Want in?" They were playing poker.

"No thanks," he replied.

The inclusion caught her by surprise. All through the day, it caught her by surprise. Her delight at *being* included also caught her by surprise. She'd always held groups in low regard. They were tribes, they were mechanisms of injustice, they were exclusionary.

But then, she'd always been the one excluded.

True, if she'd had her app set on the female version of herself, she probably would have been waved over, included, by the women's table.

She'd looked around in vain for the grownups' table.

"Do you know how to play poker?" she asked Dylan that evening.

"Yeah. But the rules are mind-numbingly simple and winning depends solely on chance and bluffing. Not my cup of tea."

Not Rev's either. But his description did seem to explain its attraction for men. Being a man seemed to be all about being a poser.

On the fourth day, someone told him that the Team Lead position was open. Another surprise. His colleagues gave him information. Which was far more valuable than a stapler. Not that a forklift operator needed a stapler.

He approached the Manager, expressed interest in the position.

"Is that like 'Supervisor'?" Even Dylan was surprised.

"No, I think it's like 'Pre-Supervisor.'"

Still. He hadn't been assertive. He hadn't shown any initiative. He'd simply shown that he wasn't incompetent.

By the end of the first week, she was tired, thoroughly tired, of the relentless competition. Men turned everything into a game, into winning and losing. Everything—*everything*—she did or said had to be either putting herself up or putting someone else down. That constant need to impress the alpha male was exhausting.

She was also tired of the superficial conversation. She'd realized early in the week that men really *weren't* very good at seeing the big picture. Their view didn't extend much past themselves and their tribe. Their standing within their tribe.

Nor were they very good at seeing detail. Women were the fussy ones. Crossing the t's and dotting the i's, so to speak. Or, rather, correcting mistakes and cleaning up.

The wonder wasn't that climate change was about to end the

world as we know it, she realized that Friday. The wonder was that it took so long.

And of course, she was tired of the misogyny. Disgusted, actually. She'd always suspected that what men said to each other was quite different than what they said to women, but 'different' didn't even come close to …

"But it's just posturing," Dylan said when she asked him about it. "Most men don't believe the shit they say."

"Even the shit they say about women?"

"Especially the shit they say about women."

"Hm." Rev wasn't so sure.

"Then why do they say it?"

"I guess it's a male bonding thing." Dylan had never said that kind of shit. He had never participated in those conversations.

"Males bond over the degradation of women." She'd known that, of course, intellectually. It was just—

She was also tired of being called a fag or a pussy every time she didn't play the misogynist Neanderthal.

"Hey, Revv, comin'?" One of the other forklift operators was waiting in the doorway at the end of the day. "We always go to Chuck's, Fridays after work."

"Oh—sure, I'll meet you there!"

She should go, she told herself. It would be good for the test, she told herself. She didn't have to say long, she told herself.

"Revv?" The Manager called out to him as he stood there, trying to convince herself to go to Chuck's. "I recommended you for Team Lead. You got it!"

"So one of the guys asked me today what I thought of the game." Monday was post-game day.

"What game?"

"What I said. He went ballistic. I told him I spent my weekend watching soap operas instead."

"He went even *more* ballistic."

"He did. So I proceeded to tell him that the soaps have more heft than the game. In both cases," Rev explained, "the central theme, and that which drives the action, is winning. In the soaps, what the players are trying to win is money, power, love, and/or happiness. Pretty substantial goals."

Dylan nodded.

"In the game, however, the players are trying to win—the game. Frankly, it verges on circularity—you play the game in order to win the game—which comes close to utter triviality."

"Did you tell him that?"

"I did. I went on to tell him that while both sets of players use strategy, often involving manipulation, the strategy of the soaps is considerably more complicated than 'Fake left, then go right.' In fact, I would venture to say that the soaps is to the game what chess is to checkers."

"And?"

"His face got red. Redder."

"I imagine so."

"Then I talked about the setting. Which at least in the soaps changes. As for dialogue—"

Dylan burst out laughing.

"There *is* some."

"I suspect players in the game speak to each other too. We just never get to hear their dialogue. Odd."

"Yeah, all we get to hear is the voice-over commentary, explaining the action. Rather like a Greek chorus."

"As patronizing now as it no doubt was then."

"In the cinematography category," Rev continued, "the game is superior for its long shots, but the soaps are superior for their close-ups. A tie. But in the soundtrack category, the soaps walk away with the prize."

Dylan nodded.

"As for sex and violence, the soaps lead on both counts. There is simply no sex in the game—unless you count the occasional ass-pat, but that's so very elementary, it hardly even counts as foreplay. And while there is a lot more physical contact in the game, of a violent-seeming nature, and while injury is therefore frequent, it's seldom permanent; in the soaps, people kill each other."

Again Dylan burst out laughing.

"One might point out that the game is real," Rev added, "whereas the soaps are not, and on that basis alone claim victory for the game. Unfortunately this very 'advantage' backfires: given the level of injury and death in the soaps, it's to its credit that it's *not* real; in the game, however, real people get hurt."

"What'd he say to that?"

"Oh, he'd just sort of walked away after my ass-pat comment."

"I said 'Nice tie' to someone today," Rev said to Dylan on the Monday evening of the second week. "And the guy said 'Yeah, your sister thought so too when I put it on this morning.' Everyone laughed. Why is that funny?" Rev asked.

"It's a guy joke," Dylan replied.

"Yeah, but what's the *joke?* Oh, wait! 'My sister is my property and so—' Nope. Still don't get it. Oh wait, is having sex with another man's sister theft? No, that can't be right. Unless he's stealing her virginity. Which he's not. He's not even taking it. He's just *ending* it. And so is she. And anyway, why would that be funny?"

"I think guys think it's funny because by having sex with someone's sister, you make her a slut."

"What?" She was absolutely flummoxed. "How does having sex with a woman make her a slut?" Quite apart from all women were sluts to begin with. "And even so, where's the humor in that?"

"He's making her damaged goods?" Dylan was struggling too. He wasn't the kind of guy who found guy jokes funny.

"Still waiting for the humor. Oh—damaging his property is getting one up on him? And it's funny to make someone one-down. Because ... ?"

"It's like leaving a banana peel on the ground for someone to slip on?" Dylan suggested. "Which is not funny."

"Speaking of guy jokes," Rev resumed a few minutes later, "why do men stop in the middle of a dirty joke when a woman shows up?" It was another thing that she'd noticed. A lot. "It can't be because they think we're ignorant of sex and therefore won't get it. Can it? I mean, assuming we're sluts means assuming we have sex with everybody, so surely we'd learn a thing or two.

"And it can't be because they think we *should* be ignorant of sex and therefore shouldn't get it. Because then—I don't know." She sighed. "None of this makes any sense."

"I think," Dylan ventured, for he himself had never told such a joke, "it might be because they don't want women to know that they think of them, every one of them, all the time, as just … cunts." He waited for her response.

"Yeah." She sighed. "I suspected as much."

On the Tuesday evening …

"One of the guys called Hurricane Sandy 'a real bitch' today," Rev said. "So I said 'Excuse me?' And the guy just looked at me. And I just didn't know … where to start."

Dylan nodded. "Men have really upped their hatred of women. And I don't know why."

"Maybe tv? First, with cable and satellite tv, the number of channels available to most people has increased tremendously. There are ten NHL stations. So it's possible now for men to watch testosterone-pumped aggressive manly sports all the time, not just on Saturday nights during the football or hockey season.

"Second, it seems that so many prime-time dramas disproportionately feature crimes in which women are the victims and men are the perpetrators. So men see men hurting women every night.

"Third, the whole reality show thing shows us the very worst of humankind. Immaturity is … celebrated.

"Put it all together and what do you get? Exactly what we have."

"But why the hate in the first place?" Dylan didn't hate women. As a rule.

"Maybe it's not so much hate as insult. Men insulting women is putting them in their place. As inferiors. Subordinates."

"And they need to do that all the time because … " Because Dylan sure as hell didn't do that all the time.

"Because they know deep down that if status were awarded according to effort, ability, or value, they wouldn't be superior all the time. So they hang on like hell to their superior-status-by-god-given-sex."

"Reminding women every chance they get of their inferior-status-by-god-given-sex. Hm."

Wednesday, she was called into Human Resources.

"Here it comes," she thought, pessimistically. Because.

"Hi Revv, have a seat," a red-haired woman said genially.

Revv sat.

"So, I've taken a look at your resume, and I have to say that you're overqualified to be driving fork."

Driving fork? But yeah, overqualified. Duh. This was where they'd tell her they couldn't afford to pay her what she was worth and suggest she seek employment elsewhere.

On top of the background 'What kind of a fuck-up *are* you that the only job you can get, with your education and experience, is this one?'

"So we'd like to offer you a promotion. With your degrees and your teaching experience—how'd you like to work here in HR, doing Employee Training? More than twice the pay, I believe, but I'd have to check ... "

"I'm going out for a bit, wanna come?" It was a nice night. And he really wanted to go for a walk. A nice long walk.

"As Dylanna?"

"No. Why?"

"Because then I'd have to be Revv."

"Why?" But as soon as he said it, he knew.

"Fuck!"

19

They'd first decided to spend Saturday biking around Saltspring Island, visiting the many artist galleries.

Then they decided to make a weekend of it and ferry over on Sunday to Galiano, with its lovely logging trails and country lanes.

Then they decided to spend the entire week, biking, hiking, kayaking, and camping. Neither of them had had a nine-to-five Monday-to-Friday job since—forever. They hadn't taken into account how terribly soul-sucking it would be. And they'd been at it for two whole weeks.

"Apparently," Dylan said, walking out onto the porch after his fourth phone call, "it's nuts to go kayaking in the Gulf Islands in February."

"But isn't the west coast climate temperate? Relatively speaking?" Rev was waiting for the sunset. Most evenings, it had been as promised: crimson and scarlet, wisps and streaks ...

"Yes, but—"

"And we go kayaking back home day before and day after ice."

"*You* go kayaking back home day before and day after ice."

"And when it's snowing."

"Yeah. That was cool. I should call Loup. But," Dylan was not to be completely sidetracked, "it's been a terribly mild and/or terribly weird winter, quote unquote, so we might be able to do it. If we stay in sheltered coves."

"Which we intend to do, right? No paddling in the ocean. The open ocean. Because sheltered coves are still ocean. *And* still ocean." She grinned. And took another toke. It had been a while. Day before, one of her forklift buddies had queried Revv as to the purchase of— because he would never have queried Rev. As to.

Dylan reached out for the offered joint and took a toke as well.

"So, have you got everything planned?" She grinned again, this time at her non-responsibilities. She loved that Dylan was their event planner. *And* that he was very good at it.

"I do, yes. Ferry reservations, bike rentals, kayak rentals, camping gear rentals, route ... "

"In just four phone calls?"

"In just two phone calls. The others were for pizza and Doritos. And cheesecake." Now he grinned.

"You thought ahead! Okay, so, you're not nearly stoned enough."

They decided it would be a no-app trip. In fact, Dylan had decided he was finished with the app. Finished with living as a woman. And he didn't want to go there. But he knew that he must. Eventually.

He'd expected most of what had happened, or would have said so if someone had asked him about sexism in the workplace. It was just that *experiencing* it first hand was ... surprisingly different.

And the cumulative effect ... *That* he *hadn't* expected.

They started with Saltspring since it was the closest, and Dylan knew Rev would want the ferry trips to be as short as possible. Because oddly enough, they felt more like plane trips than boat trips. As initially planned, they rented bikes and just biked around. It was very relaxing.

"Riding a bike is significantly different than driving a forklift."

"I imagine it is, yes."

"Perhaps especially because of the dissimilar context." Oh god, she'd hated being in a warehouse all day. Wearing earplugs.

"It would be quite stupid to drive a forklift here."

At one of the galleries, Rev saw a piece of glass art she very much wanted. It reminded her of the sunsets they'd been seeing, streaking and wisping orange and scarlet and crimson, and although there was nothing blue about it, as glass, the piece also reminded her of the water.

"Pity we can't exactly take it with us," she said, moving on.

"No, but I'm sure they can ship it home for you."

"Yeah, but—"

"You can afford it! Now."

"Damn it!" It wasn't the first time her habit of living poor had gotten in the way of relatively simple pleasures. "Yes! I can! Now."

"Okay, so next we go to—"

She looked over his shoulder to the itinerary. Prepared by Gulf Island Tours.

"You delegated!"

"Is that—wrong?"

"Yes!" It was … cheating. It was not doing your own damn work. Men thought it was a good thing. Probably because it indicated power-over.

"They had the knowledge we needed," Dylan said. "I told them 'a bit of hiking, a bit of biking, and a bit of kayaking, all on the relaxing side of the difficulty spectrum, and a bit of camping or bed-and-breakfasting, seven days, maximum quiet, minimum people, lots of beauty, lots of intrigue.' They put it all together. In an hour. Would've taken me all day."

She considered all that. It *was* a reasonable use of resources.

"And it's been good so far, right?"

After Saltspring was Galiano. Or Mayne. Or Pender. She decided she didn't really need to know. It was nice just following Dylan's lead.

The biking, the walking, the paddling. It was all so very nice, so very good. The paddling especially, when the view was nothing but still water, reflecting the shoreline, islands in the distance …

"We have one more island?" Rev asked four or five days later, as they boarded the ferry yet again.

"We do. Saturna Island." He presented it to her like a birthday gift.

"It's the least developed island," he said. "It is, and I quote, 'By far, the most remote and crowd-free refuge.'"

Which, they discovered, was really depressing. Because the remote and crowd-free refuge had its own tourism association. An association that published and distributed brochures to ferries. No surprise, campsites on Saturna Island had to be reserved in advance. Not a problem, since the tour company had done that, for two nights, giving them three days on the island. Even so.

"Local residents are complaining about decreasing property values due to changes in the ferry service," Rev said as she read *The Saturna News*. She'd put the tourism brochure down as soon as she'd picked it up. "Homes once worth $450,000 are now worth only $400,000 because the ferry to Vancouver costs $150."

She looked at Dylan then. He hadn't told her how much this week was costing them.

"Our per diem covers it all."

"But we're not using the app."

"True. But surely they don't expect us to use it every day during the entire time."

"No?"

"Okay, then, we just worked for two weeks. Full-time."

"That's true," Rev smiled. It made the forklift job worth it. If it paid for this.

She returned to the issue at hand. "Wouldn't they *welcome* lower property values? It means lower property taxes.

"And wouldn't they welcome higher ferry tickets? It would mean fewer tourists. Aren't they living here for the beauty and solitude?"

"But it also means less business," Dylan suggested. "Maybe the people living here derive their income from tourists. Or by commuting to Vancouver."

"Hm." She read on. "It's not just the ticket prices. It's less service. Aren't there several ferries a day? What do they want, a fucking highway?"

"Maybe." But Dylan shuddered too, imagining four-laned bridges connecting all of the Gulf Islands with each other and with Victoria Island and the mainland.

First day on Saturna, they went to the east point to see the orca whales. It was, apparently, one of the best land spots for whale-watching. And school field trips.

"It wouldn't be so bad if they were just sitting quietly, in awe," Rev said, seething with annoyance, staring at all the pre-teens who were posing for pictures, laughing and shouting. Every one of them was facing *away* from the passing orcas. Not to mention the dozen talking into their cell phones or checking their text messages or whatever.

It was a desecration.

Dylan nodded then to one girl standing by herself, away from the pack, watching. The orcas. Lazily surfacing, again and again. Awe on her face.

"If just one—Isn't it worth it then?" Dylan asked.

"She'll grow up to be me," Rev answered. Sadly.

Dylan nodded. Happily.

Next day, they were walking along and—suddenly Rev stopped. She stared intently into the distance. "Wild horses?"

"Wild goats." Dylan had read the brochure.

"Yeah, that would've been my second guess."

"And the sheep we saw walking on the road," Rev said a while later. "And the deer we've seen. They all get along."

"Well, they're all herbivores," Dylan said. "I did read, though, that there's some concern about the deer. Not just here but on Pender and Mayne as well. Apparently, there's up to 170 of them per square kilometer."

"Woh, that's a lot of deer!" She hadn't seen more than a dozen at home. Ever.

"Yeah. They're eating so much vegetation, the songbirds are at risk."

"I suppose they shot all the wolves. To protect the sheep. I saw an upcoming 'Lamb Barbecue' in the paper," she added with disgust.

Dylan nodded. "So they're talking about reintroducing the natural predators, not just wolves, but cougars as well, but apparently the local schools have some concerns."

"Hm. Sounds like a win-win-win to me."

"Sex is a burden," Dylan said as they lounged on a shell midden beach. It was their last day. And he'd been thinking about it all week, on and off, his reluctance to carry on with the beta test. "I have to admit that I'm glad I'm no longer driven by my libido. It was like a constant thrumming, drumming, in the background of my mind. At the time, it seemed … exciting. But now, looking back, I see that it was more trouble than it was worth."

Rev agreed. And the thrumming, drumming, in her mind probably hadn't been nearly as strong.

"And gender is a prison," he added. "That unfortunately persists long after sex is dead."

Rev agreed. Couldn't agree more.

"I wonder why so many people buy into it," she said. "It's not like it's illegal to not wear make-up."

"Three in one!" He grinned at her. "Negatives in a sentence. But yeah. Unlike the burka."

"Maybe it's just one of several things they buy into because they don't think for themselves. Or can't."

Dylan nodded. "And don't underestimate peer pressure. You've had a privileged life."

She turned to him, eyebrows raised.

"No peers. No pressure."

"Yeah, but I've still been—" No, she hadn't. Been exposed to all the media messages. She hadn't read *Teen* or *Vogue*. She'd read *Kick It Over* and *The Greenpeace Magazine.* She didn't watch much tv. Hadn't watched any at all during her university years. Didn't have the time, what with her studies *and* her part-time jobs. Yes, she'd grown up with AM radio, with its awful pop music, but once she'd discovered Pink Floyd and Beethoven and …

But she'd made choices. Yes, maybe they had been easier for her to make, but they were choices nevertheless. That others could make. If they wanted to. If they really wanted to.

Next morning, Rev's phone rang. She answered it. (Needs to be said, yes.)

"Hey, Erin, what's up?" Rev looked at Dylan.

"Is Dylan there too?"

"Yeah ... "

"Can you put me on speakerphone? We'd like this to be a sort of conference call. Dana and Kim are here with me."

"Okay, sure."

"Hey, all, what's up?" Dylan echoed Rev's greeting.

"In your last report, Rev, you said you'd be surprised if the app wasn't declared illegal. Can you elaborate on that?"

"Well, it's just that it's so subversive," Rev said. "Performing femininity ensures our subordination. If we stop—I mean, we could do that voluntarily, and I really wish we would—well, not me, because I'm already doing that, I've been doing that all my life, but I mean women. In general. In total.

"But we don't. *They* don't. But this—I'm just thinking that the ReGenderApp will somehow make it more acceptable to do that. It'll be fun at first, a novelty, a gag. But once women see, once they actually experience the difference—

"The app will give women more power than the vote. Or the right to abortion." Did they honestly not think of that? Maybe they *weren't* all women. In any case, if they were just a bunch of geeks, who hadn't even taken Psych 101 or Soc 101, let alone Gender 101—but no, Erin, at least, seemed pretty in tune to the gender politics of it all. Rev suspected it was her idea. Maybe she needed to convince Dana and/or Kim.

"Once its use is exposed, that is. If we just use it, app-men will get male privilege and app-women will get screwed. End of story. The sex-gender thing will just be reinforced.

"But once its use is exposed, well, people will never know if the person they were interacting with was using it, so they'd be careful, not to make assumptions, not to treat the person one way or the other.

"Second, if, when, they *aren't* careful, that'll open the door to god knows how many lawsuits. The app's use will provide *proof* of sexism: proof that people have responded, have made decisions, purely according to sex and/or gender. Not according to the merits of one's arguments, one's abilities, one's interests, or whatever else really matters.

"If I were you," Rev concluded, "I'd hire a really good security firm. Body guards at all times."

She heard one of them laugh. Not Erin. Dana? Kim? Whoever, must've been male. Dana. Erin's brother. That would make so much sense. Of her being the one who thought of the app in the first place. And, of course, of his laughter.

"Okay," Erin said, "thanks for the clarification. And the advice." Rev could hear her staring at Dana. Maybe Kim too.

"You know," Dylan mused as they packed their stuff, "all it would take is for men to use the app to get access to women's public rest rooms."

Rev nodded.

"That would trigger a campaign to have them declared illegal. The apps, not the men."

"Of course, the apps. And not the men." Rev said.

Then continued. "And of course, men will do that."

She sighed. "They always find a way to keep us down."

She was more ... angry/sad/tired than usual. Perhaps because she'd had a couple months of being up.

Sure enough, that afternoon, as they were waiting for the taxi that would take them to the airport—"Rev."

His tone stopped her cold.

He silently turned his laptop so she could see.

Dana had been shot. He, or she, was in critical condition.

"But—the app hasn't been released yet. Has it? I mean, we're still in the beta testing period."

"Must've been someone who—"

"Sam." Laura had gotten too uppity.

20

"S o should we keep the apps turned on for this?" Revv wondered aloud as they passed through the door to Departures. It hadn't made any difference for the taxi ride.

"Didn't they say facial recognition programs would do well with it? We could test that hypothesis." He'd recovered some of his enthusiasm for testing the app.

"Yeah, but I don't remember flights being on the list of contexts to be tested."

"Well, surely we don't have to stick to the list, do we?" Dylanna grinned at Revv. "Outside the box, remember? Kamut!""It would certainly be instructive to see what happens here," she agreed, looking at all the people, with dismay. She hated airports. There were always more people, in one place at one time, than she'd typically see in a whole year back home. She was glad they'd chosen Yellowknife instead of Fairbanks for their aurora borealis adventure.

Dylanna led the way. He liked airports. The anticipation of suddenly, relatively speaking, being somewhere else, often somewhere completely different ... They approached the check-in counter. Checked-in. Got their boarding passes. Confirmed that their carry-on luggage could be carried on. No problem.

A short distance away from Security, Dylanna did an about turn, bumping into Revv.

"We'll have to take off our jackets. And shoes."

"And ... ? Oh."

"My app-me has stockings on, but I'm wearing socks."

"Quite apart from the shoes you put on the conveyor belt won't be anything like the shoes you take off. Do you think they'll notice?"

"Of course they'll notice! They're all Security! They've been trained to notice!"

"Yeah. Okay, so we turn the apps off, proceed as ourselves, and make a note in our report. App shoes increase potential for failure at airport Security."

"We could turn them on again here," Dylan said to Rev once they'd found the right gate. He nodded to the public restrooms.

"Even if there's no one in there," Rev said, "someone might see me coming out of the women's restroom. Might see a *man* coming out of the *women's* restroom. And there's no way I'm using the *men's* restroom," she added.

"Right. Okay, so ... "

"We use the restrooms first, then go into that unoccupied alcove," Rev nodded to a spot along the wall, "turn on our apps, then casually come out."

"Come out." Dylan grinned. "How apt."

A few minutes later, they were standing near the alcove. Hard to say whether it would be better if there were a lot of people around or just a few people. Either one would probably be better than a moderate amount of people. Fascinating ...

"Okay, let's try it," Rev said. "We can block each other while we change over."

"Are we turning into vampires?"

"Well, I am."

"Women suck the life blood out of men too," Dylan said. Ten minutes later while they were waiting for the boarding call. "Some women. Those who manipulate men into marriage and kids and then expect life-long financial support."

"How manipulate?"

"Say they're on the pill when they're not. Then surprise, 'I'm pregnant.'"

"One word. Condom. And even so, the men would have been manipulated into child support. Not woman-support. Let alone marriage."

"Condoms break."

"Then don't squirt your sperm into someone's vagina. Don't take the risk if you're not prepared to lose."

"Yeah."

"Did that happen to you?"

"No. Just sayin'."

"Yeah."

They boarded the plane, nodded to the flight attendant, found their seats.

"I can help you with that," Dylanna said to a shorter fellow traveller, and started to heft a large suitcase up into the overhead bin.

"Did I ask for your help?" the man said angrily and held on. A brief tug-of-war ensued before Dylanna let go.

"Sorry," she said, then sat down.

Revv sat down beside him.

"I forgot. But women are supposed to be helpful, so how ... "

Rev thought about it. "It's not supposed to be so obvious. When we help men. Otherwise, it's emasculating."

"Ah." Dylan understood. "No wait, women are men's secretaries and PAs."

"Yeah, but in that case, it's our *job*. They *tell* us what to do. And they'd never call what we do 'help'." No, that wasn't quite right. "When it's our job," she tried again, "when we're officially some guy's assistant, that increases his status. When we just offer help, without official obligation, that decreases his status. Go figure," she added.

"But—"

"Or no, maybe it was that you offered *physical* assistance." Yes, that was it.

"Hm." Dylanna stared out the window. She was in the middle seat, and normally would have asked the window seat person, a man, if he wanted to switch, but he'd learned, already, that men are reluctant to accede to a woman's request. No matter how trivial or reasonable. She settled in.

Tried to settle in. Put his left elbow on the arm of the shared chair, but there was really only half an inch of space left, and it didn't actually work. He put his right elbow on the arm of the shared chair with Rev and found that—she was grinning. Revv had aggressively taken over the whole arm. Dylanna pressed her arms against her sides. As if she was wearing a straightjacket.

"Good afternoon and welcome aboard Best Air flight 497 bound for Yellowknife. Please fasten your seat belts and ensure that your seat backs and trays are in the upright position. For your safety, all passengers are kindly requested to turn off all mobile phones."

Dylanna and Revv looked at each other.

"Oops."

The Yellowknife airport was even smaller than the Sudbury airport. In fact, Yellowknife itself seemed smaller. Smaller than Sudbury. Not smaller than the Sudbury airport.

"It is," Dylan confirmed. "Yellowknife has one-tenth the population Sudbury has."

"Hm. For some reason I thought it was larger. Probably just because of its status as capital of somewhere. And as, virtually, the only city in somewhere."

There was no need to call a taxi. There were only three taxi services, and all three were waiting at the airport. In fact, as soon as they entered the terminal, someone approached them.

"Rev and Dylan? I'm Joe. To take you to Jill's. Got your bags?"

Initially they'd thought they'd pack their winter clothing for their aurora borealis month, but it would have added an extra bag to their travels, and honestly, they weren't sure their winter clothing would be warm enough for Yellowknife. Especially when they discovered they could rent clothing for their stay. So they asked the taxi to stop at one of the clothing rental shops on the way to the B&B. They each got a parka, insulated snow pants, winter boots, a balaclava, insulated mitts, and a really warm hat.

Dylan had arranged for them to stay at Jill's B&B. It was an off-grid floating houseboat. They would be able to see the aurora borealis right from their wrap-around deck. Cup of hot chocolate in hand.

Though at the moment, it was an off-grid sitting-on-the-ice houseboat. So the taxi drove them right up to their door.

"How do people get here in the summer?" Rev asked, as they pulled up to the houseboat.

"A canoe is provided," Dylan said. "But Jill has a motorboat as back-up. She lives in one of these other houseboats."

"That one," the taxi driver said, as Jill popped out and came over to meet them.

"Hi! Dylan and Rev, I presume?"

"Yes! Jill, I presume?"

She nodded.

"Thanks for arranging the taxi!"

"No problem." She opened the door for them, and Rev went inside, followed by Dylan, and then Jill.

"This is cozy," Rev said as she looked around. Dylan agreed. There was a fridge and a stovetop, a bathroom with shower, sink, and toilet, a table and two chairs, a couch, and a bed. No tv. Good. Internet. Good.

Jill showed them how to use everything. The big thing was not to drain the battery pack. That's why they had to use a stovetop kettle to make coffee and not a plug-in kettle.

"Do you have—" She stopped mid-sentence. It was pretty clear Rev wouldn't have a curling iron or a hair dryer.

That night they bundled up and headed out to walk around on the huge, frozen lake. Away from the houseboats into the white silence. That in itself was beautiful. Rev just stood there. Absorbing the stillness.

And then the aurora borealis appeared. At first it was just a diffused yellow streak. Truthfully, they weren't sure that what they were seeing *was* the aurora. And if it was, it was a huge disappointment.

But that was just the beginning. The streak became denser, and greener. Still, it was nothing like all the pictures they'd seen.

Then the streak started fluttering, ever so gently.

Two hours later, there were several vibrant green ribbons undulating across the night sky.

They were so busy looking up, the approaching creature took them by surprise. Rev's first thought was wolverine or something equally dangerous. She hissed. Did *not* want to be surrounded by a pack of dangerous somethings. She knew she couldn't outrun them, bundled up as she was, over snow. 'Course, maybe they couldn't do much damage either, bundled up as she was.

"It's a fox!" Dylan said, as the animal sprang back when Rev hissed, then approached again. In a dancing foxtrot sort of way. "Isn't it?"

Rev looked more closely. It was more black than red/brown. That's what had confused her.

"Do foxes come in black?"

"Foxes come with fine-featured faces and bushy tails. And inquisitive eyes."

Rev turned full circle. There wasn't a pack. Of anythings.

The fox sat down. About ten feet away.

"Good little fox," Dylan said, crouching. "Do you think it'll let me pet it?"

"Do you have a bag of fox treats in your pocket? Jelly beans, maybe?" She was referring to Dylan's role in their rescue of a baby deer in Algonquin Park. He'd calmed the little deer with lullabies and jelly beans.

"Sadly, no. Oh, oh! I have some leftover pretzel bits. Salted caramel."

"Never a good idea to feed the wildlife. Remember Billy the Bear?"

"Yeah, but." The fox sat up. Balanced on its haunches, front paws in the air.

"I didn't know foxes did that. Normally," she clarified.

Then it lay down and rolled over.

"Or that."

"Oh, you don't have to perform for your treats," Dylan said to it, then slowly took off his glove. Just as slowly reached into his pocket.

Pulled out a bag of salted caramel pretzel bits. Tossed one at the little fox. It caught it. In its mouth. Dylan tossed another one. Caught it. Another one. Caught it.

"There's only one more left," he told the fox sadly. The fox caught it deftly. Then sat down again.

And, since one place was as good as another, because all places look the same on a huge, frozen lake, Dylan and Rev sat down too. Together, the three of them watched the aurora borealis.

Next day, they asked Jill about the fox. Sure enough, it was a Billy the Bear. Well, Felix the Fox. Someone had found a fox pup one winter—probably a mix between a red fox and an arctic fox, which, although white in the winter, is black/brown in the summer—made it a warm little den in a cardboard box, and kept it fed through the winter. Come spring, knowing a good thing when it had one, the little fox had stuck around. It could catch a rabbit when it wanted to, but said rabbit tasted much better when barbecued. And you couldn't get ice cream in the wild. Though why people in Yellowknife wanted ice cream, Rev had no idea. Hot chocolate yes, but ice cream? Maybe they put it in their hot chocolate. That would be good.

That morning, Dylan emailed Dana to confess that a planeload of people now knew about the app.

"So," Rev asked, "do you think we'll be kicked out of the program?"

He looked at her. "Why would we be kicked out of the program?"

"Because—Because when women make a mistake, whenever *I've* made a mistake," she corrected, "or have had someone complain about me, I've been fired. At the very least, severely reprimanded."

"Really?"

She suspected then that men got a second chance. Probably even a third. She made a note to herself to test her suspicion.

"Well, I don't think that's going to happen in this case," Dylan said. "They'll probably just consider it advance publicity."

"Hm."

That afternoon, they walked about. Before they left, they took photographs of themselves all bundled up, then uploaded the photos to the app. Then, once outside, they discovered that the app didn't work in twenty-five below. Good to know. They made a mental note to add that to their report.

It took fifteen minutes to get to the downtown, which was actually uptown. It took only another two minutes to find a place that served hot chocolate. With ice cream. They visited the shops, found the ice falls, which weren't terribly spectacular, then stopped to knock at the red door. They'd been told that the couple who lived there would simply welcome you into their home, make you a cup of tea, and chat a while. Guess things could get pretty boring in Yellowknife, Rev thought.

They'd considered using the app for their visit, but decided there was something morally wrong about it, deceiving people who were so hospitable. They made a mental note to put that in their report as well. And a full discussion of the issue in their book. Because deception wasn't always wrong. Or not always the worst of two (or more) wrongs.

Day two, they went on a snowshoe hike.

Day three, they recovered from the snowshoe hike.

By going to the mall. Yellowknife's only mall. Jill had recommended it.

"It's small," Rev noted. The obvious.

"A small mall." Dylan grinned.

And it was eclectic. There was a used book shop, a used CD shop, a miscellaneous store with hardware, kitchen, and stationery stuff, a pharmacy, several arts and crafts shops, clearly featuring, probably exclusively, arts and crafts made in Yellowknife ...

"This has got to be the only mall in Canada without a Walmart!"

"They should bill it as such. Probably triple their business."

They stopped in at The Cookie Monster. Custom-made cookies, huge custom-made cookies, warm out of the oven, but also available for take-home. Perfect. First one chose a cookie base: plain, peanut butter, shortbread, or oatmeal. They one could add one or more flavorings: vanilla, almond, coconut, and so on. And one or more spices: cinnamon, nutmeg, ginger … . And then as many bits as one wanted, from the fruits, nuts, and seeds lists: raisins, dried cranberries, shredded coconut … , cashews, almonds, pecans … , sesame seeds, sunflower seeds, poppy seeds … .

"What, no chocolate chips?"

The woman behind the counter pointed. There was also a chips list. Chocolate, of course, milk, dark, white, and mint, but also peanut butter, butterscotch, and caramel.

And another chips list. Barbecue, salt and vinegar, sour cream and onion …

And one more list—weird stuff. Bacon bits, olives, pickles, sauerkraut. And Froot Loops!

"Do you also have Corn Flakes?"

Of course they did. Dylan bought three of each, in plain, peanut, and shortbread to send to Loup and Flaker.

"What do you think Kit would like?"

"Well since you didn't get the oatmeal base for Loup and Flaker, and I totally get that, why not get Kit some oatmeal cookies? Mix it up—coconut and cranberries in one, maybe nutmeg and poppy seeds in the other … "

"Good idea. Did you get that?" he asked the woman. She nodded.

"And … " They had yet to figure out what they themselves wanted.

Dylan got a plain cookie with barbeque chips bits and sauerkraut. And a peanut butter and pickles cookie. In honour of Peanut and Pickle, the latter being the horse he'd ridden … more or less …

Rev, ever the purist, got a cinnamon shortbread cookie. But then, since she *was* a black jaguar trying to turn into a monkey, she also got an oatmeal cookie with olives and butterscotch chips.

Days four and five, Dylan had arranged for an overnight aurora borealis camping trip. True, they'd been able to see the aurora borealis every night from their houseboat, with ice creamed hot chocolate, but the camping trip involved travelling by dogsled. Even better, they got to drive their own dogsleds.

Again, they thought about using the app, but unless they used it for the whole trip, which they couldn't, because of the cold, it would get awkward. Besides, they were pretty sure it wouldn't make any difference to the dogs.

They entered the 'Dog Sled Aurora Adventures' office, a portable building sitting on a field of snow set back from the road.

"Hi! Dylan O'Toole and Chris Reveille. We have reservations?"

"Right, hi," the woman behind the counter said. "Welcome to Aurora Adventures."

"Thank you."

She opened a file, flipped through the paperwork, then slid the last piece across to them. "Sign here, and here," she said, pointing. "It's just a waiver."

"What, in case we fall through the ice?" Dylan grinned.

"Yeah."

A couple minutes later, a young man entered the small office.

"This is them," the woman said to him, "and they're ready to go."

Rev and Dylan looked at each other.

"Normally, we have half a dozen people on a trip," she explained, "but there were some cancellations. So it's just you two."

"Great!" Rev said.

"This is Kenji. He'll be your guide."

The young man looked them up and down. "You rented that clothing here? In Yellowknife?"

"Yes."

"Good, okay. Can I see your gloves?"

They held out their insulated mitts.

"Good. I'll get you some goggles—once the dogs get up to speed, the wind can hurt your eyeballs—"

Dylan turned to Rev and grinned as the man left the office.

"Okay, let's go meet the dogs," he said once he'd returned, with two pairs of goggles.

"We're going to meet the dogs!" Dylan said to Rev. Like a kid in a candy shop.

The dogs were inside a large enclosure behind the buildings, each chained to its own little dog house.

"Perhaps if they weren't chained, they'd just take off," Rev anticipated Dylan's dismay as they approached. Though, to be honest, she figured only a really stupid dog would leave provided food and shelter. Assuming no abuse.

"They can't. Enclosure."

And the chains were so short, the dogs wouldn't be able to snuggle up with each other. Let alone play and romp about.

"Why are they chained?" Dylan asked Kenji.

"To keep them separated."

"Yeah, but—Are their little houses heated?" Dylan asked.

Kenji ignored the question.

"Back in a minute," he said once he'd led them inside the enclosure. "They're friendly," he thought to call out behind him.

Dylan introduced himself to each dog, shaking their paws, one at a time.

"Hello Thor," he said, shaking its paw, "nice to meet you."

"Nuuk," he shook the next one's paw, "nice to meet you."

"Petunia!" Dylan read the plaque on the next one's house and grinned at Rev. "Delighted to meet you, Petunia!"

Kenji returned and opened the bags he held in his hand. They were full of booties.

"Oh oh! Can I put them on?"

"Knock yourself out." He handed one of the bags to Dylan. The other to Rev. And left again.

Dylan happily sat down with the bag of twenty-four booties. Then got up and unchained the dogs. Then sat down again. The dogs crowded around. They knew. And wanted to wear their booties. Must be that cold, Rev thought. Or maybe it was just a Pavlov thing. After booties, RUN!

When Kenji returned, fifteen minutes later, he took in the scene—Dylan was in the middle of a happy pile of belly-up loll-abouts—and snorted with disgust, whether with Dylan or the dogs, hard to say.

"They're *working* dogs," he muttered. Then left again.

Half an hour later, Dylan proudly displayed his team. Thor wore one red, one blue, one yellow, and one green bootie. Jet had one orange, one red, one purple, and one green. Petunia—

"I think they were supposed to each get a matching set," Rev said, grinning. Nodding to her six, suitably attired, dogs.

"Where's the fun in that?"

Indeed. Rev was happy to see Dylan having fun again. She'd missed that. He was her silly, her spontaneous, her giggle. Helping her move beyond all her carefully considered anger.

Maybe they'd just not use the apps at all anymore. Surely they had done enough. Or maybe they could formally withdraw from the beta test. A preoccupation with sex and gender wasn't conducive to having fun. She made a note to herself to put *that* in her report. And their book.

Finally, they were ready. Kenji led his team out across the wide open frozen expanse. Rev followed with her team. And then Dylan.

A short minute later, Rev heard him yelling "Yee Haw!" and looked back to see him and his team of ecstatic dogs slaloming across the field.

Soon after their departure, it started to snow. Their route was pretty, though more stark than Rev expected. They were travelling along the edge of sparse forest rather than through the thick. She supposed there wasn't much thick forest in Yellowknife.

The real joy was seeing the dogs run. She envied them. She wished she'd been able to run that fast, that far, with that much joy. Just once.

In two hours, they'd covered the fifteen mile trek to the campsite. As Rev had anticipated, the dogs didn't really need driving. They'd done the trip so many times before, there was a clear packed path that only a fool dog would leave, and when in doubt, take the turn taken by the team in front of you.

Dylan was disappointed when they reached the campsite. He'd imagined pitching a tent and crawling inside with his dogs. Instead, there was a modest off-grid lodge at their destination. It made sense. Aurora Adventures was a business. They brought people out here all the time. In truth, Rev appreciated the outhouse. Which featured not a hole in the ground, but a composting toilet.

They helped Kenji get the dogs settled in their outdoor pen, then went inside the lodge to get settled themselves.

"An Aurora Adventures tradition," Kenji said, as he came out of the kitchen, bearing a large tray, "and a northern delicacy. Muskox balls!"

Dylan and Rev looked at the platters Kenji set before them.

When Kenji returned to the kitchen, Rev turned to Dylan. "Balls as in meatballs or as in balls balls?"

Dylan didn't want to know.

Both shoved their plates away from them.

"Guess it's hard to be a vegetarian in the north."

They filled up on fish chowder instead.

An hour later, Kenji invited them outside for a fire. And hot chocolate.

And, of course, the aurora. Rev and Dylan lay in the snow on an incline, and not a word was said once the ribbons started forming. It was an especially active night, and the swirling was like ... spilt smoke ... in lemon, chartreuse, and magenta.

21

Next day, Jill came knocking on their door.

"Morning!"

"It is, yes!" Dylan replied. Rev's brain wasn't online yet, so she had no words.

"You guys are teachers, yeah?"

Dylan often put that on his housesit applications to suggest respectability. Go figure.

"Used to be. Why?"

"They're looking for a couple people to fill in at the high school. Pete and Janet want to attend a one-week course in the UK, philosophy in the classroom or some such."

How could they say no?

"And between you and me, they're both overdue to get the hell out of Dodge for a while. I don't think either of them have ever been overseas."

How could they say no?

The two-week experience in Victoria had totally killed Dylan's enthusiasm for the testing the app, for living as a woman. But he loved teaching. Rev was pretty much done with the app as well, but she was curious, really curious, to see what it was like to teach as a man. Plus, they both felt morally obligated to justify all their app-paid Yellowknife expenses.

So they said yes.

Unfortunately, neither Pete nor Janet taught History or English, or even Society, Challenge, and Change, the additional qualification course Dylan and Rev had both taken, during which they'd first met so many, many years ago. Pete and Janet taught Phys-Ed and French.

They decided that despite her stellar performance of "Ma Belle Amie" in Salt Lake City, Rev would replace the high school French teacher. After all, she'd *taken* high school French, for five years. Dylan would replace the Phys-Ed teacher.

But they were thinking of themselves as themselves, not as male and female. In hindsight …

"You're replacing Ms. Devreau?" one student asked Revv with clear disbelief.

"Yes. Why?"

"All our French teachers have been women."

Right. Of course.

And then the real panic hit. If they found that out a man was teaching girls' gym—No wait, men often taught, coached, girls. Case in point, women's gymnastics. *Girls'* gymnastics. Which was interesting. Appalling, actually. Because men didn't even *do* the balance beam. Or the uneven bars. So how the hell were they deemed capable of *coaching* those events? At the *Olympic level*, no less?

Rev knew what would happen if a woman wanted to coach men's Olympic football … No, wait, women played football now. And hockey. And … Hm. There was no men's sport that women didn't do now. But not vice versa. *We are the champions!*

Not so fast. The pommel horse. The high bar. And what would happen if a woman presented herself to coach either of those?

Not to mention that many men coached girls' soccer, girls' basketball, and—swimming! Girls in bathing suits.

Dylan would be okay. Turned out it was co-ed gym.

Or not. Turned out the second week was to be cross-country skiing and snowshoeing. About which Dylan was sure to know more than all the kids who'd grown up in the cold, white, snowy expanse that was Yellowknife.

As for the first week ... "But I'm not doing anything different!"

She nodded.

"I'm waiting silently for them to settle, I'm making the lessons interesting, I'm asking the rude ones to please be quiet—"

Rev snorted at that last one.

"None of it's working. Now."

She nodded.

"What am I doing wrong?" he wailed the day after, pacing back and forth in the kitchen.

"Nothing." Rev was leaning against the counter. "There's just no way men will do what a woman says. No matter what she says or how she says it."

He'd known that. He'd discovered that. "But I'm their *teacher!*"

"Which makes it worse. For a man, even a boy, to take instruction from a woman?"

"But even the girls—"

She nodded. "Before, you were a man. Girls, women, do what men ask them to do."

"But—" he threw up his hands, turning in a smaller and smaller circle, then stopped. He just stopped. And looked at her.

"I don't know anymore what's personal and what's political. Maybe I'm *not* good at what I do. Maybe I've *never* been good at what I do. Maybe my travel pieces are mediocre at best, maybe they're just accepted because they're written by a man."

Rev nodded.

"How can I know?" he begged her for an answer.

She didn't have one.

"They keep challenging me, asking me to explain myself, even on the little things! And they interrupt me! All the bloody time!"

She nodded. They were trying to undermine his authority; they refused to accept his authority. Her authority. They were challenging his competence. Her competence.

"By the end of the day, I wasn't sure I knew *any* of what I thought

I knew. Sudbury *is* just north of Lake Huron, right? And the Great Lakes *are* fresh water—even though they're connected to the ocean by the St. Lawrence River?"

On Friday, he turned off the app as soon as he stepped inside their cozy boathouse and all but threw his phone against the wall. "Free at last, free at last, thank God Almighty, I'm free—"
   His grin froze. Rev's icy stare made it so.
   And it all came crashing, crushing, down on him. The relentless barbed weight of it all.

"How do you do it?" he asked a while later.
   "Do what?"
   "Keep from killing every male you see?"

He started to understand her more. She'd spent what, thirty years, defending, having to defend, every little thing she said or did. Fighting for, having to fight for, everything—everything he could take for granted. Physical space, air time. Authority, respect. The presumption of competence. The presumption of value.

And the second week ... "So how was *your* day?"
   "Good," Rev replied. "Had a field trip today. Attended a City council meeting."
   "But you're teaching French."
   "Yeah, it was already scheduled. By Janet. I think the idea was for the students to see Canada's bilingualism in action."
   "And?"
   "I got a bit vocal," she confessed. "About Canada's bilingualism. Said it was rather colonial. Said that at the very least Canada should be trilingual, the third language being whatever First Nations language is most prevalent in the region in question."
   "And?"
   And it had been such a new feeling. The feeling that everyone thought she knew what she was talking about. What *was* that? Oh! Authority! She had been perceived as having authority! They took

what she said *at face-value!*

"And after the meeting, I was approached by one of the councillors about becoming her speech writer in the upcoming election campaign. She's running for Premier."

"Of the Northwest Territories?"

"No, of Denmark."

"Right. Sorry. It's just—a speechwriter job falls into your lap just because you made some comment about our bilingualism?"

She stared at him, waiting for him to connect the dots. Nada.

"I got a bit vocal about a few other things as well," she added. "I figured, hey, teacher, role model, civic engagement ... "

"Right. See?"

"See what?"

"See what happens when you're a bit vocal!"

She stared at him again for a moment.

"Who are you and what did you do with Dylan? I've been 'a bit vocal' *all my life* and all I've gotten are death threats!"

"Figuratively speaking."

"Mostly."

And then it clicked. It was Revv, not Rev, who'd been offered a job as a speech writer.

"So ... that face you've got on ... you're not happy for me?"

"Yes, it's just that—" No! He wasn't happy for her! He was seething with resentment. And jealousy and outrage and anger.

And shame.

"You're a better person than me," he said in a small voice. "How can you even—*like* me? How can you not resent all the male privilege I get?"

She shrugged. She *did* resent all the male privilege he got. Still.

"And how was *your* day?" she asked.

"I was fired."

"Really?"

"Yeah and there might be a lawsuit. We should tell Dana ... " he trailed off.

"What happened?"

"I'd asked them, politely, not to use the ropes. I had them tied safely to the wall."

"Well, that's *one* way to control the class."

He smiled. Just a bit.

"Then I *told* them not to use the ropes. And explained why."

"Ropes bad."

"Still, one kid untied one of them and started climbing. While I was busy with another kid. As soon as I saw him up there, I told everyone to hurry and bring out the crash pads. You know, in case."

She nodded. Afraid of where this was going.

"I insisted he come back down. But he refused."

She nodded.

"Then it occurred to me that maybe he was stuck. Either paralyzed by a previously unknown fear of heights or too weak to make it back down."

"But if he made it up—Oh, right. He'd have to let go with one hand, to go hand over hand ... "

"So I climbed up after him, intending to help him down. I thought I could cradle him down or something."

"And?"

"He jumped."

"Of course he did." She sighed and looked out the window.

"What? Why 'Of course he did'?"

"You had the app on all that time?"

"Yeah, I—*Seriously?*" He replayed everything in his mind.

"You asked," Rev reviewed the event. "Okay. You explained, you gave a rational argument. Less okay. And you ordered. Definitely not okay. And then when you climbed up after him, well, you may as well have castrated him."

"He'd rather break a leg than ... accept help from a woman?"

"Men would rather kill the planet than."

Dylan considered that. Decided to back away from it, at least for now.

"So ... how do you—how did you—teach?"

She shrugged. "Someone once told me the only way women could teach was either to play the flirt, ask sweetly, bat your eyelashes, or to play the Mom, be a warm fuzzy bundle of nurturing."

Dylan couldn't imagine Rev pulling off either. Dylan couldn't imagine Rev *trying* to pull off either.

"And so ... the kid broke a leg?"

Dylan nodded.

"The principal told me I was relieved of my duties. Effectively immediately. Told me I was unable to control the class."

Rev nodded.

"But I did what I normally do. Normally it works."

"Normally you're a man."

22

"Faster!" Dylan grinned from the back seat. Kit had come to the airport to get them, and he was soooo eager to see Loup.

Kit glanced in the rear view mirror and saw that he was taking 'back seat driver' to heart by doing a full-out mime.

"This isn't a standard. No need to keep shifting gears."

"Well, that's no fun."

Rev grinned too. Delight was back.

Both Loup and Flaker were at the gate when Kit pulled into the driveway. And as soon as Dylan got out of the back seat, Loup put her front paws up onto the fencing rail and let out a high-pitched howl that was part squeal. They'd never heard her do that before. Dylan squealed back as he opened the gate and embraced her. Loup's tail was wagging enthusiastically. Dylan's would have been too.

Flaker gave a slightly more sedate greeting to Kit, then to Rev, then joined in the tumble that Loup and Dylan had become.

They spent the rest of the afternoon walking in the forest, Dylan, Loup, and Rev. They spent the afternoon after that again walking in the forest. Dylan, Loup, and Rev. By the day after that, most of the ice on the lake had melted, so Rev went out kayaking. Dylan went biking through the forest with Loup running by his side.

It wasn't until the end of the week that they thought about the app. Reluctantly. But April was part of the five-month testing period they'd committed themselves too.

"Didn't you have a plan to test the app on the local rednecks and kept women?" Dylan asked when they were having their coffee and cold pizza, in front of the fire Dylan had made. He was sitting on the floor against the couch, legs stretched out in front of him, so Loup could lay beside him, pressed against him—Loup had overcome her fear of fire enough to do just that.

"Yeah, but then I had a better idea. Thought I'd go to a township meeting as Revv. See if my two decades of requests might finally be taken seriously."

"But ... ?"

"But it has since occurred to me that they'll recognize me. If not *me*, my *name*."

"Can't you use another name?"

"Only taxpayers would be allowed at the meeting."

"Right. Of course."

"Kit!" They both said at once.

They—Dylan, Rev, Loup, and Flaker, who had been spending his days with them again, now that they were back and Kit was away all day—walked over to her place the next afternoon, late. In fact, Flaker was already on his way, and the three of them had to catch up. How did he know what time it was? How did he know when Kit would be on her way home? No matter. He knew.

"So, does the township know you?" Rev asked Kit once they were settled in her porch, Kit and Dylan with a beer, Rev with a Pepsi. "The mayor, the council members, the office staff—does anyone know you? Do they know you're a woman?"

"I don't know. I guess not. Just 'Kit'—'Kit Millereau'—is on all my stuff. Could go either way, I guess."

Dylan nodded. "You could be ... Kittredge Millereau."

"You've never paid your taxes in person?" Rev asked. "You've never called about anything?"

Kit shook her head. "I pay online. And I haven't really had anything to call about. Well, except for the trap thing, but you guys said you'd already called. Several times. So I figured … "

"You figured right," Rev said. It would have been a waste of time.

She glanced at Dylan, then made their request. "How would you like to test the app for us at a township meeting?"

Kit widened her eyes. She'd been wondering what they were after. That had not occurred to her.

"You mean, go as a man?"

They nodded.

"Rev was going to go," Dylan explained, "as a man, to see if the reaction to her many requests would be different, but they know her. So it wouldn't work."

"Right … Okay … ," Kit nodded, warming to the idea quite quickly, "Yes, I'll do it! Hell, yeah! I'll need a list of your talking points," she added.

Rev handed her a piece of paper. Several pieces of paper, in fact. After all, she'd had twenty years.

Kit grinned at her then started reading, and nodding, and reading, and nodding, and reading, and—tilting her head.

"What?"

"I use the firing range."

"Oh. Well you don't have to argue *all* my points—"

"No," she'd kept reading, "but I didn't know that every single shot could be heard by everyone in the township. So clearly."

Rev nodded. "What we've got here is a river opening up to lake that's surrounded by hills. It's like a tunnel opening up to a cave. With a pool of water in it. An acoustic disaster."

"You're right," she said. "The range should never have been allowed there."

Kit read on, then gave a sort of snort.

"What?" Rev asked, curious.

"Silencers. The guys'll never go for that. They like the noise."

Rev looked at Dylan. "See? Told you."

"Vroom vroom." He agreed.

"You're lucky they don't have cannons here."

Rev blanched.

"You've never heard of potato cannons?" Kit looked at her.

Rev shook her head. Kit added to the list. "You'll want the township to ban their use."

"Okay ... "

Kit resumed reading, and nodding. "They've already got berms, but you're right about could be indoor or underground. And no skeet shooting," she added another note. "I think that's what you're hearing most of the time. They shoot up.

"And yeah," she kept reading, "regular and limited hours. There's no need for it to be open twenty-four/seven. Especially if it puts everyone on edge, waiting for the shots.

"Chinese lanterns?" she looked up at Rev a few moments later.

"Yeah, last year people started sending them out to float over the water, from where they can then drift up over the trees—"

"What kind of idiots do you have living on your lake? Don't they know that trees are—flammable?"

"Well, I was going to say 'the lungs of the planet,' but I guess 'flammable' has to be logically prior."

Kit continued reading Rev's list, asking for clarification here and there.

"Okay, so," she'd gotten to the end and looked up, "when is the next meeting?"

"Tuesday," Rev said. "I'd better not go," she added.

"No, you'd just annoy people," Dylan said.

She glanced at him.

"Put them on alert, I mean."

"No, she'd annoy them," Kit smiled.

"I'll go," Dylan said. "I could be Kittredge's friend. I'll observe, take notes, and surreptitiously, record."

Rev gave Kit her phone, and they explained how to use the app. They waited while she uploaded a few pictures of herself, then helped her tweak the settings until she had a convincing Kittredge.

"Well?" Rev met them at the door, Flaker and Loup crowding around. "What happened?"

Dylan gave some doggy treats to Loup and Flaker—no freshly killed rabbits were handy—and offered a beer to Kit.

"Would you like some hot chocolate instead?" Rev asked, plugging in the kettle. Coffee or Pepsi, and she'd be up all night.

"No, the beer's fine, thanks."

They settled in the living room, Dylan on the floor with Loup and Flaker, Kit and Rev on the couch.

"Okay, so they'll talk to the firing range," Kit opened. "About all of your points."

"About *all* of my points?" Already, Rev was ... pissed off and happy.

"And apparently there's already a law that says jetskis have to be five hundred metres from shore—"

"But the lake at its widest is probably only a thousand metres," Rev protested, then pointed out the obvious. "So that means that all this time, they were in violation of an existing law! Except when they drove in a straight line up or down the middle of the lake. Which was never." What they did was drive in circles around and around and around ...

"Which is something my friend Dylanna pointed out," Kit grinned.

"At which point," Dylan took over the narrative, "they asked who I was. Then said that as Kittredge's friend, I had no standing and wasn't allowed to speak."

"Right," Rev muttered. "*That's* why you weren't allowed to speak."

"So I repeated what my friend Dylanna pointed out," Kit said, "word for word. They took note."

"Probably had it bronzed."

"That said, zoning the lake as motor-free or electric-motor only is a Ministry decision, but they said they'd make a petition for that decision.

"At first, they didn't believe that two gallons of uncombusted fuel went straight into the lake for every hour of jetski operation," Kit added, "so I'm glad you had the reference for that."

Rev nodded.

"Same goes for the paths through crown land," Kit continued. "Ministry jurisdiction. I reminded them that this township has one of the highest proportions of crown land to private property—thanks for that stat, by the way—and they were letting it be destroyed by snowmobilers and ATVers who don't stay on their designated trails."

Not to mention that a firing range surely alienates the wildlife, as do logging companies, and quarries ... Rev hadn't put any of *that* on her list. Hm. Next time.

"So they said they'd petition the Ministry for ATVs and snowmobiles to be restricted to the snowmobile trails."

Rev leaned back. This was too much. She'd been complaining about that for years. The Ontario government had designated 30,000 kilometres of mostly crown land for snowmobile-only use. Without asking all the non-snowmobiling taxpayers, of course. Still, snow-mobilers drove on any trail they wanted. As did the ATVers. As a result, not only did the noise and the fumes make walking, running, mountain biking, snowshoeing, and cross-country skiing unpleasant, the vehicles themselves, since the trails were used as a racetrack, as well as the erosion of the trail into a mess of exposed rocks and roots, made it dangerous.

"And the noise bylaw?"

"Well, that's tricky. They were really reluctant to say that chainsaws, leaf blowers, weed trimmers, lawn mowers, power tools, and backhoes can be used only on Saturdays, but they did seem to get the point that if they were allowed every day, all day, between 8 a.m. and 11 p.m., they couldn't promote the township, or at least the lake, which is, after all, the township's centrepiece, as 'A Place of Natural Beauty and Peace.'"

"I suggested an alternative slogan, on your behalf," Dylan grinned. "'Where the Noise Never Stops.'"

Rev grinned. Sort of.

"And the guy who sets the traps near the trails," Dylan continued, gleefully, "he's going to jail. For life."

"No!"

"No," Dylan agreed, "but he's going to be told he can't set any traps within five hundred metres of a trail. Which, since he's probably a lard-ass who can't walk more than ten metres through the bush on his own two feet, let alone drag a carcass that far, means no more traps." He ruffled Loup's fur.

Half an hour later, Kit and Flaker were ready to go home.

"Oh," Rev had almost forgotten. "My phone?"

"Yeah, about that … Can I take it with me to work tomorrow? Just one day. Please? Please please pretty please with a cherry on top?"

Rev grinned. She understood. Completely.

"Okay. But only if you stop saying 'Please please pretty please'."

"'With a cherry on top,'" Dylan added.

"It'll give you away," Rev explained. Because that was why.

"Okay, then let me put it this way," Kit said. "Give me the fucking phone or I'll blow your fucking head off."

Rev looked at Dylan. "Quick study."

"But you can't just walk into the office as Kittredge," Rev pointed out. "How will you explain—?"

"Oh, I don't intend to just walk into the office. I intend to show up on one of the trips. I want to engage with the kids. As a guy. For just one day."

"But—"

"I don't know, but I'll come up with something. I'll say I'm an intern or something."

The next night, when they went to retrieve Rev's phone, they found Kit well on the way to total inebriation. As Corn Flake indicated when he met them at the door. He returned to her side, ready to protect her while she was thus incapacitated.

"I take it it didn't go so well," Rev said. Staring at the empty beer bottles on the coffee table.

"Au contraire" Kit replied. "We know about shystemic shexism, mishogyny, and schmale privilege." She looked at Rev. "Right? I mean we *know*. Well," she tried to get up, then abandoned the effort, or changed her mind, "we don't know shit."

Rev nodded.

Dylan nodded.

"In just *one day*," she tried again and managed to get up. Then remembered what she was going to say.

"My shelf-esteem is *through the roof* now!" She punched the air with her fist. Then fell down.

They wrote their report about the township meeting the next

morning—Rev had untarped the porch and was snuggled on her couch, Dylan was on his chair, and Loup was in her nest in the corner, with one of his, her, shoes—then sent it off.

They spent the rest of the week—when they weren't out on the lake or in the forest—working on their book, organizing all of their reports into a coherent whole, adding commentary to the reportage. Afternoons, they spent out on the lake or in the forest or both. By the end of the week, they had a solid two hundred pages.

"You know," Dylan said on the Sunday morning, "I'm inclined to tell Dana, Erin, and Kim that we're done."

"You know," she replied, "I'm inclined to do that as well."

They each started preparing an email.

"Wait!"

"I see it."

A message from Erin had popped into their inboxes.

"Given the exceedingly thorough nature of your reports to date, we have decided that you have more than met your contractual obligations. Thank you for your insightful observations and comments ... "

"Cool," Rev said.

"You ain't seen nothin' yet," Dylan muttered, as he attached their two-hundred pages. Rev did the same.

"Wait! You've included our conclusion?" Rev asked. They'd written it just the night before.

"Yes. 'As hypothesized, gender is ridiculously irrational, frighteningly pervasive, and, since it is what enables sexism, truly harmful. Therefore, it should be neutralized.'"

"'Neuterized'!" Rev revised gleefully. Dylan followed suit.

"'We believe the ReGenderApp,'" he continued, "'which we suggest be renamed the TransApp—not only because it captures the confusion, the equivocation, the ambiguity, of gender and sex, but also because it conveys the app's transformative potential, not only for individuals, but for society as a whole—will be disturbingly instrumental in achieving that objective.'"

They each hit SEND.